A Penny a Shell

A WW1 Yorkshire War Story

Antony J Bell

Goldfish

Contents

A Penny a Shell

Based on the True Story of the Barnbow Lasses

By Antony J. Bell.

When greater perils men environ,
Then, women show a front of iron.
And gentle in their manner, they
Do bold things in a quiet way

Thomas Dunn English (1819-1902)

Dedicated to my Mother, my Wife and all the hard working Women of Yorkshire

Author's Note

Sarah Ann Jennings is based on my great-grandmother, who was killed in the Barnbow explosion on December 5, 1916. Cecil Jennings, her son, and her parents, James and Susannah Jennings, also come from my family history. While their existence and connection to these events are factual, their detailed interactions, inner thoughts, and dialogue in this novel are fictionalised to bring their experiences to life.

This story includes a portrayal of TNT poisoning. Although Rose Turner is a fictional character, the exact health symptoms and details of TNT poisoning in this book are taken from the real-life accounts of women and girls during this period. This element honours all workers affected by TNT exposure. It serves as a tribute to those whose lives were lost or forever changed by the terrible conditions in factories like Barnbow.

William Parkin, a real individual employed at Barnbow, and his courageous actions during the explosion are based on historical accounts of bravery shown that day.

Characters such as Thomas and Annie Brown are also based on real people connected to Sarah Ann Jennings's life. While their familial relationships are factual, the specific circumstances, characterisations, and detailed events of their lives, as portrayed here, are fictionalised to give a richer context for Sarah's journey and the hardships of the era.

All other characters—including Eliza Wren, her gang members (Lucy Atkinson, June Mitchell, Mary Sutcliffe, Hilda Morton, Nora Kershaw), and others such as Captain Miller, Miss McDowell, Ann Price, Rose Turner, and John Skinner (Eliza's landlord)—are a work of fiction. These characters and their stories discover the mixed experiences and collective spirit of the thousands of women who worked at Barnbow.

Through their voices, I hope to offer a representative portrayal of the courage, camaraderie, and sacrifices of the 'Barnbow Lasses'.

Antony John Bell

Prologue- Before the Names Were Etched in Stone

Before the names were etched in stone or lost to yellowed ledgers, it was the air that carried them first. It was thick with a gritty residue that settled on every surface—a stench that held an industrial sharpness and clung to the breath. This was the signature of a vast, hidden lung on the outskirts of Leeds—a factory inhaling young women and exhaling munitions in a never-ending, smoke-stained, death-laden rhythm.

Hidden behind fences, hedgerows, and a wall of official silence, Barnbow wasn't shown on any public map, unlike a real town. Officially, it was National Filling Factory No. 1. To the women who worked there and walked its gates, it was Barnbow.

This is an account of the Great War, but it isn't a story of trenches or mud-caked soldiers charging into the grinding teeth of machine guns. It's another front. Of factory grime and sweat, held by women whose scarred hands packed death with ruthless precision.

This is a tale of an invisible army fought in a room heavy with the stench of molten Amatol. A volatile mix of explosive TNT and ammonium nitrate, heated to pour. A sleeping concoction ready to be awakened by a single spark.

Their courage was quieter, measured not in medals but in the daily push to meet the quota. To earn a penny a shell bonus. To keep a roof over their families' heads as the world tore itself apart. This story is of the women who came from cobbled streets and soot-stained terraces, from weaving mills and a life in service and scrubbing floors—trading one kind of hardship for another. They pressed their hopes and fears into the cold brass of every shell, sending them into the endless, consuming void of war.

It's dust from a time that has long since settled. The great sheds have fallen silent, their purpose fulfilled, their secrets kept. As the night falls and winter approaches, listen closely. You can hear the echoes of laughter and songs in the hum of memory, the fear, patriotism, and names whispered in the wind.

This recounts the story of several of those names—of the lives they lived, the sacrifices they made, and the price they paid. Deep within the war-shadowed factory's roar, each woman was more than a worker.

1

Chapter 1 : Two Short, One Long

5th December 1916, Castleford

The knock at the door—two short, one long—shattered the morning quiet. It wasn't a friendly knock from a neighbour.

Eliza Wren froze, the rhythmic rocking of her body coming to an abrupt halt.

The persistent pain in her lower back, a ghost of her eight-hour shift at Barnbow, throbbed in time with her hammering heart.

It was Tuesday. Not the rent man. The knock left a heavy feeling in her heart.

Skinner.

The name hit with the power of a hammer blow. Her fingers prickled, yellow-stained skin tightening with sudden nerves.

Outside, she knew, the ground would be iron-hard with frost. For a wild second, she considered staying still... a foolish, childish hope that he might walk away. But he would know. He always knew.

The house seemed to shrink around her, frozen in that moment. The air, thick with the sour odour of damp soot and the boiled-water scent of poverty, was heavy in her lungs. The weak fire she had ignited sputtered, its light shrinking from the windows as if in fear, making the shadows in the corners deepen and twist. This was her home, her sanctuary, yet it seemed like a trap.

She went to the entrance, her stockinged feet silent on the hard slate floor of the kitchen. She drew a breath, smoothed her apron down with her trembling hand, and unlatched the door.

A blast of raw, biting air struck her, his bulk blocking the weak morning light and casting the cramped hallway into deeper shadow.

The initial impact wasn't his appearance but his aroma. It was the smoke from his pipe—not the cheap, harsh shag the pit lads smoked. Something richer, sweeter, a scent that spoke of evenings spent in warm rooms with full bellies. It curled into her kitchen, an unwelcome guest, smothering the familiar, honest scents of coal dust and black tea.

It was then that she saw him. For a landlord, he wasn't a flashy man, not really. His woollen overcoat was dark, heavy, and well-made, she could tell, but it was practical. The coat's quality was irrelevant, though.

The issue was the way he wore it, how his bulk pressed in on the air itself within the doorway, a physical, unwanted claim on her space. Her eyes dropped to his fingers. They were clean. Well-fed hands holding expensive-looking leather gloves, not resting at his sides but clasped before him, as if in judgement.

And his gaze, when it met hers, held nothing, no anger, no pity—the detached calculation of someone reviewing property.

His boots, polished to a dull gleam, sat in stark contrast to her worn front step. The collar of his thick wool coat stood high, not so much against the chill, she always thought, but more to increase his imposing air. His eyes, small and hard as pebbles, swept her cramped kitchen.

"Wren," he said, no greeting. "The payment on your husband's account, Eliza. It's overdue. Again." He paused, eyes narrowing at her hands, stained yellow.

His gaze travelled up for a moment, taking in the woman before him. She was in her late thirties, with a face that still held the ghost of a younger prettiness, but it was now overlaid with a harder quality, a strength borne of worry. Her hair was pulled back severely from a face that was all pointed, maternal focus. He flashed a condescending smile that smoothed over a hint of revulsion.

"It's a good thing you're at that factory, Eliza. It teaches a woman what a shilling is worth. Teaches you that a debt is a debt, no matter what." As his voice rose, he corrected himself and withdrew his emotion. "This isn't charity. Prices are climbing for me, too, you know. This war's no holiday for men of property."

"I know, Mr Skinner." A bitter taste lingered from the words. "I am clearing it—all the pennies I get go to paying you off—but the interest is so high."

He cut her off with a short, harsh sound, not quite a laugh. "Stan knew the terms, girl. A man's handshake—that's what it was."

A man's handshake.

Hands that had, she imagined, never experienced a day of real labour, not to the extent Stan's had. She could picture Stan's hands—knuckles scarred, nails rimmed with black dust; no amount of scrubbing could ever remove it. Those were the hands of a man whose handshake meant something, she thought, a trace of hot defiance deep inside her.

Hands that worked, that held her—hands that had once promised to work themselves to dust for her. Skinner's handshake seemed like another tool he used to get what he wanted.

That statement was a brand on her memory, a key that unlocked the moment the trap had been sprung.

Her jaw tightened as she remembered Stan coming home from Skinner's study that spring—face pale, the usual confidence gone from his eyes. He'd told her everything, his words slow and stripped of strength.

Skinner had made him stand, watching him like a predator sizing up prey. Then came the remarks—cold, disdainful—about the risk of lending to a striking miner. Jobless after a months-long strike on the picket line, heading to war.

He had laid out his terms: the full sum, steep interest—a 'wartime inconvenience fee'—and weekly repayments starting with Eliza's first wage. By default, the house would be forfeited. Not eviction, but total loss.

She recalled Stan's bitter laugh. *"He called it a 'gentleman's agreement' based on my handshake. A handshake that'll cost us dear for years to come, I reckon."* And she remembered her fierce promise, her face buried in his shoulder. "We'll pay it back, Stan. We won't let that man break us."

Her chest ached with a complex, painful knot of pride, fear, and love. The itch on her hands returned, a constant, jealous reminder from Barnbow of the man she missed.

Their love and bond, forged in hunger and humour, bound her across the miles—an anchor, a rope, a memory. And it had to hold.

"I'm doing what I can, Mr Skinner," she said in a quiet, desperate tone. "I know I'm two weeks behind on Stan's loan, but when this week's bonus comes through, I hope to clear what's outstanding within the month."

"Your best isn't good enough," he said, the polite mask slipping from his face. "I've heard your promises. They don't fill my ledger. You have until Saturday morning. Forget instalments—I want the full balance by then. Four pounds ten shillings. Not a penny less."

He leaned in closer, his voice sinking to a menacing growl that vibrated in the foul air between them. "Saturday morning, Eliza. The total amount. Let's avoid any unpleasantness, shall we?"

The sum wasn't a number; it was the unforgiving hardness of a frozen street beneath her children's feet, the sharp edge of a winter wind on their faces.

The sheer injustice of it all—that he could threaten to undo everything she was breaking herself to achieve—felt like a fresh, bitter wound.

She opened her mouth to plead again, to beg for mercy, but the words died in her throat. She remembered the town talk, the story passed over cups of weak tea in kitchens like this one. She remembered the tale of Skinner's father, a man too soft for business, who'd lost their family shop to pity and bad debt—a man broken by his own kindness. John Skinner hadn't inherited his father's heart; he'd inherited his father's fear. He wasn't just a cruel man demanding money; he was a man terrified of repeating the past. Mercy, to him, was another word for weakness—and weakness was an inherited sin. Pleading with him would be like asking a wolf not to bite.

His words stole her breath. Her mind flew to her children, to the thought of them out in the cold, and a wave of pure, protective fury burned through her fear. As her expression shifted from terror to a mother's fierce defiance, something in Skinner's own face faltered. The hard lines around his mouth softened for a single, unguarded moment. A flicker of something—pity, perhaps, or the ghost of a memory—passed through his eyes.

Eliza saw it—a crack in the armour. A wild, desperate hope surged in her chest. He was a father, too. He must understand.

"Mr Skinner, please..." she began, her voice a ragged whisper, clinging to that sliver of humanity.

But just as quickly, it was gone. He seemed to draw himself up, his jaw setting into a line harder than before. The brief warmth in his eyes vanished, replaced by a cold, deliberate flatness. It was as if a door had opened a crack, only to be slammed shut and bolted from the inside. The hope in Eliza's chest withered.

He didn't let her finish. With a sign of complete disregard, he tipped his hat in a display of complete dismissal. "No more chances. No more waiting for your Stan's money from France. This house will have tenants who pay."

His boots crunched on the frost-covered path as he wheeled around and departed.

Her gaze fell upon her hands, forever stained canary yellow. It was the colour of the poison she breathed every night to make ends meet and keep this very roof over their heads.

This wasn't a debt of laziness; it was a debt of loyalty to a husband at war and a town betrayed by the pit owners.

Eliza closed the door. A sudden, oppressive silence swallowed the sharp click of the latch. She leaned her head against the door, the flaking paint gentle and coarse against her skin, a single splinter catching in her hair.

Her breath came in shallow, ragged gasps, and she could taste something like bile or ash in her throat. The atmosphere in the narrow hallway felt thick with his presence, the sweet, sickly aroma of his tobacco smoke still a foul violation of her home.

It was no longer the chill from the floorboards seeping into her skin anymore; this was a coldness that started in her belly and spread outwards, into her very bones.

Four pounds ten shillings. By Saturday.

Her gaze darted around the small kitchen, at the stove she'd fought to keep lit. The single quilt upstairs they all shared edged into her mind.

His threat wasn't eviction. It was a promise to extinguish the fragile warmth she'd carefully nurtured to build.

In an instant, the single word was a final verdict. She felt the weight threatening to crush her, her hands shaking as she pressed them against her apron. *Impossible.*

Eliza looked at the nearly depleted coal container near the fireplace, the very symbol of her struggle against the cold. A flood of pure, hot fury burned through the despair. With a choked cry, she kicked it. The metal bucket clattered across the cold floor, spilling the last few chips of black dust in a pathetic, gritty arc.

The sharp, ugly sound broke the silence. Her breathing was steady now. The trembling had stopped. It wasn't about money anymore, she realised. It was about shells—a tally on a board.

A target to be met and beaten.

2

Chapter 2 : Winter on Bad Bargain Lane

5th December 1916, York

Six or seven miles. More work. More Thomas. The feeling was like carrying an enormous stone in her gut, heavy and cold. She turned onto the desolate stretch of Bad Bargain Lane.

All colour had fled; only charcoal and grey remained, a world sketched in soot. The harsh Yorkshire winter curled around her, the wind scouring the open fields, its mournful song rising and falling, a distant hymn in her ears.

It wasn't only a physical chill to her weary bones but a heavy psychological weight pressing on her, seeking out the gaps in her worn coat. The blackened skeletal branches of the hedgerows rattled, their clicking a contrast with the hollow crack of the frost-hardened earth beneath her boots.

With every step, the damp turned soil—a smell of rot and bitter endings—rose to greet her, a sharp difference from the pungent factory's harsh chemical odour she'd left behind.

The lane, empty and desolate, vanished into the gloom. It stirred beneath the day's worries; old memories stirred, dragged up by aching joints and the wind's hollow cry. The lane tugged at her, forcing her to remember the girl who once walked it and the chain of choices that led from a grand house in Northamptonshire to this cold, empty stretch.

It was spring in 1898. The sun was a warm blessing across her features, and at fifteen, she practically skipped beside her father, James Jennings, her laughter as light and untroubled as the bluebells nodding in the verge.

Her small case, containing a spare dress and a universe of quiet hopes, swung from her hand. Service at Sulgrave House in Northamptonshire would be her ticket to a new life, beginning something better.

"None of your cheek, Sarah." His eyes were stern. James was weathered and limped from old wounds, but he held her arm with a firm grip. "Mr Daniels won't stand for your messing about."

Mr Daniels was the head butler at Sulgrave. He had once served with her father in the 14th Regiment of Foot during the Crimean campaign. James had saved his life, taking a bullet to the knee. This scullery maid position was Daniels's way of repaying the debt.

"I'll charm 'em, Dad," she said, tossing her braid with boundless confidence.

His scowl softened then, a hint of pride brightening his weary eyes. He saw his daughter's spirit—the same fire that now carried her through the freezing fog. He squeezed her hand as the train pulled into the station, a looming beast of steam and promise.

The air at Sulgrave was thick with beeswax and age. Fifteen-year-old Sarah was a mouse in a cathedral. In the curve of a soup tureen, a girl with conker-brown hair and a smudged cheek stared back, eyes stretched with a nameless loneliness.

The door swung open, revealing Michael, the under-butler. In his gleaming uniform, he exuded simple confidence. His voice was as smooth as cream, his words a solace for her homesick heart.

"A little scullery maid, promoted to guardian of the family silver?"

Sarah recalled the blush creeping up her neck, the flutter in her stomach as he'd leaned in, his arm brushing hers, the delicate fragrance of sandalwood making her dizzy. He had seen her—or so she'd thought.

"And you've got a smile that could melt the frost off the north wing."

She had drunk in his attention like a parched field after rain, too naïve to spot the practised charm, too hungry for kindness to question where it came from.

A year later, in that same polished office, the girl, so full of adventure, was gone—replaced by a sixteen-year-old trembling with shame, her apron bulging with a five-month secret now exposed.

Mr Daniels's voice was a blade of disappointment. "Who's the father, girl?"

Michael, summoned, slouched in, his charm gone, superseded by a cold indifference that shattered her heart.

"Was only a bit of fun, sir. I'm not marrying her."

His shrug dismissed her, their child, everything.

"You're both finished here," Daniels said, his face an impassive mask. "Sarah, I will send a letter to your father."

She was sent away in disgrace, the waxed floor seeming to sneer beneath her feet as she walked away. Her father rejected her, dismissing her with a glance and a slam of the door.

The naïve girl from Sulgrave was long dead, buried under seventeen years of hardship.

Later that year, sitting in Thomas's cart beside Annie, their trip to York was wordless. Both clung to the hope that the place on Hull Road might offer some salvation. As they approached, the gaunt grey stone façade of the institution rose before them, its narrow, barred windows like suspicious eyes staring down from three imposing storeys.

A high wall topped with jagged shards of glass embedded in mortar surrounded the stark grounds, where a few gnarled, leafless trees clawed at the sky.

Inside, the atmosphere was a chilling haze of bleach, boiled cabbage, and carbolic soap—and a faint sour whiff of unwashed linen and too many bodies. The corridors stretched long and dim, lit by dancing gas lamps that cast more shadow than light.

Her stomach churned as they passed a girl no older than herself, scrubbing a tiled floor in a side passage—movements mechanical, expression pale and vacant, knuckles raw and bleeding. Only the rhythmic scraping of her brush on the tiles broke the corridor's silence.

A matron in a stiff black dress emerged from a shadowed office, her expression a picture of severe authority, keys clinking at her waist with every sharp, decisive step. She laid out the rules in a voice as starched as her collar: work for "bastardy wages", a pittance that barely covered their keep and always equated to a debt to be paid in ceaseless toil.

Babies, she explained with chilling detachment, were often taken away once weaned, especially if the mother was deemed 'unsuitable' or the meagre Bastardy Order payments stopped. Sarah would be marked forever on the parish records. Her child—a liability, a stain on her.

At sixteen, she would have little say in keeping him.

As the matron droned on, a baby's cry pierced the hall—a thin, reedy wail quickly stifled. Sarah's limbs felt like ice. Her hands formed tight fists in her lap, nails digging into her palms. Annie, watching the matron with growing horror, caught sight of the young woman with the dead eyes and turned sharply on her heel.

"We're not leaving you here." Her voice was powerful. "I won't have you treated like cattle. A mother-and-baby home—it's a bloody prison."

Sarah made her vow that night on the farm. Lying under the cover of darkness, hand resting on her belly, she whispered to the child growing inside her, "I'll do whatever it takes. I will protect you."

The memory faded, but the vow remained, burning hot as ever in the freezing yard.

A bitter flavour filled her mouth, colder than the winter air, chasing the memory away. *Charm them? What a fool I was.* The taste was of Amatol, the sharp metallic taste a constant reminder of her present reality.

There was no skipping now. Each step was a jolt through her aching body. The pain that shot up her leg was a welcome distraction. The wind whipped a strand of hair across her face, stinging her eyes. She pushed it away with a gloved hand, her fingers clenching into a tight fist inside the worn fabric.

Sarah's gaze fell on a single, hardy weed poking through the frost at the lane's edge, its leaves brittle but unbowed.

Without breaking stride, she angled her path and forced her boot down, grinding the plant into the frozen earth. The satisfying crunch sent a hot shiver up her spine, a warmth that had nothing to do with the cold.

She caught her faint reflection in a dark, icy puddle on the lane. A thin woman in her mid-thirties stared back, her face weathered and worn down by years of hard work. Her long chestnut hair was escaping its pins, whipping around a face with a look that said nothing could bother her, eyes sharp, scanning the road ahead. *That's me,* Sarah thought, not with pity but with a kind of bitter pride. *Still here.*

Her hands finally stopped trembling for the first time since her shift finished. A faster pace developed, her boots' hard rhythm a defiant counterpoint to the earth. She neared the farm, nearing home?

By half-past eight, the fog had thinned enough to reveal the Browns' Warthill farmhouse, stooped and sagging on the horizon like it was tired of standing. The rusting hinges on the gate creaked as she went through.

Thomas's prized pigpens permeated the frosty air with a familiar stench, while the yard was a mire of frozen, churned mud. As she pushed the farmhouse door open, it breathed out a weak warmth tainted by steam and sour broth.

A scene of quiet misery played out in the kitchen. Her mother, Susannah, sat by the sputtering fire, her hands, once so busy, now engaged in aimless knitting, the needles clicking without purpose. Annie, her older sister, stood at the stove, stirring a pot of watery, thin porridge, her face a mask of weary concern.

"All right, Mam?" Sarah said, her voice harsh from the cold, as she bent to kiss her mother's papery cheek.

"Aye, fair to middling," came the reply. "Oh, love, you're an half-thin."

"That's Barnbow's doing." She forced a grin that felt brittle on her mouth. "Or your porridge not sticking to me ribs."

A faint chuckle, like the rustle of dry leaves, escaped her mother. Sarah could always make her laugh, regardless of the situation.

She perched at the opposite end of the table, putting as much distance between her and Thomas as possible. Annie placed a chipped bowl of porridge before her, leaning in close as she did, her voice a whisper against Sarah's ear.

"You're fair done in, our Sarah," Annie said, her eyes flicking towards Thomas, who kept his gaze fixed elsewhere. "Is it as bad as they say?"

"Aye, and then some," Sarah murmured, wrapping her cold hands around the warm bowl. "But the pay's good, lass. It'll be worth it in the end."

The quiet exchange, filled with unspoken worry and support, was over in a second. The porridge was thin and tasteless, but the warmth of her sister's concern settled in Sarah's chest, a small defence from the room's chill.

Thomas rustled the newspaper again, his presence overwhelming in the silence. Across the table, Sarah saw The Yorkshire Post's stark, black headlines.

STALEMATE ON THE ANCRE - WINTER GRIPS THE SOMME FRONT

VERDUN DEFENCES HOLD FIRM - FRENCH COUNTER-ATTACKS REPORTED

Smaller lines underneath read: *Heavy Losses Continue. Trench Conditions Worsen.*

Her stomach turned—the Somme. Though the worst of the fighting had passed, the name remained a raw wound. Every village had lost someone—a husband, a brother, a son. She thought of Cecil, grateful he was in the Navy and not the Army.

The headlines blurred—another town, another front. More men gone. More women waiting.

She stared into the chipped bowl of weak, pale porridge, the sight vastly different from the gleaming silver she once polished until her wrists ached. Thomas pushed his empty bowl away with a scrape that set Sarah's teeth on edge. He rose from his seat, giving her a single, dismissive glance before grabbing his coat from the peg. "Pigs need seeing to." And with another disapproving look at her worn-down factory boots, he stalked out, leaving the kitchen, the door slamming shut behind him.

A hush descended as he left, the room's tension melting into calmness. Annie, still at the stove, let her shoulders drop a fraction.

Sarah watched her sister, a small, weary figure enveloped in a cloud of steam. For the first time that morning, a heartfelt smile curved her lips. "You're about as tired as I feel, our Annie," she commented, her voice edged with familiar mischief.

Annie turned, managing a weak grin. "It's the damp. Gets in your bones."

"Never mind the damp," Sarah said, leaning forward conspiratorially. "I saw Thomas yesterday, trying to teach the pigs to line up for feeding like soldiers. In the end, they all rushed past him to the trough, knocking him on his arse."

A startled laugh escaped Annie, and she quickly clapped a hand over her mouth. "Shhh... He'll hear you."

"Let him." Her eyes flashed the same defiant spark the gang at Barnbow saw every night. "Might do him good to know we're not all sitting here moping."

Even their mother, Susannah, who sat quietly knitting by the fire, raised her head briefly, a flicker of amusement passing through her before returning to work. That small, shared laugh briefly warmed the cold kitchen.

"You're terrible, you are," Annie said, shaking her head.

"Aye," Sarah sighed. "But it keeps me from going mad."

Sarah's brief smile faded as she watched her sister return to the stove, her shoulders slumped with a familiar weariness. The shared warmth evaporated once again, chilling the kitchen.

"He wasn't always like this, was he, Annie?" Sarah spoke calmer, softer now. "So... hard, I mean."

Annie paused, her back to Sarah. She stirred the thin porridge in the pot, the scraping of the spoon loud in the quiet room. "No." Her voice was distant. "Not always."

Sarah shifted forward, her tone a conspiratorial whisper. "What was he like? Before."

Annie sighed, a shaky, weary sound. She rested the spoon and turned, leaning back against the stove. A distant look filled her eyes, suggesting a vision visible only to her.

"When we were first courting... he was a different man. Quieter, maybe, but a gentle quiet. He'd just buried both his parents, you know. Rebuilt this entire farm with his own two han ds..."

A sudden boot crunch on the icy mud outside made both women freeze. Annie's eyes darted to the window, her body rigid. The sound passed. She let out a breath she hadn't realised she'd been holding, and her voice dropped to a rushed whisper.

"He'd bring me apples from the old orchard. When I was carrying Lizzie, he carved her a cradle from an ash tree he'd felled. Beamed like a summer sun, he did, whispering to his pigs about the 'little master' who'd one day take over."

"He wanted a son," Sarah stated, the pieces fitting together with a cold finality.

"More than anything," Annie confirmed, her gaze shifting towards the kitchen door. "It was all he ever talked about—keeping the farm in the Brown name. A fifth generation. That was his dream."

"And then I came home."

Annie's gaze met hers, full of deep, complicated sorrow. "Oh, love. It wasn't the shame of it, not really. Not what you think."

She took a sharp breath as the yard gate squeaked on its rusted hinges. He was coming back.

Her words tumbled out now, fast and low. "It was seeing you with little Cecil. He was the son he didn't have. Your boy is a Jennings. We kept trying, see? Each time, another girl. Our Lizzie first, and then Sally."

She turned her head down, tracing a pattern on the dusty stovetop with her finger.

"It served as a constant reminder, every single day, of the one thing he craved and couldn't have. That's what broke him. The good man I married... he just curdled. Turned to something bitter."

Annie moved from the stove, her reflection finished. The latch on the rear door rattled.

"And I suppose... I stopped being the woman he married and became another of his disappointments."

She snatched the spoon and stirred the porridge as Thomas walked back in.

He hadn't heard the story but sensed the air shift as the women fell silent. He gave them a sharp, suspicious look before sitting down and picking up his paper again.

Annie and Sarah exchanged glances. A trace of a sad, knowing smile passed between them. *A poor excuse for cruelty*, Sarah thought, but it was all he had.

As Sarah ate, her gaze settled on Annie's youngest—little Sally, two last month—crouched by the hearth, her face lit with quiet wonder as she chased a drifting mote caught in a rare sliver of winter sun. She made a small, clumsy grab for it, lost her balance, and tumbled softly onto her bottom.

Surprise danced across her features, then a pure, innocent grin bloomed on her face, followed by a delighted gurgle of laughter.

The clean, uncomplicated sound pierced Sarah's exhaustion, sparking a memory so intense it was like a physical warmth in her chest, a ghost of sunlight against the oppressive gloom of the kitchen.

Cecil, at four years old. A sense of the distant past filled her in the farmhouse's small, clean yard. It was a bright, breezy summer afternoon, and she was hanging the washing; the fragrance of lavender filled the air.

He was helping—his small hands grasping at the damp, flapping sheets, his face locked in fierce concentration. A running grab at a billowing pillowcase sent him tumbling over the laundry basket and into a tangle of white linen. Moments later, he emerged with a sheet over his head like a ghost, giggling, his dark curls peeking out, grinning from ear to ear. His laughter was the most wonderful, joyous sound in the world.

She scooped him up, laughing with him, burying her face in his neck. It had the fragrance of soap, sunshine, and pure, uncomplicated boy as it filled her senses. There was no shame or hardship in that moment—only fierce, boundless love.

CRACK.

The thud of Thomas's newspaper slamming flat upon the table shattered the memory.

Sarah flinched, her heart jolting, the sun-drenched farmyard vanishing. She had been dragged back to the smoky kitchen, the smell of sour broth from the forever stew thick in the air. Thomas was staring at her, his eyes cold, completely unfeeling.

"Day's wasting." A dismissal and an order in one. "You'll see to the yard."

Sarah looked at his hard face, the laughing child, then at her trembling, discoloured hands. As the memory dissipated, snatched away by the coldness of the stone floor, what remained wasn't love, only duty—the burden of which was etched onto her skin. She pushed her bowl aside, the thin porridge unfinished, and rose from the table. The yard was waiting.

"Looking forward to it, Thomas. It's what I live for," she said, meeting his gaze.

"Less talk, more work," he sneered.

"Give her a chance to get warm, love. She only walked in a few minutes ago," Annie sighed.

"It's alright, Annie," Sarah answered, loosing a burdened sigh of her own. "I'll get on. The sooner I get started, the sooner I'll finish."

Sarah yanked on her most battered boots—the leather caked with layers of mud and muck no scrubbing could ever quite lift, the stains holding proof of years of servitude—and pulled on her threadbare coat. It offered little defence against the Yorkshire wind.

The stench from the pig pens clung to everything—her person, her belongings, her very being—a foul perfume impervious to the strongest washing.

Her first task—cleaning the troughs, as always. Hauling icy buckets from the well, her arms already sore from the factory shift, she dumped out the slimy, half-frozen remnants of yesterday's feed. The stench churned her stomach. Her hands, raw and tender from daily exposure to Amatol, burned as cold water seeped through her frayed gloves.

From the corner of her eye, she saw Thomas emerge from the barn doorway. He stopped and watched her for quite a while, arms crossed, his face a thunderous mask.

He said nothing. Instead, he strode over to the well, where the pail she had filled sat ready. With the toe of his heavy work boot, he gave the bucket a short, sharp nudge.

It didn't tip over, but a significant amount of icy water sloshed over the rim, splashing across the ground and soaking the hem of her skirt. His eyes showed a hint of grim satisfaction as he glanced from the spilt water to her, then he turned and vanished into the barn.

His silence was more damning than any shouted insult.

Next came mucking out the chicken coop, the air sharp with the pungent smell of droppings. As she scraped the last of it away, her thoughts wandered to the advertisement she'd seen in yesterday's paper—a Leeds flat. She'd torn out the listing, a fragile square of folded newsprint, and tucked it into her pocket. It was her secret. Her dream. A small promise of escape.

Thomas reemerged then, a slop bucket in hand, his face carved into its usual grim mask. He stopped a few feet away, eyeing her work with critical detachment.

"Still at it, are we?" His tone was heavy with accusation. "A few of us have actual farm work to be doing—not playing at it before running off to make a mess with gunpowder for a king's ransom."

Sarah straightened, her back aching, chicken muck congealed on her boots. The so-called "king's ransom" from Barnbow about covered the pound he demanded for her and her mother's keep, plus the pittance she managed to stash away.

"The coop's clean, Thomas. As you asked."

He sniffed. "Reckon young Lizzie could do better—and she's half your age. At least she doesn't come back stinking of chemicals and fancy ideas."

Fancy ideas. The words sparked within her thoughts. *Fancy ideas like a life for my son? Like not being your unpaid skivvy forever?*

Injustice, confinement, and dehumanisation overwhelmed her. Why did she stay here? Why did she endure this daily humiliation?

What was the alternative?

3

Chapter 3 : The Weight of a Seashell

5th December 1916, Leeds

The letter trembled in Lucy's hands, though it was only a memory, a ghost of ink on paper. Joe's scrawl, once so familiar, blurred in her mind's eye. *"Remember, Bridlington, Luce? Waves crashing, you chasing shells?"* His last words from the Somme, scratched onto a flimsy sheet before the guns silenced him forever...

The train jolted, knocking her forehead against the cold window. She flinched, blinking hard as the memory dissolved like mist into the harsh reality of the carriage. Across the aisle, two girls from another shed cackled, their laughter sharp and loud in the enclosed space.

"Look at her—almost launched herself out the window!" one snorted, elbowing her friend.

"That's what you get for snoring through shift, love!" the other said with a smirk.

"I weren't snoring," Lucy muttered, her cheeks burning. She turned away from them, pressing her face closer to the glass, and tugged her scarf higher as if it could shield her from their careless noise.

She swallowed against the lump that had taken up permanent residence in her throat—a knot sharp and gritty as coal dust.

The other girls in Lucy's gang—Sarah, with her loud, brassy confidence; Eliza, with her quiet, unshakeable strength; Nora, June, Mary, and Hilda—had all disembarked at earlier stations. Only Lucy continued to Leeds Central.

They seemed forged from brick and brass. Lucy, only a few months past seventeen, felt like fragile paper in comparison. She saw her reflection ghosted on the dark, grimy glass of the train window: a girl with the sort of pretty that comes with youth but with a naïve, scarred look now permanently etched on her features. She was short, but not scrawny—you could tell she had been brought up right, fed well, and loved. And now... now she was this. A frightened girl in a factory uniform. As if she could be easily torn, her grief was a secret she was terrified might show.

The train hissed into Leeds Central. Steam snaked through the platform like smoke escaping a wound. The other girls rose from their seats, groaning and stretching, some lighting cigarettes with a practised flick of flint and thumb. Their caps drooped, casting shadows across their worn faces.

Lucy lingered, watching their silhouettes slip past the fogged-up glass. Outside, the city crouched under winter's gloom, chimneys coughing black smoke into a sky now choked with grey.

She stepped out, her boots squeaking on the slick stone as she walked towards the tram queue. The cold gnawed at her knuckles until they felt hollow and distant.

Inside her coat pocket, she encountered the seashell from Bridlington. She closed her hand around it, its coolness a strange comfort. It was more a hook than an anchor.

The memory did not creep in; it roared back, a tidal wave of sunlight and laughter that drowned on the grimy platform. A rhythmic promise of a different train, on a different track, emerged from the rattling clatter of the tram, this time heading east towards the sea.

It was August 1914. The world was still whole.

The train to Bridlington rattled with infectious excitement, steam curling past the window—a beckoning finger, calling to her.

Lucy, fourteen, was all elbows and dreams. She had her nose pressed so hard against the glass, watching the unfolding East Yorkshire coast pass by in a blur. A vibrant embroidery of gorse, crumbling cliffs, and then, suddenly, the breathtaking glint of sea. That etched itself onto her very soul.

Opposite her, Joe—seventeen and brimming with cocky, unassailable youth—sprawled across the seat, his foundry cap tilted at a jaunty angle.

"You'll get your mug wet if you lean any closer, Luce." He nudged her and gave that grin—the one that always made their mother sigh and smile in the same breath.

Their dad sat behind his newspaper, chuckling to himself. He glanced up, sunlight reflecting off his glasses. Harold, nearing fifty, appeared to Lucy as a gentle giant. Beside him, their mam, Agnes, fussed with a wicker basket, her love manifesting in a gentle muttering about squashed sandwiches.

"Leave her be, Joe," Agnes said, her voice possessed of a softness that belied its firm, steadying nature.

"It's her first proper holiday. She's excited, is all."

A porter shouted, his voice gruff, and the memory vanished, leaving Lucy standing alone on the slick, cold stone. She pulled her hand out of her pocket and joined the queue for the tram.

The tram arrived with a crush of bodies packed in like sardines. The smell of the Leeds folks was a suffocating scent of wet wool and cheap tobacco, and the quiet, persistent dread that had possessed the city's bones these past months permeated the air.

Lucy squeezed into a corner, her arms clasped tightly around her bag, her breath misting the glass as Leeds dragged past.

Grief-stricken, she saw narrow alleys, wounds in the brickwork. A black wreath, already wilting, hung on the door of a terraced house. Many early-morning shops were closed, their dark, vacant windows mirroring a mournful gaze.

A soldier, his loose-fitting uniform on his thin frame, limped past, one sleeve pinned where an arm used to be. A nurse helped two more, pale and drawn, into a motorcar. No one looked twice. The war had shattered the shape of ordinary life.

The sight was too much. A wave of something—nausea mingled with a deep, bone-level weariness—consumed her. She closed her eyes tightly, trying to block out the image of the boy with the empty sleeve. Her hand, buried in her coat pocket, closed firmly around the seashell. Its surface was cool and smooth against her trembling fingers, the sharp, scalloped edge a tiny, familiar pain.

Consider them a desperate voice resonating within thoughts. Not now. Think of the sun. Think of the sea. The shell's touch, the memory it evoked, drew her from the city's bleakness to happier days.

Bridlington had hit them the moment they stepped off the train—salt, fish, and sea air sharp in their noses. The harbour churned with boats, jostling like corks on the tide. Flags cracked along Prince's Parade, brass music drifted from a distant bandstand, and crowds swarmed the promenade in straw hats and light dresses. News of the fighting appeared, remote and surreal.

The sand was a warm, golden carpet under Lucy's bare feet, the North Sea a cool caress against her ankles as she danced between the waves. Joe, trousers rolled to his knees, chased her with a dripping clump of seaweed, his laughter as loud and free as a gull's cry.

"You're daft as a brush!" she squealed, splashing him back.

Children built sandcastles nearby, their buckets as bright as new pennies. Donkeys plodded past, their riders shrieking with delight. It was a world of perfect, simple joy.

Then she saw him—a boy Joe's age, his cap shadowing his eyes, transfixed by a poster sprouting like a weed from the promenade railings: JOIN UP! ADVENTURE AWAITS!

Joe followed her gaze. His grin faded, replaced by a thoughtful contemplation that chilled her more than the North Sea water.

"Reckon I'd make a fine soldier," he said, tossing a pebble into the waves.

The noise of a loud, jarring clatter from the street outside shattered the memory, the rattle of the tram's iron wheels on the track pulling her back to reality. The sun-drenched beach dissolved, leaving behind the soiled, fogged-up glass of the tram window and the chill of her weary thoughts. The smell of salt had vanished, swallowed by the city's familiar blend of damp coal smoke and wet stone.

Joe wasn't next to her anymore. Only the cold remained—and the long journey home.

She passed Mr Fischer's tobacco shop, where her dad used to buy his twist, its windows now boarded up. The façade was a gutted shell of its former self—its front smashed by thugs who decided his name sounded too German.

"War doesn't only take our lads," her father had said, bitterness sharp in his voice. "It poisons entire streets."

Then, the tram clattered past Jameson's, the butchers. A single warm light glowed on the otherwise dark street. A queue had already formed outside, curled from its door, a long tail of weary hope. Lucy's heart gave a slight, painful lurch. The rumour mill at Barnbow had it that the butchers might have bacon. Everyone in Leeds had heard the same rumour, or so it seemed.

I could try, she thought. It could be something that could coax a genuine smile from her dad. It had been so long since she had seen it: the smile Joe prompted, a significant departure from the pale reflection now etched onto his features.

The thought of her father—his quiet, hollowed-out grief—cut like a fresh wound. He tried to stay strong for them, she knew, but she saw it in the way he stared into the fire. His eyes were often fixed on a distant memory far beyond the flames. He drifted in memories and regrets, haunted by warnings no one had heeded.

The final Bridlington morning dawned with a sharp, unrelenting light.

Later, as Joe cast their father's fishing line into the North Sea, Harold squatted beside him, his eyes fixed on the endless horizon.

"Stories don't mention the stench of dead bodies." His voice was burdened by a history Joe couldn't yet know. "Burning hair. Shite in your boots. Men screaming for their mothers."

He told Joe about his grandfather, a veteran of Wellington's wars, who would wake up screaming most nights. Joe smiled—that soft, warm smile of his—full of youthful certainty and the headlines he believed.

"Why not? Someone's got to stand up. Might as well be me."

Harold turned back towards the sea, his voice lost to the wind. "Aye. And someone's got to carry what's left of you home, son."

The memory sharpened, narrowing to a single, perfect detail: the seashell she'd found that morning, its pearly curve gleaming in the sun as Joe laughed.

"Keep it, Luce. It could be good luck. Might bring us back here next year."

A sound, far from the gentle lapping of waves, startled her back into the present moment. The sun-kissed shore vanished, replaced once again by the frost-laced window and the suffocating smell of wet wool. Joe's laughing face dissolved, leaving only the reflection of her own, pale and haunted. *Next year...* The statement was a fresh, sharp blade in her heart. There would be no next year. Not for him.

On impulse, Lucy rang the tram bell, stepped into the cold street, and stood in the queue for the butchers.

The memories of that last bright summer cut through her like glass. The city's silence, its shared grief, the quiet wait for something—anything—became its kind of mourning. Her joy felt cruelly mocking, yet her mind relentlessly sought the moment the light dimmed.

Back in Bridlington on that final evening at the Spa Pavilion, its lights twinkling like fallen stars against the darkening water, the war ceased to be a whisper and became a roar. A recruiting sergeant in khaki, his voice booming over the dance band, called for men to show they were "no cowards".

The room erupted. Men stamped their feet, flushed with beer and patriotic fervour. Joe straightened, jaw clenched, eyes fixed on the crowd surging forward.

Lucy grabbed his sleeve, her tone a forceful, desperate whisper. "You're not going. You are too young."

He was snatched from the precipice by their father. "Enough, lad. Have a dance with your sister."

Joe hesitated for a second before his familiar grin broke through. He pulled her onto the floor, spinning her with a clumsy, big-brotherly charm until she giggled, her plaits flying behind her.

Wrapped in music and him, the war became just a word for a moment. Not yet a thief. The small shell held in her hand pressed into her palm like a secret promise.

"We'll come back," she said.

Joe nodded, but the recruiter's fire still burned beneath his smile, adventure glinting in his eyes—that call.

The memory retreated from her mind, leaving Lucy shivering in the biting cold, the seashell still in her hand, clutched tight in her pocket.

The line for Jameson's butcher shop moved at a glacial pace. A dozen women stood ahead of her, their shoulders hunched, their breath misting in the air—a silent congregation of weary, hopeful women.

The shop's scent—sawdust mingling with rich meat—was intoxicating, the aroma of a finer existence. The line gossip now was of no bacon left, all gone. A hushed ripple of unease passed through the women ahead of her as they whispered about it.

It was her turn. She stepped forward into the shop's comforting embrace, her eyes immediately finding the handwritten sign hanging from a hook: NO BACON. Her heart sank. Still, she held out the few coins she had, her voice small.

"A little sausage, please, Mr Jameson. And a penn'orth of dripping, if you have it."

Mr Jameson, a large man with a face as ruddy as his prime cuts, offered her a gentle smile. He knew her father. He knew about Joe.

"Aye, lass, that we can do." His voice was a quiet rumble. He wrapped two thick sausages in paper with practised efficiency. "Tell your dad I was asking after him. It's a terrible business."

"Thank you, Mr Jameson. I will," Lucy whispered, taking the tiny, valuable package.

Clutching her shopping—a win against the gloom—she ventured into the cold. Giving her father something, anything, brought a spark of purpose. But as she proceeded, the task behind her, grief crept in again. Her father's worn face rose in her thoughts—not just a memory but a weight, heavy enough to steal her breath.

She found herself inside the Bell Row kitchen, the air dense not with frost but with crushing summer 10th of July heat and an unspoken, terrible anxiety.

The grandfather clock in the hall ticked with an unnerving loudness, each second a heavy taunt against the fragile quiet of their waiting.

Everyone knew what transpired that first day on the Somme. The newspapers printed endless casualty lists, adding more names to the tally each morning. Every evening, they combed through them—her mother's finger following each column, her father reading over her shoulder, both holding their breath until they reached the bottom and didn't find Joe.

No news is good news, *they told each other—a fragile mantra against the growing surge of fear.*

"He'll be alright, won't he, Dad?" Lucy asked, her voice barely a whisper.

"Aye, pet. He's a sharp lad, our Joe," Harold replied. But he avoided her gaze, and the ensuing quiet said everything he couldn't.

Her mind shifted, seeing the moment not from inside the house but from a street perspective.

A boy was walking towards them. Fourteen years old, his uniform itching in the heat, his leather satchel heavy with brown envelopes from the Ministry.

When he signed up for the shillings, he hadn't realised that he'd become a messenger of grief, a man who heard the noise of families breaking. He paused at house number seven. The door, its paint peeling in the heat, stood crooked in its frame. He knocked.

The sound shattered the quiet inside the kitchen. Lucy froze, her pen clattering onto the table where she'd been trying to write a story. Her mother's hand flew to her mouth, a stifled cry escaping. Like a man wading through mud, her father rose with effort and yanked the sticking door open.

He stood there, a hollow-faced man in his mid-forties, looking at the boy. The young lad held out the envelope.

"Telegram, sir."

Harold took it with care, his hands already trembling. He didn't open it. He turned back inside, the door swinging half shut behind him. He walked again to the kitchen, the unopened envelope in his hand. He looked at Agnes, then Lucy, his face as grey as the Leeds dawn.

"It's Joe," he rasped, and the air in the house collapsed, heavy as coal.

Agnes sank into a chair, her apron twisted in her fists. Lucy's heart pounded—a scream trapped in her chest.

"Dad?" she said, a shallow breath of a sound.

Her mother didn't need to hear any more. A wail tore from her throat, guttural and raw, a sound of pure, animal grief that only a mother can make when she loses a child, a cry that splits the world in two.

4

Chapter 4 : A Debt of Loyalty

5th December 1916

Skinner's voice rang through the still kitchen, each word a blow. The sum was an absurd mountain she was meant to move with her bare hands. How was she supposed to find that kind of money when she couldn't even find a carrot or turnip for the pot? When the price of coal gnawed at her sleep long after her shift ended?

The injustice sat in her mouth like blood—hot, metallic, undeniable. Skinner, wrapped in his warm coat and sweet-smelling pipe smoke, held the power to snuff out the fragile warmth she fought to keep alive. He could throw them into the frozen street over a debt Stan had taken on to feed them during the strike—a debt borne of loyalty, not laziness.

The house was still and cold, and the stove was dead, with no warmth left in its belly. Eliza knelt beside it, scraping the last bits of coal from the scuttle.

Three matches flared and died before a fourth caught, coaxing a weak flame into life. Shadows danced across the bare walls of the cramped kitchen.

A feeling of queasiness rose, hot and bitter, but she swallowed it down. Her mind darted back to that meeting in Captain Miller's office only weeks ago.

The room remained cold in her mind. She remembered how the grimy windowpanes distorted the figures of the women working below, how the captain gave his rather clipped announcement: "A penny a shell bonus for every single one produced above the five-hundred quota."

It had the breath of a lifeline then—a drop of hope, a desperate possibility at a few extra shillings that might mean coal for the grate or shoes for Bobby. But even as the words left his mouth, she'd seen the trap in Miller's gaze—neutral, polished, and far too deliberate to be chance.

"It allows us to identify our most productive assets... measure peak efficiency."

A test.

A warning.

Something deep inside her twisted. She remembered leaving that office, the other charge hands shuffling out with a new, nervous hum. She could still see Miss McDowell, her face showing, her arms crossed tight, waylaying Mr Henderson in the corridor.

McDowell's voice hushed but with a blade of urgency: "This is dangerous, Mr Henderson. This is a recipe for disaster. One spark, one mistake under pressure, and it's not lost time—it's lives."

And Henderson's tired, rumpled sigh, his resignation. "The matter is out of our hands, Miss McDowell. Ministry orders... We're to follow and pray nobody makes a mistake."

Pray nobody makes a mistake... Was that the best Henderson's come up with? A prayer? It was a deep knife twisting deeper with every shell she filled. And now, with Skinner's threat also ringing in her ears, it became even more fragile. Something ready to shatter with a slight touch. The factory demanded speed for shillings; Skinner demanded shillings for their home.

And she, Eliza, stood in the deadly crossfire. For her children to keep their home, she would have to push her girls to the dangerous edge. She would have to make them chase that bonus.

It was her only hope.

Like the rest of the house, the kitchen displayed modesty—enough room to cook, eat, and exist.

A working-class woman's world, where nothing went to waste—not food, not space, not time. With effort, Eliza pulled off her boots and crossed the slate floor in her stockings.

The kettle was empty. She filled it and set it on the stove, teeth chattering, then climbed the stairs. It was already half-past eight. The children were still asleep. The staircase creaked beneath her, each step a whispered prayer to avoid waking her husband's mother.

In the bedroom, Robert, fourteen, Beth, seven, and Stanley, eighteen months, lay tangled together under a single quilt on the sagging bed. Robert, a pit labourer these past few months, slept curled in a tight ball, coal dust smudged behind his ear. His long johns were patched, his socks missing.

"Mam?" His eyes fluttered open.

"Up you get, Bobby, love," Eliza whispered, brushing his forehead.

His hair, once soft, was coarse now with coal grime.

"Time for work. Pit won't wait."

He nodded and sat up.

She gazed upon her boy, shoulders broad like his father's, which belied his age. He had a smudge of jam at the corner of his mouth; a weary confusion in his eyes revealed the boy still hiding beneath the man's responsibilities.

Eliza turned to Beth, shaking her daughter awake. "Come on, lass. School today." She tucked a stray curl of mousy hair behind her ear.

Beth stirred, blinking as she woke. "Miss said we need a new slate, Mam. Mine's cracked."

Eliza's stomach twisted. Another expense. A slate. *Where from, love? Pennies don't grow on trees, not even Barnbow pennies.* But she smiled instead.

"We'll see what we can do. Things might be easier after Friday's pay."

The girl was bright and quick with her letters and sums. Eliza was determined to give her more chances than she ever had. Stanley—'Baby Stan'—slept on, warm and damp against the frozen air.

Eliza lifted him with gentle hands, his breath steady against her neck, tiny fists curling into her shoulder. "Shhh, my bairn." She pressed a kiss to his soft curls.

That little body was her lifeline and her burden.

Robert dressed, helping Beth find her boots among the mess underneath the bed. He spoke in a hushed voice, careful not to wake their grandmother. "Mam, they're talking about doubling shifts... Lads aren't happy."

Eliza swallowed a fresh rush of worry. With the war draining seasoned hands from the pits, boys his age were worked to the bone.

More shifts meant more danger... but also more shillings. It was a bitter equation.

"Take care of yourself," she said.

"Don't be taking risks for any man. Your father always says, 'Better a live coward than a dead hero in the shadows.'"

"Aye, Mam. I'm careful."

Eliza carried Baby Stan down the stairs. Stepping over the squeaky floorboard on the landing. Her mother-in-law's door remained shut—a small mercy. When she entered the kitchen, the kettle hissed, steam fogging the window.

She brewed tea, weak as dishwater, and dipped bread crusts into it for her breakfast. For Beth and Robert, she sliced the stale loaf, also packing Robert's bait box with bread, cheese, and two hard biscuits—"Pit's hungry work," Stan used to say.

The same lunch from when he was twelve. She sent the children out—Beth to school, Robert to the pit—promising stew for tea.

"Back by nine, Bobby," she called after him, her voice soft but firm.

The words, meant as comfort, lingered in the frigid air long after the door clicked shut behind them—a proper stew. The promise now weighed heavily on her. With Baby Stan settled on a rag rug by the hearth, gnawing on a wooden peg, Eliza went to the pantry. It was little more than a shallow cupboard set into the wall, and the chill that breathed out when she unlatched it was as cold as the yard outside.

Her heart sank. The shelves were a sparse scene of want: a half-empty bag of oats, a single, lonely onion with its skin beginning to sprout, and a handful of wrinkled potatoes in a hessian bag. At the back, wrapped in muslin, sat the small wedge of salt pork she'd hoped would last the week. It was not enough—not for a real stew. It wasn't a meal that could fight off the cold and put meat on her children's bones.

She shut the door, a familiar icy dread creeping up her spine. It wasn't about tonight's tea. Her gaze fell on the coal scuttle beside the stove.

It was empty, holding nothing but black dust and a few chips of coal that wouldn't last the afternoon, let alone the long, bitter night.

Suddenly, the sheer weight of it threatened to crush her. The exhaustion of the factory, the endless, grinding worry for Stan, and now this—it was too much. Her hands trembled, and she pressed them hard against her apron, fighting back the urge to sit down and weep.

But then she looked at Baby Stan, oblivious on the floor, and the despair solidified into something else. A cold, hard anger. She was determined not to let that man win. She would not let her children feel the bite of a December wind because of his greed.

Her mind, a frantic shuttle, returned to the factory. To the tally board. To the bonus. A penny a shell. It had sounded like a pittance. At that moment, it was the only thing standing between them and ruin. The risk, the speed, the groaning press—they weren't dangers anymore. They were tools. They were the only tools she had.

But the factory was hours away. Tonight's tea was a more immediate battle. She couldn't bear the thought of Beth and Robert coming home, hungry from school and the pit, to a meal of watery porridge. The promise had been made. She would have to keep it.

Pulling her thin shawl close around her shoulders, she stepped out into the biting cold of Albany Terrace. The corner shop, run by Mrs Higgins for thirty years, was two doors down, its bell jingling a cheerful, lying welcome as she pushed the door open. The air inside was a warm, cluttered haven of scents—carbolic soap, sawdust, and the faint, sweet aroma of the aniseed twists in the big glass jar on the counter.

Mrs Higgins, whose face was as welcoming as an apple and eyes that didn't miss a thing, raised her gaze from the counter.

"Eh up, Lize, love. You alright, how's Stan?"

"For a bit of rest before the night shift," Eliza said, forcing a brittle smile. She approached the counter, her heart beginning a fast-paced drumbeat. She hated this. She hated the feel of asking, of being a burden.

"I was wondering, Mrs Higgins... if I could get a few things on tick? Till Friday. The wages from the factory... they're steady."

Mrs Higgins's friendly expression faltered—so slightly it was almost imperceptible. She sighed long and wearily. She picked up a cloth and began wiping the counter.

"Eliza," she started, kindness woven through each word, which was worse than a flat refusal. "You know I would if I could. I've known your Stan since he was a lad stealing gobstoppers. But times are hard for everyone. My suppliers want to be paid on the nail. And I heard... well, I heard Mr Skinner was doing his rounds this morning."

A silence stretched between them. The embarrassment was a hot flush on Eliza's cheeks. Of course, the entire street knew. A town crier might have announced Skinner's visit as well.

"I can pay you Saturday morning, first thing," said Eliza, her voice a desperate whisper. "A few potatoes. A carrot, maybe. Whatever you have."

Mrs Higgins looked at her, her gaze softening with a pity that made Eliza want to scream. She looked around her small, cramped shop at the half-empty shelves. With another heavy sigh, she relented.

"Alright, love," her voice low and resigned.

"Go on, then. But what do you need for tonight's stew? And not a word of this to anyone else, mind. I can't have the whole town thinking I'm running a charity."

"Thank you, Mrs Higgins," Eliza said, the comfort so powerful it left her light-headed. "I won't forget it."

She took the small, precious vegetables—two carrots and a turnip that were soft but would do—and hurried out of the shop, her cheeks still burning. The kindness was a balm, but the shame was a fresh wound. It was another debt, another obligation, another link in the chain that bound her to this desperate fight for every penny.

With a new, grim resolve, Eliza returned to the larder. She took out the five small potatoes and the single onion. It wasn't the stew she'd promised, but at least it would be hot. It would be something. As she carried them to the sink, her movements shed their weariness—now sharp, efficient, the actions of a woman preparing for battle.

The letterbox clanged. Eliza froze, a piece of bread crust halfway to her mouth. Her heart didn't leap. Not at first. It stopped.

For a terrifying second, all the air left the room. A letter from France. It could be anything. It could be from a chaplain, full of careful, devastating words. It could be from a friend, the handwriting unfamiliar, the news unbearable. She walked to the door as if wading through water, her hand trembling as she reached for the single letter on the mat.

And then she saw it. The handwriting. Not a stranger's, not a chaplain's. *His*. Stan's familiar, cramped scrawl, the loop on the 'E' of her name a little too big, like always. Her breath came back in a rush, a dizzying wave of relief so strong her knees almost buckled. She carried it back to the table, her fingers tracing the smudged postmark. The paper felt fragile, and she could almost smell the journey on it—the damp of the boats, the grime of the mail sacks.

It was a fragment of him, a ghost of his touch that had somehow found its way home. She smoothed the envelope on the table, hands still trembling, and read:

My dearest Eliza,

I hope this finds you well and not too tired.

Things here are slow but steady. We lost a lad last week. God help me, it never gets easier. Yes, I'm eating well enough, love.

Don't worry. I think of you every night.

I know things must be hard with Mam, the bairns, and Skinner sniffing about. But you're doing more than most generals. You're holding the line from your side of the Channel.

Tell our Bobby I'm proud of him. Can't wait to see the man he's becoming.

I miss your hands. Your laugh. The sound of you banging pans when you're cross. Keep your chin up. With the way things are going, I don't see this show lasting much longer than it already has.

Here's hoping.

All my love,

Stan

Eliza read each line as if the words themselves might vanish from the page. Seventeen years married, and still, his voice, his humour, wrapped around her like the warmest wool. She thought of the boy he once was instead of the tired man in the letter. She saw him at sixteen again, grinning through a film of coal dust, the lad who'd once made her laugh outside the company office.

That grin. It pulled her back, the crude scent of her cramped kitchen fading, replaced by strong black tea and ink. The rattle of the windowpane became the pit carts clattering right outside.

23rd April 1901, Pontefract

The Prince of Wales Colliery sprawled across Pontefract's edge, its slag heaps black against a bruised sky. Sixteen-year-old Eliza sat in the colliery office, her pen scratching wages into ledgers, each figure as neat as her pinned-up hair. The room smelled of ink and tea, while the clatter of pit carts rattled through the open window.

Stan Wren, also sixteen, pushed through the door, pit tallies clutched in coal-stained hands. His eyes, bright despite the dust, found hers.

"Miss Eliza, you'll ruin those dainty hands with all that scribbling," he teased, leaning close to point at the figures.

She flushed, hiding a smile. "Better than mucking out pit ponies, Stan Wren. Got your tallies right this time, or shall I fix 'em again?"

He laughed, bold and warm. She felt a change within her, like a mechanism hitting true.

At the St. George's Day dance in the Town Hall that night, he found her under gaslights, his boots polished, his shirt patched but proud.

They waltzed, her cotton dress brushing his calloused hands. They walked and chatted, and by the River Aire, he stole a kiss while sharing a pie from a street cart.

"You're my lass now, Eliza," he said.

She didn't argue.

With Eliza's father's permission, they courted through spring, walking cobbled lanes. Stan spun tales of cave-ins and pit ponies with names like Bess. Eliza spoke of a shop—sometimes even a house with a proper range—her voice fierce despite her mam's warnings:

"He's a pit lad, nowt more. You'll be scrubbing coal dust forever."

But Eliza saw Stan's heart—steady, kind, fierce for her. He saved sixpence a week for a ring, proposing under a gaslit bridge in winter, his breath clouding the bitter air.

"Marry me, love," he said, hands rough but warm. "I'll work my bones to dust for you."

First in the pit's darkness, and now in the mud of France. A chill settled in her chest. Now it was her turn. Her turn to grind herself down in a place that reeked of poison instead of coal to hold the line he trusted her to keep.

But the boy who had proposed beneath that gaslit bridge wasn't the man who'd written the letter lying on her table.

The war had scraped the softness from his words, even in his efforts to sound cheerful. She read it between the lines—a weariness more profound than coal dust, a hardness born of horrors he'd never speak aloud.

The boy had promised her a life. This man was promising only to survive.

She looked down at his letter, then at her yellow-stained hands. He was holding his line in the tunnels of France; she was holding hers here, in the heart of Barnbow's roaring noise. They were both fighting in the trenches now.

She folded the letter, its creases as familiar as the lines on her own hands, and pressed it to her lips.

5

Chapter 5 : The Cuckoo in the Nest(Part 1)

5th December 1916, Warthill

She gripped the handle of her shovel, her knuckles white. The memory hadn't filled her with despair; it had filled her with an iron-willed purpose. She worked with a new ferocity, her movements sharp and efficient.

Every swing of the axe, every bucket hauled, was a blow struck for her son and the two clean rooms in Leeds she could see so clearly in her mind.

But as the morning wore on, her body betrayed her will.

With a queasy slant, she leaned against a rough timber post, her breath escaping in ragged gasps.

Her hands trembled on the wood, not from the cold but from something more profound, harder to shake. She hid it as best she could. Pressing her fingers to her temples, she tried to dull the gum ache and the ringing in her ears that Barnbow had gifted and never taken back.

The physical distress brought with it another memory, sharp and unsolicited as the factory fumes themselves.

A vision of Rose Turner appeared in her thoughts, as clear as if she were standing there in the yard, her skin bearing that unmistakable, lurid yellow hue, her bright hair bleached almost white where the powder had settled.

Sarah was watching her that night, a knot of unease tightening in her chest. Rose looked worse than usual under the unforgiving lights, her hands trembling as she tried to guide a shell.

Then, the almost imperceptible sway, the way Rose's breath caught and stalled over the factory din before she... dropped. Not a cry, not a stumble, but a sudden, sickening crumpling, like a puppet whose strings had been cut.

The dull thud of her body hitting the concrete floor sliced through the noise of the machinery. For a heartbeat, there was the sight of her, a crumpled heap of blue smock upon the ground. Sarah stood frozen. Hilda gasped. Nora's eyes flashed with alarm. From across the room, Ann Price sneered, "Told you she was weak."

Then Eliza's voice cracked out, cutting like a knife. "Stop the line!" She was already moving, dropping to her knees beside Rose. "She's out," Eliza said. "Sarah, June—help me."

Together, they lifted Rose's limp body, the noxious fumes clinging to her. They half-carried, half-dragged her to the medical hut.

A squat nurse, her sleeves rolled up, didn't bother to look away from her ledger. "Rose Turner. Filling team, Room 42," Eliza said, breathing hard. "Collapsed. Skin's gone golden."

"Set her down," the nurse demanded.

They eased Rose onto a narrow cot, the wool blanket already stained from the yellow dust surrounding them.

The nurse pressed two fingers to Rose's wrist. "She's breathing, but not right," she said. "I will call the doctor. She'll need the hospital."

The nurse returned to her ledger, scribbling a line—name, section, time—as if Rose were another number.

"If she doesn't wake proper in the hour, she's off to Leeds."

They left her there, surrounded by the silence of the hut and the scratch of the nurse's pen. Whispers of jaundice and liver failure followed them. They returned one woman short, and Eliza stepped into Rose's post herself, her countenance a grim mask, pushing them to make the quota.

Sarah could still see Rose's pale face against the stained blanket, another victim fallen, another space at the bench, terrifyingly empty.

Another lass fallen, she had thought then, the words a bitter echo of factory whispers. *Marked. We're all bloody marked by it. How long before it's my turn to drop, to be carted off like damaged stock?*

The thought was so cold it froze her to the spot. She slumped against the rough timber post of the woodshed, her breath coming in ragged, shallow gasps. A wave of dizziness, familiar and unwelcome, made the bleak farmyard tilt at a sickening angle. *A moment*, she thought. *One moment to allow the world to stop spinning.*

Thomas

The barn door creaked open. Emerging, Thomas carried a swill pail in each hand. Then he stopped. He saw her there, her face pale, struggling for breath.

For a fleeting second, the hard lines of his face softened. He didn't see the defiant factory girl but a younger, more fragile version of his wife's sister. A thought, unwelcome and weak, flickered through his mind—to tell her to go inside, sleep before her shift.

But it was extinguished as quickly as it came, smothered by a familiar, sour resentment. He'd been wrestling with a stubborn sow since five this morning, his own back aching with a pain that never left him. She could earn her keep.

Their eyes met across the yard for a long, heavy second. He didn't shout. He didn't speak. His expression was a flat, cold assessment, as if she were a lame horse or a patch of blighted crops. There were no concerns. There was only contempt.

He slammed the trough into place, metal clanging in the cold. He'd caught the look she gave when he nudged the bucket—defiant, just like her mother. The Jennings's arrogance stemmed from a refusal to accept their position. He'd taken them in out of duty, for his wife's sake, but any gratitude had long soured into what he saw as entitlement.

Thomas Brown worked best when he was fuelled by anger. The heat of it settled in his gut, a familiar fire that warmed him against the biting Yorkshire wind. He moved through the pig pens, his boots sinking into the thick, familiar mire. This was his domain. The pigs were simple, candid creatures.

They understood their place. They knew the hand that fed them. They didn't fill the house with the chemical stink of a factory or carry themselves with an unearned pride bought with "Barnbow brass".

He scattered the feed, the pigs snorting and shoving with a greed he could understand. It was straightforward. Honest. He thought of her in the yard, her hands stained that poisonous yellow, and the memory of a conversation in Pocklington surfaced, sudden and intrusive.

At the Pocklington livestock market, surrounded by mud and stink, the gossip started—sharp and never-ending, cutting into Thomas's pride. Farmers' wives muttered "Jenning's girl" and "bastard boy," their eyes full of judgement.

Shopkeepers said in tight, careful voices: "No ring, no shame—thinks she owns the place." One farmer's mocking laugh stung the most: "Brown's got a cuckoo in his nest, eh?"

Thomas stood frozen, his face tight with rage as the insults rained down.

At first, he tried to brush it off—lifted his chin, focused on the pigs—but the laughter clung like muck to his boots.

One butcher, a man he'd known since school, clapped him too hard on the back. "Watch yourself, Tom. Raise someone else's pup, and folk'll think it's yours."

That stuck.

With the memory gone, it left him looking back towards the farmhouse. His house. His land. His name was carved into the deed. But it felt... invaded. Compromised. For a moment, his anger at Sarah was complicated by a different, older ache.

He remembered Annie from years ago, before all this. Before the bitterness had set in, he remembered her laughing, her face flushed from the sun as they'd worked together to mend a fence, her hand warm and capable in his. He had won her affections with a quiet, steady resolve, and she had seen the good man in him, the man who adored this plot of land more than anything.

He kicked at frozen mud, bitterness rising—that man he used to be was gone, buried under years of letdowns. Sarah, turning up pregnant, had started it all: the whispers, the silence that crept between him and Annie like thorns. He blamed her—her bastard boy—for wrecking the dream he once clung to.

Sarah believed her factory wages made her independent, but to him, they were just another sign she didn't fit—another thing beyond his control. Every shilling she brought home reminded him of the son he never had and the burden he resented being asked to carry.

His resentment wasn't just about the work or the money; it was about how he was treated. It was about the name... the future. It was about the sour, bitter knowledge that the legacy he tirelessly worked for—this soil, this farm, this life—would not pass to a son of his own.

He threw the last of the feed into the trough with a sharp, angry flick of his wrist. The pigs squealed and fought for their share. At least they were grateful.

With a shake of his head, a gesture of pure dismissal, he turned and stalked back towards the barn, his heavy boots crunching on the frozen mud.

6

Chapter 6 : The Cuckoo in the Nest (Part 2)

He hadn't said a word to her, but the message was as clear as a slap to the face: '*You are weak. You are failing. You are not worth my time.*'

The silent dismissal, the sheer indifference to her struggle, was a feeling she knew all too well. The sense of being invisible, of her hard labour being seen but not valued, of being treated as something less than human.

Her throat started burning, wrenching her away from the memories. The taste was metallic—the taste of the factory, the taste of poison. *This is how it starts*, a crisp voice whispered in her mind.

A bit of shaking, a sick gut... like Rose. She saw her again, a collapsed pile of blue smock on the grey floor. For one horrifying second, Sarah felt the strength drain from her legs.

But then anger, hot and clean, surged in its place. Anger at the place that marked them like cattle, anger at Thomas for making this her only option.

No, she thought, her jaw clenching so hard it ached. *I'm not Rose. I'm not some poor, fallen lass. I'm Cecil Jennings's mother, and I've a flat to secure.*

The thought of the flat, of a clean room with a door she could lock against the world, was a lifeline. Clinging to it, her hand dove into her coat pocket, her fingers closing around the worn, soft fabric of Cecil's blue handkerchief.

The familiar texture was an anchor in the dizzying wave of sickness and fear. The embroidered "CJ" stitches were a faint, raised map under her thumb, a tangible link to the boy who was her world.

The feel of the cloth was a trigger, pulling her from the grim yard into a memory so vivid it was a balm to her frayed nerves.

In 1914, at the age of fifteen, he enlisted in the Royal Navy, bound for HMS Ganges, the training ship.

"I can't stay, Mam." He clutched her tight. "Not with him."

Sarah's heart shattered, but she nodded, pressing her St. Christopher medal—hung on a gold chain, a gift from her father before she had left for Northamptonshire, from this very station some sixteen years earlier—into his palm. "For protection." The cool metal was a tether to her love.

Cecil's eyes glistened as he drew a blue handkerchief from his pocket, embroidered with "CJ" in careful stitches, crafted in a back-alley shop in Pocklington with his scant pennies.

"For you, Mam," he said, voice breaking.

They clung to each other, the gifts a vow against Thomas's cruelty, until the train's whistle tore them apart. Sarah's tears fell only once the smoke faded, his absence gnawing at her bones. That night, she wept alone in the darkness of her room.

She knew his leaving was the right thing to do. Not for him. For both of them.

A wave of dizziness brought her back to the present. The memory slipped away, leaving a deep, aching tenderness that only made her more determined.

That handkerchief wasn't a memory of his getaway but of how he had endured Thomas's house for her, that she now endured Barnbow for him. Her fingers brushed the talismans in her pocket—the scrap of newsprint advertising the flat and the folded letter from Ganges. With purpose, she stepped into the farmhouse kitchen.

The hearth sputtered, its smoke curling like the fog she'd trudged through that morning. Cecil, now seventeen, hadn't returned. His Navy letters were sparse but alive. She sat by the fire, unfolding the worn paper. She didn't need to read the letter; she knew it by heart. But she needed to see the words on the page, to feel the tangible proof of his promise, to hear his voice in her head again.

My dearest mam,

I hope this letter finds you well and that you aren't worrying too much. The training here is hard graft, no doubt about that, but it's proper work and they're making an honest man of me. The instructors shout a lot, but I'm learning to tie knots I never knew existed, and I can now climb the rigging like a monkey. You should see it, Mam. When you're up high, you can see the entire world, all the water and sky. It makes you feel you could sail anywhere.

The food's not a patch on your stews, but it fills a hole. There's a lad in my mess from Leeds, and we have a good laugh sometimes, taking the mick out of the lads from down south. So, you see, I'm getting on alright.

The best part, though, is the pay. It's not a king's ransom, but I'm saving every penny I can. Proper saving, in a tin under my bunk. It won't be long, I swear it. You're in my thoughts every night, and I promise I'll have enough put by soon. Then I'll come and get you away from that place, away from him. We'll have our little room somewhere, like you always wanted—a proper home for us.

I keep the St. Christopher you gave me tucked in my breast pocket. I hold on to it tight when I think of you. You hold on a little longer, Mam.

All my love, always,

Your son, Cecil

Sarah clung to the dream of a home of her own, a room for Cecil, an encouragement to bring him back. Barnbow's pay—twice that of a maid's wage—promised it, despite the factory's toll. Her joints groaned and her head spun, but she would endure—penny by penny.

She pulled the scrap of paper from her pocket, the newsprint worn soft from her constant handling. As her eyes scanned the words, "Two rooms, city centre," her eyes blurred, making the letters swim for a terrifying second.

Her hands shook uncontrollably, a constant trembling that wouldn't cease. She willed her hand to be still, to obey, but the tremor only intensified—a terrifying flutter she couldn't hide or control.

The poison is winning.

The thought was cold and sharp. Time was running out. This wasn't a dream of escape; it was a race.

Leeds.

The word gleamed in her mind like a new-minted coin, a proper home to lure Cecil back—the seventeen-year-old adrift within the ranks of the Royal Navy—to bring him home after two years away.

7

Chapter 7 : A China Doll in a Boiler Room

5th December 1916, Leeds

The walk home felt stretched, each step heavy with cold and fatigue that sank deeper than muscle. The fog wrapped around Lucy's legs like a shroud. Her street appeared through the gloom—red-brick terraces standing shoulder to shoulder, a silent line of mourners.

Their house sagged mid-row, soot-blackened, slumped under the weight of four months' grief. The front garden was choked with weeds; the iron gate, taken for the war effort, left a jagged gap like a missing tooth. Lucy shoved the door—it stuck, as always. She leaned her shoulder against it, and it gave way with a groan.

The house no longer smelled of home. The air hung thick, not with warmth but with a suffocating stillness. Pain now lived here, settled deep within the walls. There was no bright sting of carbolic soap, no polish on the front step. Only the flat scent of coal, boiled cloth, and something else—the smell of sorrow left too long.

"Mam, I'm home," Lucy said, with only a breath.

Her mother, Agnes, stood at the sink, a dishcloth limp in her hands. Her distant eyes found Lucy's for only a moment before drifting away. The cloth slipped from her fingers into the murky water with a faint splash.

"I can see that, love," said Agnes, her voice a faded version of what it once was. "Get your boots off. You'll muck the floor."

Lucy kicked them off, mud flaking onto the linoleum. She walked to the kitchen table, where her father, Harold, sat cradling his favourite mug, his work jumper and boots still on, as though he was ready to go to work. However, it was well past nine, and he was just sitting there. He hadn't stirred. His eyes, dulled by the same grief that hollowed Agnes, met Lucy's.

"I stopped by Jameson's, Dad." Her voice lifted with a fragile hope. "I've got you some sausage and dripping for your tea." She set the small, precious parcel on the table and leaned in to kiss his forehead.

Harold looked at her then, really looked, for the first time in what felt like days. A tired smile ghosted his face—the same weary curve she remembered from when Joe used to come home from the foundry, full of stories and life.

"Lovely. You alright, pet?" he asked, his voice raspy, the cheer leached from it, leaving only a shadow.

"Knackered, but fine," Lucy lied. She wanted to tell him about the noise, the fear, the way her hands shook when handling the Gaines, but the words stuck in her throat. She couldn't add to their burden.

"You shouldn't be at that mardy place," he murmured, his voice too quiet to start a row—a man swallowed by helplessness.

Agnes, who had been standing silently at the sink, turned at the sight of the delicate, prized parcel. A glimmer of her former energy stirred.

"Sausage?" she declared, her voice a little stronger than it had been all day. "Give it here, lass. You'll have a proper bit of supper before you sleep. You're too thin."

Before Lucy could protest, her mother took the package and was already moving to the stove, her actions suddenly full of purpose. It was a gesture of pure, fierce maternal love—a need to nurture the one child she had left.

Harold watched his wife, then turned his gaze back to Lucy, his eyes filled with a profound, weary sadness.

"You should be at your studies. Writing those stories of yours," he said, the roughness in his voice catching like sandpaper.

The mention of her stories made Lucy's throat tighten into a painful knot. *Stories?* The word felt like it belonged to another girl, a girl from a different life. She hadn't written a single line since the telegram came.

She pushed the feeling down. She reached out and put her hand on her father's arm.

"It's alright, Dad. The work's steady, and the pay's good. I'm... I'm doing my bit. For him."

The unspoken name lingered between them. Harold placed his calloused hand over hers and gave it a single, tight squeeze. He said nothing more, but in that touch, Lucy felt all his love, his grief, and his guilt.

A few minutes later, Agnes put a plate on the table with two sizzling sausages and a piece of bread glistening with dripping. It was a feast. They shared it in the kitchen's hush, the minor act of eating together a fragile communion against the silence that had consumed their house. For a moment, it felt almost normal.

Agnes moved from the sink, her steps slow and deliberate. She paused by Lucy, her hand hovering briefly before resting gently on her daughter's shoulder. The touch was light, but it carried the weight of the world.

"You're a good lass, Lucy," she whispered, her voice thin as worn linen. "Doing this for us... for Joe."

The words, intended as a comfort, caught Lucy off guard, and the memory they triggered was as grey and merciless as a winter dawn.

It was the morning after the telegram arrived—her seventeenth birthday. The house was silent—no clink of dishes from the kitchen, no cheerful hum from her mother.

She woke in her room, tangled in a woollen blanket that belonged to Joe, its familiar warmth now a lie. She lay staring at the cracks in the ceiling, willing the day to pass unnoticed. No one would sing "Happy Birthday". She wouldn't want anyone to. Life wasn't real—not with Joe gone.

She dragged herself into the kitchen, plaits loose, eyes raw and red. Agnes stood at the sink, gazing into the distance, her hands idle. Harold was at the table, his Yorkshire Electricity jumper crumpled, his mug cold. The room reeked of dying embers. Her birthday, once a day of jam tarts and Joe's teasing, was stained beyond repair, drowned in loss.

Her father looked up then, his eyes red, the faint smile he always saved for Joe flickering and then vanishing.

"You're seventeen, Lucy," he rasped, his voice ragged as torn cloth. "We'll need to think on work now, pet."

The words landed like stones at the pit of her stomach. Work. *A cruel intrusion, a profanity against the fresh, gaping wound of Joe's absence. How could the world demand it when her world had ended?*

But amidst the shock, a sliver of understanding had pierced: money. Joe's apprentice's pay had helped. Now there was a hole, not in their hearts but in their meagre finances.

She thought of the posters plastered all over Leeds, the determined woman in overalls. YOUR COUNTRY NEEDS YOU!

Joe would have wanted her to be strong and do her part. The thought—small and shaky—took root. If she could help Mam and Dad, keep them from sinking completely, perhaps that would honour him. It would be a way to continue going.

"Aye, Dad," she said, her voice catching but steady. "I'll... I'll manage. I'll find something."

Back in the present, her mother's hand squeezed her shoulder—a brief, firm pressure—before she turned back to the dishes. The quiet clink of crockery was the only punctuation to a grief too immense for words.

Lucy stood up from the table, the memory solidifying her purpose, a sad, heavy resolve. This was why she went back to that terrible place each night. It was her duty. It was her penance. It was for Joe.

She climbed the stairs to her room, leaving her parents to their silent haunting below.

Her feet were burdened, her spirit more so. With its single window framing the grey Leeds rooftops, the draughty nook was her only sanctuary. Joe's old woollen blanket lay on her bed, still holding the slight shape of her body from her last failed attempt at sleep.

She wrapped it around herself, its familiar weight a comfort almost too painful to bear. She pressed her face deep into the wool, breathing in the faint, clean fragrance of him that still clung to the fibres—a ghost of soap and wind and boy.

She breathed it in, desperate to banish the other scent that now clung to everything she owned: the strong, chemical odour from the factory. The smell of Amatol had seeped into her clothes, hair, and skin, and in this sacred, grieving space, it appeared as a betrayal.

She lay down still dressed to rest her eyes. An hour, maybe two, before she had to face it all again.

Sleep, a shy and fleeting visitor these days, slipped past her once more. Her mind churned—*Joe, Barnbow, Joe, the girls, Joe.* She remembered her first night in that hell over a week ago, after Rose Turner had fallen. She'd been trained in Room 5, painting shells—a quieter, cleaner world. Nothing had prepared her for Room 42.

The memory was not a gentle recollection; it was a raw, sensory assault, still sharp enough to make her breath catch in her throat.

The air hit her first. It was thick, almost viscous—a choking murk of scorching oil and the strangely sweet, acrid tang of molten Amatol, tasting like fear on her tongue. Strained yellow gaslight cast long, dancing shadows, making the vast, high-ceilinged room feel like some infernal cavern. Women, their faces pale or sallow beneath their tight caps, moved with a frantic, desperate energy that was terrifying to behold.

Eliza Wren, the charge hand, had looked her up and down, a brief, assessing glance that missed nothing. Her face was etched with a weariness that went deep to her bones.

"You're Atkinson? Rose's replacement?"

Clutching her pass like a holy relic, Lucy had only managed a jerky nod, her voice caught in her throat.

"Keep pace, love," Eliza had said, her words clear and steady, reaching through the factory's roar. "No chatter. Watch Sarah Jennings—follow her lead. And don't get in the way."

The bluntness was a further shock. Then Sarah herself—brassy, a whirlwind of almost aggressive confidence—had clapped her hard on the back, making her stumble.

"This one looks sturdy enough, Lize! We'll keep 'er!" Sarah's ear-to-ear grin flashed a mouth full of white teeth in a face already tinged yellow, but her eyes held something else as they swept over Lucy—a grim assessment, a sizing up of another lamb brought to the factory's altar. The look made Lucy feel small, breakable, like a china doll in a boiler room.

She was shown her station and handed a pile of wiping cloths. As she stood there, completely overwhelmed by the sensory assault, Mary Sutcliffe, passing on her way to the capping machine, saw the terror on her face. She paused, leaned in close, and shouted into Lucy's ear over the roar, her voice rough but not unkind.

"You'll get used to the noise, lass. Don't fight it. Let it settle in your bones. You'll go mad otherwise." Mary gave her a firm, quick pat on the shoulder and moved on.

Nora Kershaw approached as Lucy, frozen with terror, tried to absorb the advice. She caught Lucy's eye, offered her a slight, reassuring nod, and pressed something into her palm—a folded, clean handkerchief, still warm from being kept in a pocket. The simple, unexpected kindness was so profound it almost made Lucy cry. It was a silent message: 'I see you. You're not alone.'

The line lurched forward. The first pressed shell arrived at her station, heavy and cold, as Lucy's trembling hands closed around its casing. A realisation, sharp and icy as the steel itself, pierced through her fear: A shell such as this one. *It wasn't an abstract thought; it was a sudden, sickening vision of this very object screaming across a field in France.*

Was it a similar shell that took Joe? Did a girl like me, tired, scared, send it on its way? *Her breath hitched, and for a terrifying second, her fingers went numb. The shell felt far too heavy, a dead weight not of metal but of grief and a terrible, hard-won understanding.*

She remembered the overwhelming fear of dropping something, of making a mistake that could... could what? She hadn't dared even to form the thought.

The proximity of the other women, their swift, sure movements, and their easy, often coarse banter only highlighted her terror and ineptitude.

She was an outsider, a frightened child in a world of hardened, formidable women who danced with death each minute of their shift.

That first night, every second had stretched into an eternity of noise, heat, and the suffocating terror of the unknown. She had wanted to run, to scream, to find Joe somehow and tell him she couldn't do this, couldn't bear it. But she hadn't.

For him. For her parents. She had picked up that first cloth, her hands so slick with nervous sweat it was a wonder she hadn't dropped it.

Lucy sat up in bed now, her heart fluttering with the memory of that panic. It wasn't only a memory; it was a premonition of the night to come. She had to get tougher, or the line would chew her up and spit her out. The ache of missing Joe twisted like a knife in her ribs.

She reached for the battered tin writing box on her nightstand, her movements slow and reverent. This was her only real sanctuary. She opened it with care.

Inside lay the archive of a life cut short—her stories, Joe's letters, and a photo of him on a camel in Egypt, looking so happy in those silly sunglasses, his grin wide and carefree against a foreign sun. She thumbed through the pages of her writing—scraps of poems, a half-finished letter she'd never sent.

"You see more than most, Luce," he'd said once, his eyes bright with a belief in her she had never found in herself. "You just don't believe it yet." Without him, she felt lost, her own words nothing but faint scratches on a page.

Her fingers found the last letter he'd sent from France, the paper soft as fabric from being read so many times. It was full of jokes about the food and the mud, but she could feel the weariness in the cramped handwriting.

In the house's highest reaches, as her thumb traced his signature, the grief-stricken attic room vanished, the perspective pulling away, across the Channel, across the months, to a place of mud.

She had heard the stories of the first day of the Somme from the returning Leeds men, the injured, their tales running through the city like a hot knife. Tales of uncut wire under a sky still smoking from a week-long bombardment, the Pals standing by Gospel Corpses near Serre.

For what she didn't know, her imagination filled in the rest...

July 1st, 1916. The Leeds Pals stood on the fire-step. Joe stood with his friends, his rifle gripped tight in his trembling hands. The air tasted of bully beef, cordite, and the stink of death.

The constant mind-numbing pounding of the guns had seeped into their bones. He thought of his mother's shepherd's pie, the thick gravy, the crusty potatoes—a memory of warmth in this cold, wet hell.

The shelling stopped. The silence that followed was worse, a ringing, hollow void soon filled by the sharp, shrill blast of a whistle.

He climbed the ladder. He ran. A line of boys in khaki, their faces pale beneath their helmets, surged into the smoke and fire. No-man's-land opened before them, a cratered hell of mud and blood. Bullets raked the earth like claws. George, his mate from the foundry, went down with a bloom of red on his chest.

Danny crumpled without a sound. Joe ran on, his lungs burning, mud clawing at his boots. The wire was still intact. The German guns were constant. A shell screamed, and the air tore open. A round struck his arm, twisting him to the side. Then two more hits, in his chest and side. He fell.

He couldn't breathe. The sky swam above him, a smudge of indifferent grey. He tried to call out, but the sound snagged in his throat. His last thoughts were of the cast-iron pan from the foundry, the one his mam used for her shepherd's pie, always on the stove. "Mam..." he said to the mud.

That morning, 233 of the brave 500 Leeds Pals were killed in the first five minutes. Joe was one of them.

The memory—a truth Lucy would never know—faded, leaving only the profound, aching silence of her small room. She stared at the letters in her lap, at the cheerful, lying words he had sent to protect her. She grabbed a blank sheet of paper from her writing box, the pen scratching fast across the surface, a sudden, desperate need to speak to him, to bridge the impossible distance.

Dear Joe,

The fog was so thick today that I couldn't see the Jameson's butcher's window. Got sausage and dripping for Dad—the rumours were true, a proper treat. Barnbow's hard graft, but I'm learning. The girls I work with are great, but scary and good-hearted.

I keep thinking about the last letter you wrote. You said the food was decent, your mates were good men, all. I'm glad you were with friends.

You didn't say anything about the fear.

Were you scared? Did you die alone? Were you in pain, Joe?

I hate that I don't know.

I hate that no one does.

Her hand trembled, and a single tear dropped, pooling at the edge of the sentence, making the ink bleed like a fresh wound. She folded the paper carefully, hesitated for a moment, then slid it back into the tin with the others. She wasn't ready to let him go. Not yet.

She got up and prepared for the night ahead. She went downstairs and swept the hearth, the rhythmic whisk of the brush a slight act of order in a house consumed by chaos. She packed her small lunch: bread, a sliver of beetroot, and half an apple. She stoked the fire and stood at the window, watching the early night and the fog roll in. It was turning 6:30 PM.

The knot in her stomach returned, tight and familiar. It was time to catch the tram again. Time to return to her other life—the one filled with noise, danger, and women she didn't quite understand.

Her grief for Joe was a raw, open wound, but it was also now a strange source of strength. She was doing this for him. For her parents. She buttoned her coat, and with the weight of her lost world settled deep in her bones, she stepped back out into the night. She didn't feel ready. But she had to be.

8

Chapter 8 : Nowt to Worry About

5th December 1916, Castleford

A floorboard creaked on the stairs, jangling Eliza's already frayed nerves. Her mother-in-law appeared in the kitchen doorway, a thin, worn shawl clutched around her shoulders, her face pinched with suspicion.

"Was that Skinner at the door?" she asked, her voice sharp and brittle. "I heard a man's voice. Shouting."

Eliza didn't turn away from the stove, where the kettle was hissing. "It's handled, Mam."

"Handled?" The old woman shuffled into the room, her eyes darting from Eliza to the front door and back again. "He'll leave us without a home, Eliza. For all your fancy wages from that powder factory, we're still in his grip. I told Stan when he took that loan, I told him no good would come of owing that man—"

"I said it's handled," Eliza repeated, her voice flat with a weariness deeper than muscle. She turned then, and the look in her eyes was enough to silence the old woman's rising tirade. It was a look of such profound exhaustion and grim resolve that it rendered further conversation unnecessary.

Her mother-in-law sniffed, pulling her shawl tighter. Her eyes rested on the baby still held tight in Eliza's arms. "Well, give me the bairn before you drop him. You need your sleep if you're to be gallivanting in those gunpowder sheds all night."

The transfer was not a tender, grandmotherly gesture. It was a duty performed with resentful hands. Eliza watched her husband's mother carry Stanley away, his small, warm weight leaving a cold absence in her arms. Now she was truly alone with the impossible task ahead.

She headed upstairs, lay on her bed, remaining in her clothes, and pulled the warm blanket over her. She shut her eyes, summoning the images of her children, their hungry, hopeful eyes warring with the chemical stench and danger of Room 42, Stan's mud-filled tunnels, and Barnbow's perilous bonus.

Stan's letter sat folded in her apron, ink smudged, his words still warm: *"I'll come home, lass."* Her chest eased; a smile appeared on her lips. Sleep offered no rest—another factory, this one filled with Skinner's grin and the stench of the poorhouse. She ran, children ahead, but the ground turned to mud, dragging her down. She snapped awake, heart pounding.

After three hours of fragile sleep, the factory's flames flooded the darkness behind her eyes, and Eliza jolted awake. Her mouth was dry, tasting of ash, and a sharp pain lanced behind her eyes.

The sleep hadn't been restful; it had been a shallow dive into a sea of anxiety, and she'd surfaced more tired than before. Darkness pressed in, and winter's chill was biting. It was time.

She splashed cold water on her face, the shock sharpening her senses. Then, she pinned back her hair and slipped into her worn work clothes before she descended the stairs to the kitchen. Stanley sat quietly on a blanket, gnawing on a wooden spoon.

She buttoned her fraying coat as the door creaked open. Robert stepped inside, coal dust streaking his face, exhaustion carving deep lines on his fourteen years.

"All right, Mam?" he asked, shaking off flakes, his voice rough but warm.

He looked at her hands as she buttoned her coat, his brow furrowing with a worry older than his fourteen years.

"They're gettin' proper yellow, Mam. Does it hurt?"

Eliza tucked her hands away, forcing a briskness she didn't feel. "Don't be daft, it's a stain. Nowt to worry about. Go on, get your stew before it's cold."

Robert hesitated, his gaze still on her hidden hands, his expression unconvinced. He knew better than to argue when she used that tone, but the unease didn't leave his eyes. He gave a slow nod and moved towards the stove.

"Put wood in 'ole, love!" his grandmother shouted from the kitchen. "I'll catch me bloody death!"

She nodded, forcing a smile. "Go on, get washed. Stew's on the stove. Nan's got the little un. Help Beth with her reading. Bed by nine, aye?"

"Sure, Mam." He stepped aside, lanky but sturdy, a man's weight settling on a boy's shoulders.

Eliza lingered in the doorway. "I'm proud of you," she said, voice quiet but loving.

He turned to say, "I love you," but she was already going out the door.

She hurried along Albany Terrace, her boots crunching over frost, passing a queue of pale-faced women forming outside the butcher's. A faded recruiting poster of Lord Kitchener flapped on a lamppost, its slogan feeling like an "old lie". The yellow chemical stain covering her hands—Barnbow's mark—itched beneath her gloves, a constant reminder of the hours spent in Room 42.

She reached June's house just as the garden gate groaned open and June Mitchell emerged, bundled for the shift. June's face, which was usually quick to smile, was a pale mask of worry.

June, late twenties, wore the look of a woman who had seen too much hardship. There were faint, blueish shadows beneath her eyes, the mark of a mother who had spent the night listening to a child's feverish rattle. She seemed to have shrunk inside her thin coat, her shoulders slumped with a weariness that had nothing to do with the factory.

June stopped short as she saw Eliza, her breath misting in the cold air. "Lize, you alright, love?" Her voice, once bright, carried a sharp edge of concern. "You look like you've seen a ghost."

Eliza's composure, held together all day by the thinnest of threads, frayed. The words she'd held back tumbled out in a desperate, whispered rush. "Skinner came this morning. He wants every penny Stan owes by Saturday—or we're out. All of us." She gripped the strap of her satchel, her knuckles whitening. "I don't have a clue how, June... not unless we pull a massive bonus this week. Every last shell..."

June's face tightened with fierce understanding. The wind whipped a wisp of hair across her eyes. She reached out, her gloved hand briefly gripping Eliza's arm.

"That bastard," June said, a spark of anger cutting through the cold. Her gaze hardened. "My Tom's on his knees as it is, and now they're on about double shifts at the pit. Pushing the lads 'til they drop for next to no pay. He'll work himself into an early grave..." Her voice faded away, the unspoken fear hanging between them.

June looked ahead, her desperation mirroring Eliza's. "Right then, Lize. We make that bonus. We bloody have to."

A bleak, shared resolve passed between them—a silent acknowledgement of what was at stake. That was all that needed to be said. The shell line waited, its acrid fumes swirling, Sarah's defiant laugh echoing, Lucy's quiet tremors trembling, and the constant, ticking threat of a single spark.

Eliza squared her shoulders, Stan's last letter a fragile shield over her heart. With a grim nod to June, she stepped into the deepening frozen night, the factory's insatiable hunger dragging them both forward.

9

Chapter 9 : A Telephone Call to Leeds

5th December 1916, Warthill, York

Thomas's sharp voice cut through the quiet from the table: "Yard's waiting."

Sarah's resolve hardened.

She worked for one more hour to complete the tasks Thomas had assigned her, and now she had a choice. She could get some much-needed rest or go to the Pocklington post office, request the terms, and schedule an appointment for Saturday.

It was two in the afternoon. In the freezing washhouse behind the farmhouse, Sarah prepared herself. This wasn't her usual quick wash after finishing in the yard; this was a deliberate, almost desperate, cleansing.

She was going into Pocklington, a place she hated, where every glance felt like a judgement and the whispers followed her like a shadow. But it was equipped with a telephone, and she had a call to make.

She stripped off her work clothes in the flickering lamplight. The faint but unmistakable yellow stain on her skin mocked her. Today, she was attempting to erase two whole lives embedded within her, and she loathed both.

One was the sharp, chemical tang of the factory—a poison that clung to her hair and lodged deep in her lungs. The other was the cloying, earthy stench of the farm—of muck and damp hay—that permeated the rough clothes she wore for her chores. They were the twin stenches of her cage.

She grabbed the stiff brush and carbolic soap, scrubbing hard. Her hands moved fast, furious, attacking the saffron stains like they were the enemy. She wasn't only washing off dust; she was trying to scour away the vision of Rose Turner falling and the tremble in her hands that wouldn't stop.

The water in the stone basin turned a sickening, murky yellow-brown. *The colour of my existence*, she thought. The poison from Barnbow mixed with the filth of Warthill.

She stared at the foul puddle, a gasp escaping her lips. This was what she was made of. How could she ever build a tidy, safe home for Cecil when she was steeped in this? The dream of the flat in Leeds—of clean curtains and polished floors, a hope that had felt so distant—seemed like a silly fantasy, a world away from this grim reality.

She scrubbed until her flesh was raw, but she knew it was useless. The poison was deeper than her skin. It was in her aching gums, the constant ringing in her ears, the dizziness that threatened to fell her in the yard.

And the smell of the farm was a ghost she could never exorcise; it clung to the fabric of her worn-out dress, a constant reminder of her servitude to Thomas.

The tremor in her hands seemed to get worse. She looked down at their yellow stain. The poison was winning. Time was running out. It was impossible for her to wash this life away.

She had to cut it off, escape it completely. If she were to get that flat, if she were to build that safe harbour for him to come home to, she couldn't wait. It had to be now.

Her resolve, fuelled by desperation and the memory of Cecil, burned like a fever. She thought of the post office in Pocklington. It was a good six-mile slog, and she hadn't slept, but it had a telephone.

A chance to call the Leeds landlord she'd seen in that advert.

It was a mad risk walking all that way to a town full of gossips, but it was a gamble she had to take.

Halfway there, she had to stop, leaning her full weight against a frost-slicked gatepost, her breath coming in ragged, painful bursts. The bitter January air burned in her lungs, and a familiar wave of nausea churned in her gut.

She closed her eyes, fighting it down, her gloved hand clutching the newspaper clipping in her pocket like a holy relic. *Just a little further*, she told herself, the image of Cecil's face giving her the strength to push off the post and force her aching legs to move again.

The winter fog, dense and cloying, resembled the town's malicious whispers, muffling countryside sounds and isolating her in a grey, featureless world. Her limbs felt like lead, each step an effort of will. Dizziness, a familiar, unwelcome companion, swayed her; the frozen ruts blurred and shifted before her eyes.

A hundred and twelve extra shells. She'd overheard Eliza say it quiet like at the end of the shift, as if speaking it too loud might curse them. It wasn't much once split—over a bob and a bit—but Sarah clung to every coin as if it were the key to a front door she could lock behind her.

By half-past three, Pocklington's cobbled streets emerged from the gloom. Thc gaslights sputtered weakly, casting an eerie, jaundiced glow on familiar storefronts as darkness fell. The post office crouched in the shadow of the market square, its grimy windows shrouded in fog.

The worn stone threshold seemed etched with the weight of each whispered judgement, each sidelong, scornful glance Sarah had ever dodged in this godforsaken town.

She forced open the heavy door. The bell jangled above her, and a blast of heat hit her in the face. The air was heavy with the bitter, earthy tang of animal dung clinging to farmers' coats and the sweet, saccharine scent of cheap tobacco—a smell that always curled in her throat, making her want to cough.

Talk, once subdued and soft and stirred with energy, fell quiet, hushed enough for her to feel the shift, the sudden awareness of her presence.

She didn't have to look to know their eyes were on her: the farmers' wives, mouths pursed tight with disapproval; the butcher's sharp-faced girl, glances cutting like bone. *Jennings's girl. Bastard's mam. Swanning 'round with her Barnbow brass.* The words hung unspoken but as real as the fog outside.

Sarah didn't flinch—not today. Too much was at stake. She walked taller than she felt, chin set with defiance, though her stomach churned. Each step on the worn floorboards echoed in the sudden hush—a small, solitary challenge. She reached the telephone booth, a cramped, dark cubicle smelling of stale smoke and desperation.

The weedy clerk slid the battered ebonite receiver towards her with a look like he was handing over a dead rat. She pressed a hard-earned Barnbow penny into his waiting palm.

The line hissed and crackled. "Miss Jennings, Warthill," she stated. "The two-room flat you advertised... in Leeds. I'm calling about the terms."

The man on the other end was clipped and uninterested. "Deposit one month and one month's rent upfront. Three pounds, three shillings total. No lodgers, no pets, no children under ten unless arranged beforehand. No exceptions."

She had enough saved. Using this week's bonus, she could get some nice furniture and make a proper home for Cecil, like she had always dreamed. A tremor ran through her legs, but she spoke firmly. "I'll take it," she said, the words a lifeline. "I... I'll be there Saturday with the deposit."

A Leeds flat. Two rooms. Enough for her and Cecil if—*when*—he came home. No farm, no watching her mother grow smaller by the day, no filthy looks from Thomas or whispers from the village wives. Quiet. A clean room. A bed that was hers.

Another four nights like last night and she'd have enough to pay the deposit. It wouldn't matter if it were a yellow coin or blood-earned, so long as it was hers.

She replaced the receiver, her hand leaving a faint, damp smudge on the polished counter. Turning, she felt the warmth of every pair of narrowed, curious eyes now openly tracking her.

As she headed for the door, a thick-ankled woman near the entrance, wearing a moth-eaten fox-fur collar, muttered to her friend loud enough for half the post office to hear, "No shame, that one."

The words struck her, not as a fresh wound but a final spark on dry tinder. In a blinding flash, seventeen years of humiliation ignited in her mind.

Michael, shrugging his dismissal: "Was only a bit of fun, sir." Her father's face, contorted in fury, the slam of the door echoing in her soul. Years of Thomas's quiet contempt, the sneer in his voice, the way he looked at her son.

No, she thought, a silent roar rising inside her. *No more.*

She stopped. Mid-stride, mid-breath. The air in the post office snapped taut as a breaking wire. She turned, slow and deliberate, locking eyes with the speaker. The woman's smug, self-righteous face faltered under Sarah's unwavering stare.

"Is there summat you need, love?" Sarah asked, her voice bright on the surface, sharp as a broken bottle.

The woman blinked, mouth opening and closing like a stranded fish. "Pardon?" she stammered, confidence drained.

"Only you keep staring like you've lost summat valuable." Her voice carried through the silent room. "I can help you look for it, if you like. Could it be your manners that've gone missing?"

A choked, suppressed chuckle broke out near the scales. The woman's cheeks flushed a mottled, unbecoming red.

Sarah didn't wait for a reply. She swept past, head held high, and pushed open the heavy door—the bell jangling above, sounding for all the world like applause.

Back at Warthill by five thirty, the farmhouse's oppressive, smoky, animal-scented air bothered her less now. She was on her way out; nothing, not even Thomas Brown, could stop her.

He loomed in the kitchen doorway as she stepped inside, blocking the weak light.

"Where have you been then?" he asked, his voice stern.

"I went to Pocklington—to the post office, if you must know—to use the telephone," she said, her tone level and defiant. "I've found a flat in Leeds. For Cecil and me. I'm moving out."

Thomas blinked, shocked, then his features tightened into a mean sneer. "Leeds? Thinking of flitting, are we? Good riddance, I say! I'll even help you pack your rags!"

Though her legs trembled with exhaustion and a new onset of dizziness made the room spin, Sarah faced him, her resolve hardened into armour. "Yeah, I'm leaving, Thomas. So you'll have to find someone else to be your skivvy from now on."

Annie appeared behind him in the doorway, her face pale, pleading. "She's earned it, Thomas, love. Sarah has worked hard."

Thomas's eyes blazed, fury that had simmered for years boiling over. "Fine. Out by week's end, or I'll throw you to the bloody lanes myself! And you can take her and all!" He jabbed a finger at Susannah, lashing out in fury at the thought of losing his pound-a-week workhorse.

His threat of eviction and destitution loomed like a bitter winter frost. But Annie shot him a hard, steady look—one that said: *'If you're thinking of throwing my mother out, think again.'* Thomas lowered his head and stalked from the room.

With her hand on the cold iron latch, the metallic tang of her anger tasted the same as it had two years ago. The last time that man's cruelty had threatened to take everything.

1914. The air in the same kitchen was saturated with a younger, sharper rage. Thomas's face was hardened like a mask of thunder, but his fury wasn't directed at her. It was aimed at a fifteen-year-old Cecil.

"Don't you take that tone with me, boy!" Thomas roared, jabbing a finger towards him. "Not in my house."

Cecil, all sharp angles and seething defiance, stood his ground between Thomas and his mother. "She's done her work. Leave her be."

A harsh, joyless laugh escaped Thomas's throat. "She's done her work? She brought you into this house. You eat my food, you sleep under my roof. But you are a Jennings, boy. A cuckoo in this nest. And you'd do well to remember it."

The colour drained from Cecil's face and gave way to a pale, hard mask. He looked at his mother, at her tired, protective stance, and then back at the man who would never see him as anything but a burden. The fight left him, replaced by a sudden, chilling certainty.

"Fine," Cecil said, his voice quiet, stripped of all emotion. "Then I won't be a burden any longer. I'm joining the Navy."

The words stunned the room into silence. Sarah's hand quickly covered her mouth to stifle the shock. Thomas stared, surprised, then gave a dismissive snort and turned away, mumbling, "If they'd have you," as he left.

Later, after Thomas had gone out to the pigs, grumbling about ungrateful whelps, Sarah found Cecil in the small room under the eaves. He was already bundling his few belongings into a canvas sack.

"I have to, Mam," he said, his voice cracking.

Sarah's resolve didn't waver. In the tense silence that followed, her mother, Susannah, shuffled over from her position beside the hearth. Pouring tea from the stewed pot on the stove brought her screaming back from that memory.

She walked over to Sarah, put a hand on her shoulder, and placed the mug into her trembling hands. "Here y'are, love," she said, her voice soft as moth wings. "Might warm your hands."

Sarah accepted the mug, their chapped fingers brushing against each other. "Thanks, Mam. You shouldn't have."

Susannah's gaze was distant, but for a moment, it sharpened with worry. "His temper's been a foul thing these past few weeks. Be careful, Sarah. Don't provoke him more than you must."

Sarah's jaw clenched. The warning, meant as kindness, felt like another bar on her cage. "I earn my keep here, Mam—more than. And soon," she added, her voice fierce with promise, "Cecil and I will have our own place. And you can come with us. Away from him. Away from all this."

A glimmer of fear, quickly masked, crossed her mother's face. "Oh, love... that's a grand dream." She patted Sarah's arm, a hesitant, bird-like touch, before shuffling back to the fire.

Later, as she prepared to leave for Barnbow, forcing down what little she could of Annie's watery stew, her mind was clear. The stakes were laid bare. She had to earn that bonus this week, or she and her mother would be on the street. Her war against Thomas Brown and the public war effort had now merged into a single, desperate fight for survival.

Annie pressed a hunk of bread into her hand, eyes full of unshed tears. Her mother murmured a blessing from her chair by the fire.

"Good lass, Sarah. Be careful." It was a faint, fragile balm.

As her boots scraped on the frozen path, dizziness hovered like an unwelcome but constant companion. Sarah Jennings prepared once more for the journey to York Station, then to Barnbow's hungry, waiting jaws.

She wasn't a weary worker or an enduring victim. She was a soldier heading to the front line, with everything to lose and a hard-won victory ahead. And she would not be defeated.

10

Chapter 10 : Cross Gates

5th December 1916, Castleford, Leeds, York, Barnbow

The carriage's gaslight hissed, casting a weak, jaundiced glow on the frost that spider-webbed across the windowpanes. Outside, the skeletal trees of the West Riding flashed past in a black, unforgiving blur. The air inside had a sooty tang of coal smoke from the engine.

For a few precious minutes, there was only the steady, rocking rhythm of the journey, a brief rebellion of warmth and quiet against the cold, roaring night that awaited them.

Eliza felt the train's monotonous clatter not in her ears but as a deep, weary vibration in her bones. She pulled her thin coat tighter, the chill from the hard wooden bench seeping through the fabric.

Beside her, June Mitchell was a portrait of quiet tension. She stared out the window, but her gaze was distant, lost in a worry far from the noise and grime of Barnbow.

She leaned against the icy glass, soot-smeared fields flashing by in a streak of black and grey. "I keep telling myself," June said, her voice a thin counterpoint to the rhythmic racket, "if this weather turns much colder, I'm bringing the kettle from home. We could make a cup of tea right on the train."

Eliza managed a faint smile that didn't quite reach her tired eyes. "I don't think the train company would like you setting the bloody thing alight to keep warm."

They both laugh—a brief, surprising crack of warmth that faded almost as soon as it arrived.

"Still," June continued, flexing her stiff, chapped fingers, "doing 112 was helpful for our bonus number, Lize. Another shilling in the tin will do us all some good."

"Yeah, indeed," said Eliza, the idea of her own stretched budget tightening her chest like a vice. She counted every penny, evaluated each purchase, and a constant, silent calculation played in her head.

A nervous silence fell, interrupted solely by the click-clack as the train rolled along. June, who had been about to launch into a story, stopped mid-sentence and glanced over her shoulder, as if expecting to see a dark suit in the aisle.

"They were inside Shed C last night, the men from London, doing the efficiency study," Eliza said, speaking so it wouldn't be overheard. "Watching Gladis Hirst. Her lad's been sent to the front, and her hands were shaking something awful. Dropped a casing twice."

A visible shiver passed through June. She attacked her bootlaces again with renewed nervous energy. "That's all it takes, isn't it?" Her brow contorted across her forehead. "One bad day, one slip, and another girl takes your place. You're out on your ear with nothing but a rumour of 'inefficient movement' for a reference."

The work was dangerous, the yellow tinge on their skin a badge of pride and peril. But the fear of the production line was nothing compared to the terror of losing it. The wages were more than money—they were daily bread, medicine for the sick, a fragile shield against the world's harshest edges.

June sighed, a sound almost lost beneath the clatter of the wheels, and began rubbing her chapped hands together. "My fingers are aching something awful tonight." Her voice was thin. "Feel like they'll snap clean off if it gets any colder."

Eliza nodded, flexing her own stiff, stained fingers on her lap. "It's the chemicals. Dries them out. Then the cold gets in. It's a bad mix."

"Aye, that it is," June said. The forced cheerfulness she wore had fallen away, leaving her looking tired and thin.

Eliza watched her for a moment, the silence between them now heavy with unspoken anxieties.

"You're a long way away tonight, June," she said. "Is it Margaret again?"

June startled as if pulled from a bad dream. She turned slowly from the window, her eyes shimmering with an exhaustion that went deeper than a single shift.

"Aye, it's that rattle, Lize," she whispered, her voice tight and raw. "A dry sound, like rustling paper deep within her. And she's so warm. I put a damp cloth on her head, but the fever seems to absorb it. The house is so cold... not a lump of coal left in the scuttle. Tommy... he just sits there, staring at the grate. He's a proud man, you know. He hated me taking every bit of the provisions you brought over, but what could we do?"

She swallowed hard, a moment of sheer panic in her eyes.

"This bonus money... it's not for her tonic anymore. I think it might have to be for a doctor."

As she spoke, a mental picture of her kitchen flooded her mind, so vivid it blotted out the train window. She could make out Tommy, hunched and helpless, and hear the faint, papery rattle of Margaret's breath from the cot by the dying fire.

*****

The cold in June Mitchell's kitchen was a living thing. It crept in through the ill-fitting window frame and rose from the stone floor, a damp, persistent chill that the dying embers in the grate could no longer fight. It settled deep in the lungs, a thief who stole breath.

June knelt beside the small cot she had dragged into the kitchen, the warmest room in the house. Inside, her daughter, Margaret, slept a restless, shallow sleep. June leaned closer, listening, her entire world narrowing to the sound of the little girl's breathing. It was there—a faint but unmistakable crackle on every exhale, a wispy rattle that sent a fresh wave of fear through her.

She placed her hand on Margaret's forehead. Still too warm. The fever was holding on with a stubborn, cruel grip. She tucked the thin, worn blanket tighter around the slight frame, a useless gesture against a cold that came from within.

Across the room, her husband, Tommy, sat hunched at the table, staring into a mug of lukewarm tea he'd long since forgotten. His pit-stained hands were clasped so tightly together that his knuckles were white. He had said little all evening. There was nothing left to say.

His shift at the pit had been cut short again, and the extra work he'd been promised had vanished. It was the same story over all the pits in the country. They were cutting the skilled men's time but working the young lads like Bobby Wren to death for half the wage. His silence was not anger; it was the heavy, suffocating weight of a good man's helplessness.

June looked from her daughter's feverish face to the empty coal scuttle by the hearth. She thought of the doctor's house, of the shilling fee for a visit—a sum as unobtainable as the moon—of the bonus. The thought was a frantic, desperate prayer.

The tally board at the factory wasn't just numbers to her; it was a bag of coal. It was a bottle of tonic. It was the price of a doctor's visit. It was the cost of that terrible rattle leaving her daughter's chest.

"It's not right, Junie," he rasped, his voice raw with a pain he couldn't hide. "Me sat here like a useless lump while you go to that place."

"We do what we have to, Tommy," she whispered, her voice fierce. "You dig the coal that keeps the furnaces burning, and I pack the shells. It's all the same war. We have to win ours."

*****

The fear of a child's fever in a cold room. The words were a key, unlocking a door in Eliza's mind that she tried to keep bolted shut. *Judith.* Her bonny lass, not yet a year old, her smile bright as a summer morning. The memory was not a thought; it was a physical blow.

Eliza could almost feel the ghostly weight of a small, squirming baby in her arms and smell the faint scent of lavender soap on a flannel. She pictured Judith's tiny chest struggling to breathe in that freezing house, the cough—so much like the one June had described—robbing her of breath.

Stan had been broken by it, but she... she had built a wall of stone around that grief. A wall that was now crumbling. She remembered the helplessness, a feeling so profound that it had nearly drowned her.

"No." Her voice, suddenly fierce, startled June with its intensity. She reached out and gripped June's arm, her fingers digging in with a strength she didn't know she had. "That will not happen. Not to you. Not while I can help it. We'll get that bonus, June. I'll run the girls ragged if I have to, but we'll get it."

Eliza saw June flinch, her eyes wide as she took in the passion in Eliza's stare. Eliza didn't look away. There was fear in June's face—but also a flicker of understanding, as the weight of her promise, and the pain behind it, sank in.

June gave a small, shaky nod, seeming to draw a little strength from Eliza's vow. "Alright, Lize," she agreed, her voice no louder than a breath. "Alright."

A brief, nervous hush descended upon their corner of the carriage, the clatter of the wheels suddenly seeming louder.

The train's brakes shrieked, a jarring sound that pulled Eliza from her thoughts. The carriage groaned to a halt, and a guard's voice bellowed from the platform, his words swallowed by a hiss of steam: "Cross Gates! This stop's Cross Gates! Change here for Barnbow!"

As Eliza and June joined the surge of women pouring onto the platform, they were met with a chaotic influx from the newly arrived Leeds train, the metallic sound of the nearby tracks underscored by a babble of noise as the two streams of workers merged.

Laughter from one group mixed with the weary complaints of another, a river of tired humanity flowing towards the waiting Barnbow train.

"Come on, love," Eliza said, keeping a firm hold on June's sleeve. "Let's find our lot before we get swept away."

They pushed through the throng towards the platform. As they waited on the steps, two men in dark, immaculate suits stood further down, their polished leather boots a stark contrast to the worn-out, scuffed shoes of the women around them. They looked deeply uncomfortable in the crush of bodies, their expressions a mixture of impatience and distaste.

Eliza froze for a heartbeat, a jolt of pure dread shooting through her. It was them—the efficiency men from London. Mr Finch, whose glasses seemed to magnify his lack of emotion, and the grim-faced Inspector Harper, a man who looked as though he'd never smiled in his life.

As they stood waiting for the train from York to arrive, a ripple of silence spread across the platform. The ragged chorus of 'Keep the Home Fires Burning' faltered and died. Laughter was cut short, conversations trailing off into nervous whispers. Every woman there seemed to stiffen, their shoulders tightening as they recognised the men who held their livelihoods between the ticks of a stopwatch.

Eliza knew immediately what had happened. They were looking to board at the wrong end of the train. The front two carriages were for management, watchers, and inspectors—a small, quiet world of authority. The back three were for the workers—a loud, cramped, and entirely separate kingdom.

Mr Finch's lips thinned with annoyance as he took in the crowded, noisy area. He exchanged an irritated glance with Harper, then, without a word, they began pushing through the horde. Their shoulders carved a narrow path as women instinctively shrank back. They were heading towards the front of the train.

Their passage created a wave of silence. As they passed Eliza, now joined by Lucy, Mary, Hilda, and Nora, the girls huddled together as if for warmth, their small group a temporary protection. Finch's gaze swept over them, cool, measuring, and devoid of sympathy. He looked at them not as women but as components, assessing their value with the eye of a butcher.

His eyes lingered for a fraction of a second on Lucy's pale, nervous face. Eliza saw him make a small, deliberate tick on his clipboard before moving on. *Leave her be, you bastard,* Eliza thought, a hot surge of fury rising in her chest. *She's a child.* The gesture was as loud as a gunshot on the now-quiet platform.

The men disappeared through the crowd and stood with the management, but the chill of their presence remained. The singing did not resume. The light-hearted atmosphere had been completely extinguished, replaced by a tense, watchful quiet that felt heavier than the threat of the work itself.

Eliza looked around at her team, her protective instincts on high alert, a charge hand assessing her girls before a battle. Her eyes landed on Lucy first. The girl stood hunched next to Nora, her knuckles white where she gripped her satchel strap like a lifeline. Her face was pale and drawn, her eyes holding a fragile, haunted look that never seemed to leave her.

Grief's a heavy load for shoulders so young, Eliza thought, the memory of Lucy's brother Joe, lost at the Somme, a constant, silent presence. The girl was trying so hard to be strong, to do her bit, but Eliza could see the terror shimmering beneath the surface. The thought was less a decision and more a settled weight of responsibility.

Her attention was then drawn by Mary Sutcliffe, who, catching her eye, offered a paper-wrapped parcel of bread with a slight, almost imperceptible nod.

Eliza shook her head in thanks, her eyes catching the way Mary shifted her weight, favouring the leg the looms had ruined years ago. *Solid as a rock, that one,* Eliza thought, a flicker of respect cutting through her worries.

Mary never complained; she endured the pain as a fact of life, as she endured the factory. A stout woman in her mid-fifties, short and solid, years of hard work etched into the lines around her eyes, she had a look that said she had seen and done it all, but there was a deep kindness there, too. She stood quietly, a mindful, steady presence who never spoke unless she knew her words would mean something. Every shilling she earned, every ounce of strength she spent, was for her Sam, digging his way under France. The rest of them were background noise to that single, fierce purpose.

Then her gaze drifted to Hilda Morton, who stood ramrod straight beside Mary, adjusting her scarf. Hilda was a tall, slim woman, taller than most of the girls, with blonde hair tucked neatly under her cap. She pushed her small, round glasses up with a habitual finger, wrinkling her nose as she did so—the very picture of the precise schoolmistress she once was. The schoolmistress from Wakefield, by way of County Clare. Eliza saw the quiet formality that set her apart, the soft Irish lilt she tried to hide when she spoke.

Eliza knew the posture was a shield, built to conceal a grief as sharp as her own. She wasn't here for the wages, not really; she was here to fight a private war for her brother, Albert. Every shell she filled was a piece of her old life, a measured tribute on the altar of duty.

At last, her eyes rested on Nora Kershaw, huddled by the window, her thumb tracing the simple wedding band on her finger. With her shock of red hair escaping her cap and a dusting of freckles across her nose, Nora was beautiful. There was a natural warmth to her, the look of someone born to be a mum, her expression full of a kind, considerate hope for the future. Her thoughts were far away—somewhere on a battleship rocking in the cold, grey Atlantic.

Nora spoke of her fears, but every carefully seated fuse was a quiet prayer sent out to sea, a small act of love to keep her Will safe. She was their gang's steady, gentle heart, and Eliza felt a sudden urge to protect that fragile hope at all costs.

The York train was seen approaching, its lamp and Cyclops eye cutting through the gloom. The women looked up, their faces breaking into relieved smiles. With a series of nods and shuffles, they gathered their things and made their way over, squeezing in beside Eliza and June towards the front of the platform.

Lucy and Nora followed, drawn into the orbit of their small gang. For a moment, huddled together, a small pocket of familiarity braced against the noise and the long night ahead.

A new cloud of steam billowed down the platform as the much larger train from York groaned to a halt. There was a rush to get on board. The air in the carriage, already thick with chatter, grew louder as women gathered their bags and pushed towards the doors.

"Right then, girls, this is us," Eliza called out over the din, her voice steady and clear. "Stick together. Shout out if you spot Sarah or a seat!"

They moved as one, a small, determined unit flowing into the river of workers pouring onto the train. The junction was a controlled chaos of hissing steam, shouted orders, and the clatter of boots on timber.

And there, framed in one of the open doorways, was Sarah Jennings.

Eliza saw her at once. Even in the dim station light, Sarah's energy stood out. Her coat was unbuttoned despite the cold, and she stood with one hand on her hip, her head thrown back in laughter at something a girl beside her had said.

She had a defiance that the factory, the long hours, and the hardships at home could never quite extinguish.

"There she is," June said beside Eliza, a note of affection in her voice.

Sarah spotted them then, her grin widening. "Took you lot long enough!" The shout came across the platform, her voice carrying easily over the noise. "Thought you had all slept in! The bonus won't wait for you, you know!"

With a final push through the crowd, Eliza led her team aboard. They found a small space in the carriage, the seven of them squeezing onto the benches, their shoulders pressed together, a silent reinforcement of their bond.

Sarah immediately launched into a story, her voice loud and brassy, and the familiar rhythm of their gang settled over them.

The guard's whistle blew, sharp and piercing. With a mighty lurch that rattled the windows, the Barnbow Special began to move, pulling away from the junction. All of them were now together. The last leg of the journey had begun.

11

Chapter 11 : The Barnbow Special

5th December 1916, Barnbow

The train from Cross Gates shrieked into Barnbow Halt, its brakes howling like a scalded beast, but moments before, inside the carriage, there was a different world. It was a brief, raucous rebellion against the creeping dread. With its wooden benches hard and unyielding, the carriage rocked with desperate warmth and defiant mischief.

Lanterns swayed overhead, their flames flaring and forming soft, golden halos over flushed faces, shadows dancing in the corners like mischievous sprites.

The atmosphere was a dense murk—a cloying blend of damp wood, the acrid tang of coal smoke, and the ever-present, faint sting of chemicals clinging to their clothes and skin.

June sneezed, a dry sound. Mary, without looking up from a loose thread on her cuff, passed her a handkerchief. A faint nod passed between them—an unspoken acknowledgement. It was the smell of their lives now, a scent they carried together.

Eliza noticed Lucy... and felt a pang of sympathy. For the girl, the sheer, sprawling scale of Barnbow, now materialising through the pre-dawn gloom, must have pressed on her like a physical weight. Eliza watched as the shadowed buildings rolled past, hulking and grim.

"It's... It's like a whole city, isn't it?" Lucy murmured to June Mitchell, who gave her a weary smile, her voice only a mist in the cold.

"All those sheds, and the blast walls... like ancient castle walls. And so many of us."

June nodded.

Sarah snorted at the view. "Aye, it's a whole bloody city, love," she said, waving at the scene blurring past in the window. "Built on secrets and our sweat. They say there are sixteen thousand of us now, and they need thirty trains a day to haul us in and out like cattle. All this..." She gestured dismissively at the passing sheds. "...from nothing in less than a year. All for their bloody war."

Eliza could see Lucy trying to absorb the number, but it was too vast. The number was overwhelming even for Eliza, enough to make anyone feel like fragile paper caught in a whirlwind. She could tell from Lucy's demeanour that her grief for Joe, a secret she was terrified of showing, was there even amidst the noise.

At the centre of that noise, naturally, was Sarah Jennings. Perched at the end of a bench, her patched coat thrown open despite the drafts, she was leading a scandalous rendition of Mademoiselle from Armentières, her voice like cracked slate—bold, brazen, and unbothered by pitch or propriety.

"Mademoiselle from Armentières, parlez-vous!
Mademoiselle from Armentières, parlez-vous!
The officers get all the steak,
and all we get is the bellyache.

Hinky dinky, parlez-vous!"

She belted it out, her grin sharp and wicked as she scanned the faces of her gang. A ragged but enthusiastic chorus of women from up and down the carriage roared back, *"She had four chins, her knees would knock, parlez-vous!"*

"And her face would stop a cuckoo clock!" Sarah sang, leaning in and lowering her voice conspiratorially. *"Hinky dinky, parley-Voo!"*

June Mitchell threw her head back and laughed, a genuine, hearty sound that cut through the gloom. Beside her, Mary gave a wry roll of her eyes, though a small smile twitched at the corners of her mouth; she'd seen Sarah's performances a hundred times, and they never lost their rebellious spark.

"Again!" someone shouted from further down the carriage.

"Oh, aye!" Sarah crowed, her eyes glinting. She caught Lucy's startled gaze and gave her a theatrical wink before launching into another verse, this one aimed at the blushing girl.

"Mademoiselle from Armentières, she's never been kissed in forty years! Hinky dinky, parlez-vous!"

Lucy's cheeks flushed a deep crimson, and she stared intently out the window.

June, sitting beside her, gave Sarah a look. "Leave her be, Sarah. She's only been on the line a week, still finding her feet, bless her."

Sarah just laughed, a gust of sound like wind through a barn door. Her laughter was a performance, a whirlwind of defiance against the exhaustion she refused to show. But then, for a moment, as the song ended and another girl sighed about missing her bairns, her grin faltered.

Eliza saw the mask slip. In her eyes, the shadows of Warthill's drudgery, of Thomas Brown's stony stare, and of Cecil's far-off, beloved face flitted across them. She could see the weight of Sarah's punishing schedule pushed down like a physical force. Just as quickly, the smile returned, and she had shoved it away.

"Right then, who's next?" She snapped back into character. "Another chorus to wake the dead, eh?"

"Don't you worry your pretty head, love," Sarah said, her voice pitched just for Lucy, a grin full of mischief. "We're all still here, aren't we? Well, almost all."

"Almost?" Lucy echoed, the word sticking in her throat. Her gaze flicked to Eliza, who stared out the window, her profile silhouetted by the passing landscape. "What do you mean 'almost'? Do girls... Are we missing someone?"

Noticing the genuine terror she had now caused in Lucy, Sarah quickly broke the tension in the only way she knew how. She caught Lucy's eye, twirled a finger near her temple, and nodded towards Mary.

Mary, ever sharp, shot a wry, almost imperceptible look back. "I saw that, Jennings," she said, voice dry but warm, a smile playing on her lips.

To Sarah's delight, a nervous giggle bubbled out of Lucy—the first real ease they'd heard from the girl.

Sarah's grin faltered for a second, replaced by a more serious, knowing look. She exchanged a quick, dark glance with Mary across the carriage.

It was June who leaned in, her words soft, a fraction above a breath. "Some girls, love, they get sick," she said quietly. "The chemicals. They can get inside you. Make you sick."

"Like our Rose," Sarah added, her voice now stripped of its earlier humour. "She was at our bench last week. Skin like lemon peel and shaking like a leaf. They took her off to the infirmary. Haven't heard a word since."

The specific name, the tangible fate of one of their own, lingered. Eliza could see the colour drain from Lucy's face. The thought of Rose 'vanishing' made them all feel that way.

Eliza, without turning, gave Lucy a slight, knowing nod. "The rules are there to keep us safe, Lucy," she stated, her tone calm and unwavering, a counterpoint to the train's mounting rhythm. "Follow your training, do your job right—you'll be alright. And the pay's decent. Hard to argue with that."

But as she offered reassurance, the sight of Rose, who had been gone for over a week now, was sharp in her mind. Rose, the very girl Lucy had replaced, her skin a sickly yellow, her breath shallow against a starched pillow.

Did I push Rose too hard? The question, familiar and unwelcome, coiled in Eliza's gut.

She'd seen the signs, hadn't she? That deepening yellow. Her laugh thinned into a rasp. But the quotas never eased. The pressure from above was never-ending.

And Rose had needed the money, like all of them.

"I am a bit tired, Lize," she'd said with a forced smile that didn't meet the eyes. "I'll be right as rain after a good kip."

But she hadn't been. And Eliza, as charge hand, had needed every pair of hands. Bonus or not, they had to meet demand.

She'd mentioned Rose to Miss McDowell, saying she looked peaky. But what else could she have done? Forced her to go home? Cost her a day's pay? Risked her job for slowing the line?

The factory had a logic all its own. Brutal. Impersonal.

Some girls really did disappear—swallowed by the factory's appetite. And with each one, fresh guilt washed through Eliza.

She handled their output, yes. But wasn't she responsible for them, too?

The thought of Lucy—so young, already heavy with grief—ending up like Rose made an icy dread bloom inside her.

The memory of Rose, the fear for her current gang, twisted like a blade beneath her ribs, mocking her words of comfort.

Eliza stared out the dirty window, the memory of Rose cruelly mocking her words of comfort. She leaned closer to June, using the rhythmic clatter of the wheels as cover.

"It's not just the powder, June," she whispered, her voice tight. "It's the machines."

June looked up, her fear mirroring Eliza's. "What do you mean?"

"My press." Her gaze locked on the dark, passing fields. "It's been making a noise all week. A high-pitched sound when it's under full load. Like a scream."

A shiver ran through June. "I've heard it," she breathed. "Like a trapped animal. I thought I was imagining it."

"You weren't," Eliza confirmed, the words feeling like grit. "And if that thing gives way on us, we lose the whole shift. The tally falls, the bonus vanishes... and Skinner..." She didn't need to finish. The name lingered between them in the air, heavy and cold as iron.

A rough, quiet voice cut in from beside them. "It's not the valve screaming."

Eliza and June turned. Mary was staring straight ahead, her gaze fixed on nothing, but she had clearly heard every word. Her own hands were clenched tight in her lap.

"I've heard that sound before," Mary said, her voice low and raspy. "It's the main bearing. It's grinding itself to dust. Heard it for a month straight at the mill. When it went, it seized the whole drive belt. Ripped a man's arm clean off."

A cold, heavy silence fell over their corner of the carriage.

Mary didn't look at them. She just shook her head slowly. "A drop of oil won't fix that, Lize. That thing's a bloody time bomb."

June's hand clenched in her lap. "And with them London men watching every move we make... they'd have us out on our ear for 'damaging factory property'."

Eliza just nodded, her breath fogging the glass. The deadline with Skinner was a frantic, ticking clock in her skull, and now every pull of the press lever felt like a gamble.

The songs and laughter masked it all, but the air on the train thickened with more than tobacco smoke. Whispers about the Ministry inspectors fluttered like startled birds.

"A lass from early shift said they were in Shed D today, them fellas from London," a woman from Selby muttered, her voice breaking the silence.

"Marking names down. Said Mrs Prosserwitch was slowing the line... said she was... surplus." The word landed, stony and clinical.

June's attempt to start another song faltered.

"Surplus," Sarah muttered, voice tight with sudden anger. "Work us to the bone for their bloody war, then toss us out like old rags if we can't keep their impossible pace." She snorted, shifting on the hard bench as if the thought made her physically uncomfortable.

"Place is full of 'em," she said. "Watchers, inspectors, now efficiency bods, all on five quid a week, can you imagine? You'd think we were stuffing the bloody crown jewels, not four an half-inch howitzers for blowing Fritz to bits."

"Overheard Miss McDowell speaking with a charge hand from another shed only yesterday," June said. "New timings... not meeting the mark... warnings issued." She gripped her coat lapels at the thought. "Warnings. The first step towards being made dispensable."

Her worn coat couldn't hold out the cold, like her words to Lucy couldn't quite keep the truth at bay.

Dispensable. That word settled like a rock in the belly for Eliza.

Eliza knew June's situation. If her pay stopped—if she were let go for being too slow—it wouldn't be June and Tommy who paid the price. Margaret's cough was worsening, dry and ragged. Coal was already stretched. A doctor? Out of the question. And Tommy's boots were worn through the soles.

"And them experts they've sent—well, who knows our remaining numbers when they're done counting. Last hired, first fired. War or not, women've always been first to go."

Her tone was flat, but beneath it was heat, resentment, dread, and something more dangerous: conviction. Years of scraping by now strained under the factory's pressure and this new threat of being measured and cut loose.

The others were silent. Sarah, quick with a retort, sat motionless, a cigarette forgotten between her fingers.

"This war's changed things," June said, her voice rising, tight and unsteady. "Now they need us. And they're paying us like proper workers—more than we ever got scrubbing floors or spinning in the mills." She took a breath, chest heaving, a flush of anger on her cheeks.

"They think we'll go back to a few bob a week once it's over? Not likely! We've shown we can do this work—dangerous, skilled, vital work. They can't unsee that when it suits them," June finished.

Her defiance cracked the silence like a match in the dark. Eliza watched the passion ignite in June's eyes.

But Hilda Morton shook her head, deliberate. "It's about what must be done. This bonus... it's not for a new life."

"It's not about what they'll let us do, Sarah," Hilda continued, her voice quieter than the others, the soft lilt of her Irish home more pronounced when she was tired.

"That bloody Lloyd George promises the earth to them suffrage women, but we will get nowt when this is all said and done," June said, her voice tight with a cynical anger that mirrored Sarah's. "He'll get his shells, and we'll get sweet nothing. The vote they're talking about is for women over thirty who own property. How many of us is that, then? They're happy for us to die for them but not to vote for them."

Eliza, sitting opposite, reached out and gently touched June's knee. A quiet plea for calm. But her eyes, when they met June's, held no rebuke—only understanding. And something else. Pride.

Mary listened to the debate with weary patience, watching the fire leap in June's eyes. It was the same fire she remembered seeing in the mill girls' eyes years ago, before their hope was ground down by dust and debt.

She remembered her husband, his quiet endurance at the looms, and the dry, persistent cough that rattled within his chest—the cough he always waved off as "a tickle". She had exchanged the looms for Barnbow, but the bargain felt the same.

Her eyes landed on her hands, discoloured yellow. *Your body for their wage. Your strength for their survival.* She thought of her son, Sam, in a muddy trench in France, and the thick woollen socks her bonus money would buy him. Her war was a quiet one, fought at the kitchen table with a jar of liniment and amidst the clamour of the factory with a steady hand.

Her eyes, full of fatigue that seemed ancient, met Eliza's. "You're alright." Her voice was arid, cutting through the chatter. "And you're all wrong. They need us now, so they talk of heroes and pennies. They'll forget us when they don't need us anymore. They always do. Patriotism, pay, politics... It's all different words for the same thing. It all costs the same. And we're the ones who pay."

A woman from Pontefract sighed heavily. "And where would we go, June love? You know how it is with the Munitions Act—can't change jobs without a leaving certificate from the factory. We're tied to the place, like pit ponies to the cart."

"Aye, tied—and likely whipped if we don't pull hard enough for their liking," Sarah chimed in, her voice lacking its usual cheer.

A woman from Selby leaned across the aisle, her face etched with lines of worry, straining to be heard over a raucous verse of a song from the train rear. "Heard owt from the Front, love?" she asked Eliza softly. "My Alfie's near Arras. Not had a letter in three weeks. Said the mud's so thick it fair swallows men whole."

Eliza shook her head, her smile faltering as she thought of Stan—a bird of anxiety fluttering in her chest.

"Nothing new, Poll. The usual. No news is good news, eh?" But the platitude felt threadbare, worn thin from overuse.

Inside the carriage, seven women from Eliza's crew sat close—not quite friends but bound by Room 42, by danger, by bone-deep exhaustion.

June, practical as ever, leaned in. "Three pounds a week, Lucy. A young un like you ought to be saving most of that. There won't be wages like these after the war, mark my words." Her voice, stripped of fear now, was maternal, seasoned with the wisdom of someone who knew the worth of every farthing. "Keep it for your wedding, or a rainy day. Lord knows they come often enough."

Lucy nodded, the advice taking root.

Eliza listened, thinking, *Yes, my wage is also good at four pounds a week—but with Skinner's outrageous interest, income tax at 25%, and prices climbing sky-high, it's still a stretch.*

But for a girl like Lucy, June's words were sound. The war would end, and women would be pushed back into mills and into service.

"Sarah?" Lucy began, emboldened by the relative privacy of the train carriage. The rhythmic clatter of wheels became a comforting shield. "Your... hands. And some of the others... they look a bit..." She trailed off, unsure how to voice her concern without sounding rude or alarmed.

Sarah tugged her tattered coat tighter, as if fending off a chill that came more from within than out. She flexed her fingers, the yellowing around her knuckles and under her nails stark in the dim light, like old parchment.

She gave a quick shrug—too fast, too practised. "Mustard yellow. Just earning our keep," she said with a lopsided grin. "Occupational hazard, love. The factory leaves its mark." Her voice was a scrape of dry humour, her chuckle more gravel than mirth. "Or maybe we've been hittin' the piccalilli too hard."

Eliza noticed that Sarah's eyes didn't quite meet Lucy's. Whatever flickered there wasn't amusement.

Eliza, watching from her seat by the window, caught the exchange. She gave Sarah a small shake of her head, almost imperceptible. A silent warning: '*Not now. Not in front of the new girl.*'

Sarah had laughed it off. "*Mustard yellow... Just earning our keep.*" But to Eliza, the lie had tasted sour.

The memory of Rose—pale and collapsing—was too fresh.

Eliza listened to the rising tide of resentment and fear, the cold knot of anxiety tightening in her stomach. The pressure from Skinner layered another, more personal dread over the government's demands.

A new quiet fell over the carriage—tense, watchful, and heavy with unspoken fears. The rebellion was over. The battle was about to begin.

12

Chapter 12 : The Halt

5th December 1916

The train's brakes howled, and with one last, shuddering groan, it came to a halt. The singing died. Cold climbed into Eliza's boots as she stepped onto the frost-hardened timber of the platform.

Around her, the night shivered with movement—a river of weary humanity spilling from the carriages, coats bundled tight, the rhythmic clack of heels and worn boots consumed by the frigid air.

Above, the sky hung swollen and still, thick with snow clouds that pressed the gas lamps' glow into a watery, submarine light. The usual boisterous laughter of arrival was absent, substituted with a padded hush, thick with unspoken anxieties of the men with clipboards and stopwatches.

Eliza's eyes scanned the crowd, searching for her girls. She saw Lucy and Sarah stepping down, their faces pale in the gloom. A glance passed between them—too brief for words in the throng but enough to say: '*I see you. I'm here.*' The surge of bodies pushed them apart before more could be said.

At the platform's end, the permit house loomed, and a queue was already forming. Girls stamped their feet against the biting cold, their voices low and nervous.

Sarah, however, swaggered forward and slapped her pass down with theatrical flair. "Evenin', love." She flashed a crooked smile at the young, stone-faced guard. "Hope you have your long johns on under that handsome uniform. Wouldn't want frostbite on those knobbly knees."

He sighed, a hint of a smile playing on his lips. "You again, Jennings."

"Every bloody night, love. Someone's got to keep spirits up," she shot back, though her spirits felt as brittle as the rime underfoot.

*****

As Hilda Morton underwent the cursory inspection at the permit house, her fingers checking that every wisp of hair was tucked beneath her cap, she felt a familiar sense of calm. The rules, the order, the strict removal of anything that could hold an electrostatic charge—it was a discipline she understood. It was a universe away from the chaos of her family's farm in County Clare, a place she had fled six years ago.

A guard grunted as he checked her pass, his uniform reminding her of another. She suddenly remembered the photograph on her nightstand: Albert, her brother, grinning in that same khaki, his eyes full of a life extinguished in the mud of Ypres. She remembered the angry letters from her uncle, the words like acid on the page: *"Let him die for the Crown that starved us."* But her loyalty was to Albert, not a flag. She had traded the quiet order of a classroom for this roaring hell, and every perfect shell that passed her inspection was a line of Euclid, a tribute to the boy in the silver frame. This was her duty.

*****

Eliza followed, her pass half-frozen in her hand. She endured the perfunctory inspection—pockets upturned, buttons checked. No matches, no coins, no excuses. Danger, she knew, wore the mask of innocuous things here.

A new poster had been plastered beside the gate. It showed a bright woman in perfect overalls holding a shell beneath bold words: "*WOMEN ARE DOING THEIR BIT - LEARN TO MAKE MUNITIONS!*"

Its pristine heroine looked nothing like the yellow-stained women trudging in frost. The chill was biting harder now, and the women of Bench 12 huddled closer, linking arms as they walked. Lucy, her mind elsewhere, stumbled on a patch of black ice. Sarah's arm tightened around her, holding her steady.

"Easy, love. Got you," Sarah said, her voice raspy, stripped of its usual mockery.

Eliza, walking just ahead, paused and looked back, her gaze sharp but not unkind. She observed the flash of terror in Lucy's eyes, followed by a rush of shame. "You're alright, Atkinson," Eliza said, quiet but firm, a clear note of command that was also meant as reassurance. "Just find your feet. You've been steady all week."

Lucy gave a grateful nod, her shoulders relaxing a fraction. The brief praise from their charge hand provided a small measure of relief.

Sarah, seeing the moment, couldn't resist a grin. She nudged Lucy with her elbow. "See? The boss said you're grand. Now stop trying to break your neck before you've earned us our bonus. I've got ideas for that money."

A trace of a genuine smile graced Lucy's lips, and for a single moment, all three of them—the leader, the defiant heart, and the fragile newcomer—were bound by a thread of shared understanding as they moved towards the canteen.

Sarah snorted, dry as cinders, her eyes riveted on the smiling woman on the poster. "Doing our bit and getting poisoned for it. How come she's not yellow like us?"

"Or smelling like Amatol," Mary said, her voice flat. "She looks like she works at a bank."

"Check those arms." June nudged Hilda. "She's built like a navvy. Reckon she's eating more than milk and stew."

Hilda adjusted her scarf, her gaze lingering on the poster with a thoughtful, almost sad expression. "It's for morale," she said, her Irish lilt soft but clear. "A symbol. I suppose it's something the country needs right now."

Sarah let out a short, sharp laugh, devoid of any humour. "Morale?" She said the word as if it were something tasting bitter. "That's a word for men in offices, Hilda. For men who've never had to scrub yellow from their skin till it's raw, only to wake up and find it's still there, a part of you. Morale doesn't put coal in the scuttle. It's a pretty picture to stop us thinking too hard about the fact they're killing us for a few pennies a day."

Her words hung in the cold air, sharp but true.

June, whose desperation was a tangible thing, nodded, her eyes still on the poster as if trying to draw strength from it. "She's right, though," she said almost to herself. "It is a symbol. I look at that and I don't see morale... I see a doctor's fee. I see a winter coat for Margaret.

If looking at that pretty lie gets another hundred shells out of me, and that gets me the bonus... well, I'll stare at it all bloody night."

The raw honesty of her confession silenced them for a few steps. It was a truth they all understood. The poster wasn't selling patriotism; it was selling hope, in its cruellest and most necessary form.

It was Mary Sutcliffe who broke the quiet. She hadn't looked at the poster at all, her gaze fixed on the path ahead. "Symbol or shilling," she concluded, voice as dry as dust, "it all costs the same in the end. Come on. Our milk's getting cold."

A symbol of what? Eliza wondered, pulling her thin coat tighter. *A symbol of a clean, strong woman who doesn't exist. Not here. Not with the yellow staining our skin and the dread that settles in our gut like undigested lead.*

13

Chapter 13 : A Thousand Hands, A Single Fear

5th December 1916

Through the long corridor, Mr William Parkin sat hunched in his cramped booth in the warmth of the mechanics' office, a quiet island of order in the chaos. The air smelled of old ledgers, faint pipe smoke, and a metallic, sourness. His pencil stub scratched the page with steady purpose.

"Well, girls," he said, his eyes fixed on the ledger, "ready for another stab at glory? Or just trying to look busy for the new overseers?" His attempt at jest fell flat in the tense air.

Sarah, undeterred, winked as she leaned over the table. "Looking sharp, Mr Parkin. Got a sweetheart canary waiting after the shift? Or is it us you're trying to impress?" Sarah leaned in, irrepressible as ever, her grin flashing in the dim light. "But that moustache needs some extra wax, Mr Parkin. It's flopping like a dead cat."

"Enough of your cheek, Jennings," he said, mock stern, though a ghost of a smile tugged at his lips, softening the creases around his tired eyes. "Anyway, not bloody likely, I have you lot to look after," he added. "And mind your pace tonight, Jennings. Word is, they're not only counting shells anymore."

As Sarah moved on, Lucy passed like a shadow behind her, the clock card trembling in her hand.

Parkin's eyes softened. "Evening, Miss Atkinson."

She blinked, startled, and gave a shy "Good evening, Mr Parkin" before disappearing through the door like smoke.

"Anything that needs fixing at your bench, Eliza?" he asked, but his tone was more pointed than usual. He leaned forward slightly, his voice dropping.

"I was doing my rounds last shift, and I heard a high-pitched shriek from your press. It sounded as if the pressure valve was struggling. Are you sure it's alright?"

Eliza's heart gave a hard lurch. He knew. Of course, he knew. He missed nothing. For a split second, she was about to tell him the truth—to confess that the groan was getting worse, that the lever had been sticking. The words were on the tip of her tongue.

But then two images flashed through her mind, jagged and brutal as broken glass. The first was the faces of her children, their cheeks pinched blue with cold in the morning half-light. The second was Skinner's voice, a low growl vibrating in the rotten air between them: *"Saturday morning, Eliza. Let's avoid any unpleasantness, shall we?"* The memory of his threat was a physical thing, a cold dread that seized her gut and squeezed the truth from her throat.

Over Parkin's shoulder, she saw a trace of movement down the long corridor. It was Mr Finch, the man from London, his stopwatch glinting. Downtime meant no bonus. No bonus meant Skinner would win.

The lie came out thin and brittle. "No, Mr Parkin, all's fine. Only the usual moans and groans. Maybe a drop of fresh oil on the lever, if you get a moment. Keep it singing."

He held her gaze for a long moment, his eyes tired but perceptive, any hint of a smile he'd had earlier gone.

"That's not singing, Eliza," he replied, any prior jest now missing. "That's a scream. You be careful."

He knew she was lying. She could feel it in the pressure of his stare, see it in the slight tightening of his mouth.

His perceptive gaze made her shift in her seat, uneasy. The brief, tense silence dragged her back to a memory from a few months ago—a night when the central drive belt had snapped.

She'd shared a cup of tea with Parkin in his cramped booth while they waited. He'd seen the same weariness in her eyes then.

"You carry a heavy load for this lot, Eliza," he said. "More than a charge hand ought to."

"We all have our burdens, Mr Parkin," she replied.

"Aye, that you are," he agreed, a sad smile touching his lips. "It's a funny thing, this war. The ones who want to go can't. The ones who shouldn't have to bear the brunt of it."

He paused then, his eyes losing focus.

"I tried to sign up myself, you know. Back in '14. Lads half my age were marching off, and I was stuck here fixing looms." He gave a short, humourless laugh. "They wouldn't have me. Said I had a flaw in my chest, a whisper in the lung from my days in the mills. Not fit for the trenches."

He tapped the wall of his booth. "Came here instead. Figured if I can't fire the shells, the least I can do is try to keep the lasses that make 'em safe."

The memory of his quiet decency made the lie she'd just told him feel like a fresh betrayal. He let out a slow, drained sigh, the fight going out of him.

"Alright, Eliza." His voice was now flat with a resignation worse than any argument. He looked her straight in the eye again, his expression deadly serious. "But you give me a shout the *second* it makes that noise again. Don't you be a hero for their quotas. That machine gives way, it won't only be the tally that gets hurt. Understood?"

"Yes, Mr Parkin," she said, the guilt a crushing burden in her stomach.

He nodded once, then turned back to his ledger. "Off to the canteen with you lot for your milk."

His words now formed the nightly ritual for the Barnbow lasses.

The canteen—tall ceiling, corrugated walls—held three rows of eight tables, enough for two hundred girls, a cavern of jaundiced light and echoing noise. Milk and barley water lined one side, the hulking 'Jackson' boiler puffing tea steam from the other as they filed in from the biting cold.

Mismatched enamel mugs clinked against dented trays, and weary voices murmured beneath the hum. A heaviness was present in the air with the sour scent of milk, damp wool, and a metallic tang that clung to the nostrils. The smell of fatigued routine overlaid with a sharp tang of collective nervousness was familiar.

Conversations were muted, heads bent closer together. Eliza's gang settled at their usual corner table.

Sarah Jennings slammed her mug on the table with a clatter that made Lucy jump.

"Right then," she announced to no one in particular, a wicked grin spreading across her face. "Another glass of the finest milk and water a woman's penny can buy. What I wouldn't give for a proper pint of ale."

"You'd be asleep on the line before the first trolley was done," Mary Sutcliffe said without looking up, her voice dry as dust.

"Aye, but I'd be dreaming of a better life," Sarah shot back. She took a theatrical sip of her milk and shuddered.

"A better life?" June said, swirling the thin milk in her mug. "I'd settle for a life without a cough in it. One where I'm not counting pennies for a bag of coal to keep the damp out. That's good enough for me."

Hilda Morton, who had been sitting straight-backed, added, "That bonus isn't for a better life. It's to see this work finished. My brother, Albert... he chose to wear that uniform. The shells are for him. For the boys like him."

Sarah snorted, though with no real malice. "That's a fine thought, Hilda love, and I hope you're right. But patriotism pays no rent. That bonus money is a roof over my lad's head. Simple as that. Nowt to do with bringing boys home, more to do with giving mine a home to come back to."

Sarah leaned forward, her eyes glinting with mischief. She winked at Nora, who offered a small, hesitant smile.

*****

Nora Kershaw, watching Lucy with a gentle, knowing smile, patted the seat beside her. "Don't you mind her," she commented, her voice a whisper. "Sarah's bark is a good deal worse than her bite. Are you alright, love? You look tired."

As Lucy mumbled a reply, Nora's gaze drifted, though her mind was miles away. Her thumb traced the smooth, cool surface of her wedding band. That simple, unbroken circle was her compass. She thought of Will on the vast grey beast of the North Sea and pulled his last letter from her pocket, the paper soft from being read repeatedly.

She didn't need the words; she knew them by heart. *"I keep that little pebble from Filey in my pocket,"* he'd written. *"It's you, that stone. Soft around the edges, but solid right through. Won't crack, no matter what."*

She kept her work at Barnbow a secret from him. Her letters back were a tended garden where only good news grew—cheerful anecdotes about helping a neighbour or a new recipe for stew.

He had enough monsters to fight; he didn't need to picture her wrestling her own in a roaring factory. Her war was fought in silence, and her hope was that the money hidden in the tea caddy was a deposit on a life waiting to begin.

*****

"Come on, girls, let's have a song before the real work starts. How about a rousing chorus of 'Mademoiselle from Armentières'?" Sarah cleared her throat and sang in a loud, brazen voice, *"The officers get all the steak, parlez-vous!"*

Hilda looked positively scandalised, muttering, "Sarah, honestly, not in here."

"Oh, listen to her! All proper, our Hilda. You can take the girl out of the convent school, but you can't take the convent school out of the girl, eh?" Sarah teased. "It's good for morale! Better than those dreary hymns Hilda's always humming."

Lucy eyed her mug of the so-named "TNT tonic" with suspicion.

"Drink it, lass. Supposed to help with the fumes. The poison. Doesn't do much for the taste, mind—like watered-down whitewash," Mary said, her voice rough and hushed.

"They say this stuff stops the poison from taking hold. I think it's a plot to make us too miserable to notice," Sarah chimed in.

Lucy's eyes were fixed on her mug, fingers clenched tight. Fear stuck to her like dust.

Poor lamb. Ready to bolt, thought Eliza. Barnbow would either break her or forge her. Eliza hoped for the latter, for all their sakes. Her thoughts wandered to Stan. She hoped he was getting something better than chalky milk in those tunnels.

"Don't know what they're feeding those cows. "Chalk, by the looks of it," she said with a grin. "Hundred and twenty of 'em and still can't get a drop o' decent milk. It's a bloody mystery, that."

Eliza took a small sip, the chalky liquid coating her tongue. Her attention was snagged on the lowered voices from a nearby table.

"Is that her at Wren's table? The quiet one with the dark hair," one woman said.

"Aye, that's her—the new girl who lost her brother at the Somme. Poor girl. Still looks half a child herself. Tragic, it is."

A third woman sighed, voice carrying. "And it never stops. The Somme's still going, killing more boys every day, they say in the papers. My nephew's got his papers for France. I'm dreading it, I am..."

Eliza's gaze flicked to Lucy. The girl had gone still, her small hand frozen around her mug. The warmth from the milk couldn't possibly be touching the chill that had spread across her face, leaving it pale and pinched. Eliza heard the murmurs from the other table again and caught the glances cast in her direction.

The new girl. The one who lost her brother. The words were a brand, weren't they? A label attached to her that made her grief a public spectacle for strangers to whisper about over their tea. The thought of it—the sheer unfairness—made something hard and protective tighten in Eliza's chest.

As if feeling her stare, Lucy looked up and tried to offer a brave smile. It was a pathetic, watery thing that didn't reach her eyes. She took a small drink of her milk, but her hand trembled so badly that some of it splashed over the side, unnoticed.

As Lucy tried to regain her composure, Eliza leaned towards Mary Sutcliffe, her tone a low, worried whisper masked by the canteen's din. "Look at her, Mary. She's going to drop one. I can feel it. Her nerves are shot to pieces."

Mary's gaze followed Eliza's to the pale, trembling girl. She said nothing for a long moment, her weathered face unreadable as she sipped at her milk.

Eliza pressed on, the words weighing like guilt on her lips. "I'm thinking I need to talk to McDowell." Her gaze fixed on Lucy. "See if they can move her into the paint room. It's not safe... for her or for us."

Mary turned, her tired eyes meeting Eliza's. She didn't disagree. She simply offered a slow, resigned nod. "Grief is a heavy load," she murmured, voice arid. "And this place offers no comfort." She paused, her gaze sweeping over the tense faces at their table. "You do what you think is right, Lize. You're the charge hand. It's your burden to carry."

From a nearby table, a pale woman leaned in, her face drawn and eyes rimmed with red. She held up a folded *Yorkshire Post*, a finger stabbing at a grim headline.

HEAVY FIGHTING ON THE SOMME - ARTILLERY DUELS DOMINATE

"My Bill's out there." Her voice echoed in the sudden lull. "Last letter said they're firing shells faster than we can make 'em. Thousands a day. To hold the line."

The words landed like pebbles into the canteen's nervous quiet. The war—vast and hungry—surged closer with that single page. Suddenly, the numbers on the tally sheets weren't only numbers; they were meaningful. They were lifelines.

"Oi, Jennings!"

The call cracked through the room like a dropped shell. Ann Price stood with her crew, her posture an obvious challenge.

"Heard your lot could only manage six hundred." Her voice was loud enough to carry. "We hit six-fifty, and the London brass said we were a 'model of efficiency'. Best see that your gang doesn't drag their heels. Wouldn't want anyone labelled... 'surplus to requirements'."

The word—*surplus*—hit Sarah like a blow to the gut. If these London men cut her loose, the flat in Leeds would vanish like smoke. *No, I won't let them.*

She turned, her grin sharp as a knife. "Six-twelve, Price! And every one of 'em spot-on, not like the shoddy duds your lot chuck out. It's quality they want, not just a mad dash. Let's see who's surplus when they check for that."

Ann Price grinned, a sharp, knowing smirk. "Listen to her, all high and mighty. Gettin' right mardy, are we, Jennings? Big talk for a lass goin' canary. Hope your hands hold steady when they're timin' you or there'll be nowt left of thee but a yellow smudge and a foul smell."

A wiry girl from Ann's crew, her face sharp with nervous energy, leaned forward and said, "Aye, our Ann's right. We heard them London men sayin' they're lookin' for speed. Not slow coaches."

Sarah's eyes narrowed on the girl, her grin turning venomous. "And you look like a powerful gust of wind would blow you over, love. Best hope they're not measuring for backbone or you'll be the first one out of the gate." Sarah was getting into her stride and ready to unleash a flurry of insults. "I've seen more meat on a sparrow's kneecap than's on you."

"Don't mind Ann Price," June whispered to Eliza, nodding towards the other table. "Heard her father was one of the men laid off last month. She's got her whole family riding on that bonus. It's made her sharp as a razor."

Eliza watched the scene unfold, an icy dread warring with a surge of fierce pride. Part of her wanted to let Sarah fight their corner, to put Ann Price and her cronies back in their box with a few well-aimed insults. Sarah was good at that. But her eyes darted towards the watchers' table near the door. Any real row, any shouting that drew official attention, would be a black mark against Bench 12.

Finch was looking for any excuse to label a team inefficient, and a public brawl in the canteen would be a gift-wrapped present. She had to shut this down. It was her duty as charge hand, even if it meant swallowing their pride.

She didn't flinch. Her voice, when it came, was cold steel, now directed at all of them. "Alright, Price. Come morning, we'll see who's counting pennies and who still has a place on the line."

Ann's bravado faltered for a moment under Eliza's cool, unwavering gaze before she shrugged and turned away with a final laugh meant for the whole canteen.

Eliza tapped the rim of her mug, drawing their focus back to their own table. "Right, listen." There was no volume to her voice but no mistaking the steel in it, cutting through their private anxieties. "Last shift, we hit six-twelve. That's a hundred and twelve over."

A pause. Murmurs of approval, though less enthusiastic than usual. Boots shifted, backs straightened, eyes darted nervously around the canteen.

"That kind of number means coal on the fire, bacon on the pan." *And a roof over our heads*, she added in her thoughts, Skinner's threat a raw wound.

"We keep that pace, Friday's payout won't be scraps." Eliza met their gazes, one by one. "But steady. No rushing, no cutting corners. Not with those... visitors about. Understood?"

A heavy silence fell, punctuated by distant clatter.

Lucy nodded quickly, her eyes wide, fixed on Eliza like a lifeline.

Nora's lips pressed into a thin line, her hand resting on Will's scarf—a silent vow of care.

Hilda gave a curt, military dip of her chin, her schoolmistress precision already calculating the balance between speed and safety.

Mary Sutcliffe's gaze was unreadable, but her weathered hands gave the faintest clench; she'd seen too many accidents born of haste.

June forced a wobbly smile. "Steady it is, Lize. Can't have us blowing ourselves up before we get our hands on that bacon, eh?" Her lightness didn't chase away the chill settling over them.

Only then did Sarah, ever brazen, raise her mug. "To bacon and coal and to not ending up 'surplus to requirements'."

Her bravado now carried a sharper irony.

*****

The others raised their mugs, a fragile, temporary solidarity under the pressure-filled circumstances. Mary Sutcliffe, however, only stared into her cup of chalky milk. She sipped slowly, the taste like whitewash on her tongue. She'd seen this all before—the impossible targets, the talk of bonuses, the way desperation was sharpened into a tool to make women work faster. It was the same rhythm as the looms that had taken her husband's health and ruined her leg.

Her thoughts wandered from the noisy canteen to the quiet of her kitchen table and the aroma of the strong-smelling liniment she worked into her calf each evening. The pain was an old injury, a price paid long ago for a different wage. Her husband, Tom, had paid his price, coming home from the mill with his cap dusted with cotton he could never fully shake and a dry, persistent cough he always dismissed with a flick of his hand. He had endured the looms for her and their boy. Now, she endured this roaring factory for that same boy, her Sam, somewhere in the mire of a French trench.

She looked at the younger women at her table, at their fierce hopes and raw fears. Her bonus money wasn't for a new beginning; it was for another pair of thick woollen socks, for a bar of his favourite carbolic soap to put in a parcel.

Her pain for his comfort. It had always been a fair trade. The industrial whistle shrieked, a piercing command that shattered her thoughts. Mary placed her mug down with a soft, final click. The moment had arrived to pay the price.

*****

The time for talk was over.

Eliza stood, pushing her mug back. "Right then," she said, calm despite the turmoil she knew churned beneath. "Let's get to it."

They rose together, a small band of women, their aspirations and anxieties now bound to a dangerous promise made weeks ago.

As Eliza's gang rose, Ann caught her eye again from the opposite side of the room. Her expression had changed. The hard bravado was gone, replaced by something that looked unnervingly like desperation. She made a slight, unsure gesture. "Eliza, can I have a word?"

Eliza paused as the other girls passed by, giving Ann a wary, questioning look. Ann walked over, stopping a short distance away, unable to make eye contact with her.

"I'm sorry about all that." Her gaze fell to her boots, a rare, half-ashamed apology. "It's... My dad has lost his job. Laid off from the colliery last month. My mam's trying to take in washing, but it's not enough to keep the fire lit." She looked up, and Eliza saw a raw fear reflected in her eyes that mirrored her own.

"This bonus... it's not meant for looking good for these efficiency sods. It's the only way we'll have fuel for the fire next week. I had to... I had to show my girls we were fighting for it."

Eliza gave a measured nod, the anger she'd felt moments before dissolving into a quiet understanding. She looked past Ann to her crew, at June's worried face, at Sarah's fierce defiance, at all the hopes and fears gathered under this one vast, humming roof. Every woman in this factory was fighting her own desperate war.

As they made their way towards the changing rooms, their boots clattering on the cleanway, Eliza felt the pressure of that promised penny settle over them—heavy and real, as oppressive as the chemical-laden air that awaited.

The whole frantic, terrifying race had started in that stuffy little office back in October. It seemed a lifetime ago.

14

Chapter 14 : A Whisper of Victory

October 28th, 1916, Barnbow Canteen – Night Shift

By late October, a restless energy—sharper than the usual pre-shift murmur—buzzed through the canteen. For days, rumours had swirled like smoke: talk of new targets, a significant push from the Ministry of Munitions, and most tantalising of all, a potential bonus scheme.

The whispers grew louder with each newspaper headline reporting the grinding horrors of the Somme. Since July, the offensive had chewed through men and ammunition with the same merciless hunger, and still, the guns roared on across the Channel.

Then came the summons. All watchers, charge hands, and inspectors from every shift were ordered—no one used the word "invited"—to report to Captain Miller's office.

Each group was called just before their shift began, like a changing of the guard. Eliza stood among the night shift leaders, shoulder to shoulder in the narrow, smoke-stained corridor outside Miller's door.

The air was thick with tobacco and tension, with the tired scent of boot polish and worry.

Captain Miller's office loomed over the factory floor like a watchtower, a glass-fronted perch with a commanding view of the factory below. Inside, the air held the stale weight of pipe smoke and dusty ledgers—the distinct smell of bureaucracy and war.

Every surface was brushed with a fine yellow powder, and the dust was inescapable. The office was functional, not a place of home comforts.

Captain Miller stood at the head of the room, hands clasped behind his back, his face unreadable. The familiar scent of his pipe was absent today. In its place was a tension Eliza could feel, sharp and nearly tangible.

"You've done great work, ladies and gentlemen," he began speaking, his voice calm. His gaze drifted across the room, resting for a moment on each face.

Eliza felt her stomach clench.

"But the army's hungry for more. Desperately so. The Somme offensive is consuming ammunition at a rate we've never seen. I have reports of entire gun batteries firing non-stop for a week straight, their barrels warping red-hot from the constant use, their men left deafened by the roar."

He stopped and looked around the room at the women's faces.

"Millions of shells fired, and still, the demand is rising. The Ministry of Munitions is under immense pressure. Mr Lloyd George desires a business-oriented administration and will not tolerate another scandal like that of 1915."

He paused and let the silence stretch.

"It's a national imperative. The boys in France—your sons, husbands, brothers—they need every shell we can turn out."

He stepped forward.

"From today, production increases. The Ministry has authorised an additional incentive—a one penny bonus for every shell produced over the five-hundred quota, per gang, per shift."

A ripple passed through the room. Eliza heard the quickened breaths and saw muted glances. She felt the mood shift to a combination of hope and dread.

A penny a shell. The offer hung in the stale air of the office. It sounded like nowt—an insult. But as the other women shifted and murmured, Eliza's mind was already racing, the numbers falling into place.

It wasn't a fortune, but it was *something*.

It was boots for Bobby. It was a full scuttle of coal. It made all the difference. It was a chance, however slim, to chip away at Skinner's debt. A little more time before the knock came. A chance to serve something better than bread and dripping to the children.

But five hundred shells in eight hours was already demanding—already a grind. Already dangerous. Her thoughts flicked to the filling rooms, the fine powders in the air, the aching joints, the delicate fuses.

Every step faster meant a step closer to mistakes. The kind that exploded. She'd heard the stories—blasts in other factories, arms and lives gone in the blink of an eye.

Still, her hands curled into fists. She had a promise to keep.

Miller's voice cut back through her thoughts, now harder, colder.

"This isn't only about the coin. This is your bit for victory. Every extra shell brings our boys home faster. This bonus isn't a reward—it's a duty."

Then his tone shifted—calm, administrative, detached.

"And, of course," he said, "it allows us to identify our most productive assets. The Ministry is keen to ensure all 'National Factories' are running at peak efficiency. This scheme will help us measure that."

His words landed like lead weights. A reward. A test. A warning.

Eliza's blood ran colder—peak *efficiency.* The words sounded less like remuneration and more like those a pit manager used right before a round of sackings, a cold way of saying that some would be kept on and some would be cast aside. This wasn't about earning more. It was about not falling short and not being the one who couldn't keep up.

Her heart gave a sharp, anxious thud. Another hundred shells a shift—what would that mean for her girls? For Rose, already running herself ragged, her cough deepening by the day. Could they handle it? Could she make them handle it?

The image of Skinner's face swam unbidden to the front of her mind—tight-lipped, unyielding, calculating. The cost of falling short with him was unthinkable. A shiver traced her spine, one that had little to do with the autumn chill creeping through Miller's draughty office.

Miller's language had been clipped, impersonal. But to Eliza, the meaning was clear—and chilling. The talk of bonuses and patriotism was a veil. This was a measurement. An assessment. A test of who could endure and who would fail. A penny a shell, yes—but maybe also a quiet way to thin the ranks.

Beside her, she saw Miss McDowell shift on her heels, arms crossed tight over her coat, mouth drawn into a hard line. Eliza caught her eye and felt they shared a silent, grim understanding. They knew exactly what this was.

"That will be all, ladies and gentlemen," Miller said, turning back to the papers on his desk, dismissing them like a schoolmaster.

The charge hands and watchers shuffled out, quieter now, their earlier buzz replaced by a nervous hum.

As the charge hands dispersed down the cleanway, their faces a mixture of grim determination and anxiety, Miss McDowell lingered by the doorway. She saw William Parkin waiting further down the corridor, his wrench in hand, his expression already troubled. He'd seen the faces of the women coming out; he knew something was wrong. She walked over to him, her posture rigid with contained anger.

"William," she began, her voice above a whisper, "what are your thoughts on a penny a shell bonus?"

Parkin wiped a greasy hand on a rag, his eyes meeting hers with a look of profound weariness. "My thoughts, Miss McDowell, Edna? I think the machines are already running ragged. The maintenance windows between shifts are barely long enough to oil the main drives, let alone check for real wear. Pushing for more speed..." He shook his head with hesitation. "It's asking for trouble. It's asking for one lass to make a mistake."

"My thoughts exactly," McDowell confirmed, her lips tightening. "But it's out of our hands. Ministry orders."

"It always is," Parkin said, his gaze hardening with a specific worry. "And there's something else. That press on Bench 12, Eliza Wren's bench. There's been a sound coming from it for a week now. A high-pitched shriek when it's under full load. That's not only a groan of old machinery, Edna. That's a pressure valve screaming for mercy."

A knot of cold dread tightened McDowell's stomach. She had noticed it herself—a discordant note in the factory's symphony. "I've heard it. I've put in a request for a diagnostic."

"A diagnostic won't be enough," Parkin insisted, urgency threading through his hushed words. "It needs to be taken offline. Stripped down. But with these new quotas and Finch and his stopwatch breathing down everyone's neck..." He let the sentence hang in the air, the implication clear.

McDowell nodded, her resolve hardening. "Thank you, William. You've confirmed my fears. Leave it with me. I will speak to Captain Miller about it myself. That bench will not run tonight if I believe it to be a danger to my girls."

Parkin just gave a slow, fatalistic nod. "Let's hope he listens, Edna. Let's hope someone does." He turned and headed towards the noise from the factory floor, leaving McDowell alone in the corridor with the gravity of his warning.

Eliza walked on, her chest tightening with a potent blend of hope and dread. The bonus might be their lifeline, a glimmer of relief from Skinner's looming shadow, a few more meals, and a roof held secure, at least for now.

It was a possibility, albeit small. But the war, like the factory, never stopped taking its toll. And now it demanded more than muscle and care—it wanted proof of usefulness, measurable and merciless.

She pictured Stan deep in some muddy tunnel beneath France, carving his way forward without light. Another type of danger. An alternative kind of courage.

She would match it. She had to. For Bobby. For Beth. For little Stanley. For their home. For their survival.

Eliza pushed through the canteen doors, the weight of Miller's announcement heavy on her shoulders. She saw her gang at their usual corner table. Sarah Jennings was holding court, making Rose Turner give a weak giggle. June, Hilda, and Nora looked up as she approached, their expressions a mixture of curiosity and apprehension.

June, ever thoughtful, slid a mug of milk towards Eliza as she sat with a heavy sigh.

"Well, Lize?" Sarah asked, her usual bravado edged with impatience. "Spit it out. Has old Miller decided we're heroines, or is he handing us more grief?"

Eliza took a slow sip, gathering her thoughts, her eyes sweeping across them. "He had news," her voice serious. "Good news, he called it—for those willing to earn it. And work hard."

They leaned in. She watched their faces, seeing a reflection of her fragile hope. "The quota's still five hundred shells a shift. But starting tonight... there's a bonus. A penny for every shell a gang finishes beyond five hundred."

Silence fell. Then Sarah's eyes sparked with a fire Eliza had expected.

"A penny?" she said, the disbelief sharp. "A whole bloody penny per shell over? By God!" A slow whistle slipped through her teeth. "If we put our backs into it—six hundred, could be more—that's proper money! Enough for some good furniture in that flat in Leeds I've been dreaming of!"

Sarah burned bright, Eliza thought, but an icy knot of dread formed in her stomach. This place, this work... it would take more than dreams if they pushed too far.

June gasped, her hand to her mouth. "A penny... Are you sure?" she said, and Eliza could see the hope and fear warring in her eyes.

"Even an extra fifty a night... That's real help."

It's always the bairns, Eliza thought, her mind flashing to her own. *That's what drives a woman to places like this.*

Rose, looking paler than ever, coughed into her hand. "But over five hundred, Lize?" she asked. "We're already breaking ourselves to reach that. My hands... they're shaking something awful."

A pang of concern, sharp and familiar, went through Eliza. The yellow tinge was creeping deeper into Rose's skin. At this pace... if they pushed harder, it might finish her.

She kept her voice even, though she knew the girls could likely see the strain in her eyes. "Captain said we'll need to aim for forty-five seconds a shell. That's the pace if the bonus is to mean anything."

A collective gasp rose, quickly muffled. *Forty-five seconds.* It sounded cruel—impossible.

She saw Nora say nothing, her lips tightening into a thin line as her fingers twisted the edge of her faded blue scarf—Will's scarf, Eliza knew. *She'll drive herself to the bone if she thinks it'll keep him safe,* Eliza thought. *But at what cost?*

"We've done it before," Eliza stated, her voice piercing the rising murmur. "We know what we're capable of. We're the best gang in this factory, and we've got the numbers to prove it. We stick together, we keep our heads, we do the work exactly like we've done. And Hilda, you're right—every shell has to be perfect. We prioritise efficiency without compromising quality. We're Bench 12. We watch out for one another."

Her gaze lingered on Rose. "Rose, if you're not up to it, you tell me. We'll manage. But if we can do this... it might make a difference."

A fragile silence settled. Then Sarah raised her mug.

"To a penny a shell—and to hell with anyone who said we can't!"

One by one, they echoed her, their voices soft but resolute. June smiled, a fierce mother's hope on her face that Eliza understood all too well. Even Rose gave a slight nod.

The factory whistle shrieked. Eliza stood.

15

Chapter 15 : The Watchtower

5th December 1916, Barnbow, Room 42

From her glass-fronted office above the floor, Miss Edna McDowell watched the night shift arrive—a river of blue smocks streaming down the cleanway into the noise. The machines roared beyond the glass, not loud but constant, a guttural growl that vibrated in her chest, a buzz that never left her teeth.

At forty-seven, after two decades teaching in Tadcaster—days of chalk dust, quiet order, and the tidy comfort of literature—she'd believed herself beyond youthful anxiety. She was wrong. Here, unease clung to everything—a fine yellow dust in the air, coating every surface.

Her desk was a battlefield. On one side, stacked with grim precision by Mr Finch's clerk, sat the Ministry's latest targets. Cold numbers. Ruthless logic. No trace of the weary faces she saw below.

Across the desk lay her sister's last letter—worn, creased, ink-smudged from too many reads. Grief clung to every line, as if the paper might tear under its weight. McDowell's eyes locked on one line—her nephew's words, passed on by his mother, now etched in her mind.

"We need more shells, Aunt Edna. We can't hold them back without the shells."

Horace. Not the soldier in the photo but the ink-stained boy in her Tadcaster classroom—brow furrowed, writing about a robin. He'd loved stories. He was gentle. And now, his last correspondence from the Front had begged for the very weapons these women were being driven to make.

A surge of cold, bitter fury washed over her, of such force that it caused her to feel a little sick for a moment. *Is this the victory he died for? A factory floor that mirrors the trenches in its reckless consumption of life?*

The bonus scheme—praised in London as patriotic—was poison. She'd seen it at once. Just yesterday, she'd stormed into the captain's office, the Leeds Infirmary report clutched in her hand.

"It's Rose Turner, Captain." Her voice was tight with an apprehension that was proving prophetic. She placed the paper on his desk. "Toxic jaundice. The doctor said her liver is failing. She will not be returning."

Miller read the report, rubbing his face. He looked worn-out—uniform hanging loose, eyes dark from sleepless nights. "That's the third this quarter, Edna," he replied, all command gone from his voice.

"Rose is twenty-one," McDowell said, her tone icy. "We're poisoning them. For what? So Mr Finch can brag about a two per cent boost? The girls are exhausted. They're slipping. And when they slip, people die. We're packing death, Captain—not biscuits for a church tea."

He looked up from the report. "The Somme is a gaping maw, McDowell. My brother-in-law was lost last month. The letters I receive are no different from the ones you do. The targets are not mine to set." He tapped a stack of Ministry directives on his desk. "They must be met."

And now there were the men from London to enforce it. Mr Finch, with his cold, glinting spectacles and the incessant, unnerving click of his stopwatch, a sound like a deathwatch beetle ticking in the walls. And his shadow, Inspector Harper, whose grim silence was more intimidating than any shouted order.

Predators in this ecosystem were what they were. Their talk of "peak efficiency" and "surplus workers" reduced these women—her girls, she couldn't help but think of them as—to components in a cold, unforgiving equation. They spoke of human beings, of hopes and fears and tired bodies, as if they were faulty cogs to be measured, timed, and discarded.

The factory whistle screamed, a piercing, an undeniable order that cut through the relative quiet of her office, making the teacup on her desk rattle. The time for reflection was over. Her duty began.

Edna McDowell stood, her back straightening into the familiar, rigid posture of the schoolmistress. She put on the mask of authority, worn like armour, and stepped out of her office. The factory's loud noise hit her like a physical force, a flood of heat and noise that always stole her breath for a second.

She began her patrol, her eyes already scanning the benches, checking the lines, her heart a tight knot of dread.

She wasn't looking only for mechanical faults anymore. She was praying, with a desperation that felt unprofessional and entirely necessary, she wouldn't find the disaster she felt brewing in the heavy, chemical-laden air.

16

Chapter 16 : The Cauldron

5th December 1916, Barnbow, Room 42

The changing rooms at Barnbow were a place of transformation, a brief, liminal space between the outside world and the inferno of the factory floor. The air was cool and damp, thick with the chemical scent of soda used to scrub the magazine gear and the faint, human smell of weary bodies. Here, under the stark, unforgiving glare of a few naked bulbs, the women stripped away their civilian selves, folding their coats and skirts, their own lives, into small metal lockers.

They emerged as a uniformed army—long flannel bloomers, practical cotton shifts, and the pale blue smocks that marked them as workers.

"Christ, look at these things," Sarah's voice boomed from a few lockers down, making several girls jump. She held up the standard-issue bloomers with theatrical disdain. "More flannel than a preacher's sermon. They do everything they can to make sure a lass forgets she's a woman in here, don't they?"

A few nervous titters rippled across the benches. Lucy Atkinson, her back to Sarah, felt her cheeks burn a deep crimson as she fumbled with her uniform, hoping to become invisible.

On the other side of the room, Hilda Morton struggled with a stiff, uncooperative button on her clean, pressed smock. Her fingers, stiff from the cold journey, refused to work the small disc through the tight hole. A flicker of prim frustration crossed her face, a silent, internal battle against the stubborn fabric.

Mary Sutcliffe, who missed nothing, saw the struggle. Without a word, she stepped over to Hilda. Her own gnarled, capable fingers—used to far more complicated work—guided the button through the hole in one smooth, practised motion.

"Thank you, Mary," Hilda said, the formal gratitude in stark contrast to Sarah's boisterous complaints.

Mary gave a single, almost imperceptible nod, a silent acknowledgement of a shared duty, before returning to her locker.

Eliza saw it all. She saw the easy way June and Sarah joked as they tied their caps, the practised movements of Mary helping Hilda, the quiet, almost reverent way Nora folded her clothes. And she saw Lucy, hesitant and unsure, her gaze carrying a fear that clung to her like mist.

Hair was pinned tight and tucked into close-fitting caps, every stray wisp a potential source of disaster. Corsets with their metal stays, hairpins, rings—any small vanity or personal treasure that might carry a static charge—were strictly forbidden. The ritual was one of removal, stripping them of their individuality until they were a collective of blue-smocked figures, their only distinction the somnolent hope or sharpened dread in their eyes.

Sarah caught Lucy's final hesitation as they prepared to leave and leaned in, voice low but dry. "No rush, love. We're not lining up to join Saint Peter yet." She offered a quick wink.

A faint, grateful smile touched Lucy's lips, and Eliza saw some of the tension leave the girl's shoulders. These were her girls. Her responsibility. And she was on the verge of leading them into a new, more dangerous battle.

Behind them, muffled voices leaked from the supervisor's booth: "...German advances near Ypres... Ministry pushing for more... Review can't come soon enough..."

They stepped out of the locker rooms and onto the cleanway, a long, timber-raised path that snaked between the monolithic, corrugated walls of the sheds. They passed Nell Clark from Eliza's street.

Nell's face, once warm with a neighbourly smile, was now pale and slack, her clothes hanging as though the woman inside had thinned and dimmed. Her firstborn, John, had been killed on the Somme two months earlier.

"Evening, Nell," Eliza said, her voice softer than intended.

Nell's eyes, shadowed and slow to focus, met hers. "Alright, Eliza, love. Back for the graveyard shift?"

"Aye, bloody knackered," she replied, the words heavy with weariness. "How's things with you?"

"Day shift now, two til ten, next three weeks. I just volunteered for this double shift. Filling in for a girl pulled off the line for rest, only for tonight." Nell's voice fell to a near whisper, tight with urgency as she leaned closer. "Have you heard anything more about those blokes from London? The ones with clipboards?"

Eliza felt it again—the icy knot within her, like a fist tightening around her heart. "Rumours, Nell. Best not to dwell on it." She touched Nell's arm through her glove—a slight, fleeting warmth amidst the chill. "You need anything, love... give us a knock."

Nell's eyes shimmered with unshed tears. She nodded, brave and jerky. "Keep safe, Eliza."

"You too, love." Eliza turned and moved quickly to rejoin her shift.

The familiar walk, filled with the last vestiges of canteen chatter or quiet, personal thoughts, felt different tonight.

As they passed another checkpoint, Hilda adjusted her cap, checking that no stray hair had escaped. "Every one of us checked for so much as a stray hairpin," she said, more to herself than anyone else. "Static's a cruel mistress."

Eliza watched her, struck again by the woman's unshakeable precision. Even in this hell, she carried herself as if she were still in a classroom. Or perhaps a chapel.

They passed one of Miss McDowell's new posters, its bold letters stark under the caged lights: *MAKE IT A GOOD ONE FOR THE HUN!*

Sarah snorted. "Reckon McDowell knows owt about what to do with a Hun, good or bad?" The jest earned a few nervous chuckles, but the tension remained, a tight wire humming beneath the surface.

Eliza heard them. Her gaze was fixed further down the cleanway, where a figure had just emerged from the mechanics' shed, wiping his hands on a rag. Mr Parkin. Her stomach clenched into a cold, hard knot. She instinctively slowed her pace, letting June and Sarah get a few steps ahead, a childish urge to hide in their shadows.

The memory of her lie in his small, warm office felt like a fresh duplicity. His tired, trusting eyes. Her own voice, thin and false, assuring him the press was fine. She felt a hot flush of disgrace. Here she was, about to lead her girls into that roaring room, preaching caution, while knowing she herself had concealed a danger, all for a handful of shillings to keep a wolf like Skinner from the door.

It was her duty to keep them safe, and she had gambled their lives on a lie. Parkin turned then, heading down the adjacent corridor towards Shed B without a glance in her direction.

A surge of relief so intense it nearly made her dizzy engulfed her, and the shame that followed was even worse—the shame of being grateful she hadn't been caught.

The air was charged with a new, unspoken current—a mix of hope and raw fear that flowed between the seven girls of Bench 12.

The distant, muffled roar of the factory was a beast waiting to be fed, and the path ahead felt like the narrow track leading to its maw.

*****

Meanwhile, in Captain Miller's office, the air was thick with stale pipe smoke and unspoken tension. Miss McDowell stood before his desk, her hands clasped, her posture ramrod straight. Captain Miller sat in his chair, his gaze fixed on a stack of production reports. Mr Finch stood by the window, looking down on the factory floor, his back to the room.

"Captain," McDowell began, her voice calm but firm, "I am formally requesting that the hydraulic press at Bench 12 be taken out of service for immediate and essential maintenance. Mr Parkin has confirmed my observations. The primary pressure valve is failing. It presents a clear and unacceptable safety risk to the women on that line."

Miller ran a hand over his face. "Edna, the Ministry..."

"The Ministry is not on the floor listening to that machine scream, Captain," she cut in, her patience fraying.

Finch turned slowly from the window, his glasses glinting off the gaslight. His tone, when it arrived, was smooth and cold as a slab of granite. "A 'safety risk', Miss McDowell?" he asked, as if the concept were a quaint indulgence. "Or an excuse for downtime from one of your most efficient teams? Your charge hand, Wren, has exemplary numbers. Taking her press offline now would have a significant, and noted, impact on this shift's output."

"An impact on output is preferable to an impact on my workers' lives, Mr Finch," McDowell said, her voice dropping to a dangerous chill.

Finch gave a thin, unfriendly smile. "These machines are robust. A 'scream', as you put it, is just a sign of it working at capacity. Effective charge hands manage their equipment. She keeps it running. We need women who can handle the pressure. All of them." He glanced at Miller. "The Ministry will not tolerate interruptions for non-critical issues. I trust my report will reflect that this matter was handled with due effectiveness."

The threat was unmistakable. Miller fidgeted in his chair, his face pale. He would not overrule the London official. His eyes fell upon McDowell, his expression a mixture of apology and defeat.

"Keep a close eye on it, Miss McDowell." His voice was subdued. "That concludes everything for now."

McDowell stood frozen momentarily, her hands clenched into tight fists at her sides. A furious, helpless rage washed over her. She gave Finch a glare of pure contempt, then turned on her heel and walked out, the door closing with a sharp, definitive click behind her.

*****

Their rubber-soled shoes made a soft, cadenced shuffle on the wooden planks, a sound too quiet for the dread building in Eliza's chest.

Shed A loomed ahead, its dark form stretching into the dimness like the side of a silent, waiting warship. Room 42 was halfway down—one of the most dangerous in the entire complex. As they neared the heavy door, the air shifted, growing warmer and thicker, with a cold metal and chemical scent. An icy dread ran down the back of her neck, sharper tonight than ever before.

She paused, making the others stop with her. She glanced at each woman's face, her gaze lingering for a second on each one. She saw Lucy, ashen and fragile in the shadowy, caged light, her eyes locked on Eliza as if she were a lifeline. She saw Sarah's jaw set with a reckless, thrilling determination, her thoughts no doubt already on a deposit for a place in Leeds.

She saw the worry etched around June's tired eyes and the silent, prayerful vow in Nora's posture.

The memory of Miss McDowell's urgent whisper echoed in her ears: *"No mistakes tonight, Eliza. Especially with the extra eyes watching."*

The weight of her promise to Stan—to keep them safe—pressed down on her, a physical weight that made it hard to breathe. It warred with the brutal weight of Skinner's ultimatum.

"Right," Eliza said, her tone calm and deliberate yet carrying an intensity that made them all focus. "Listen to me." She waited until she had every eye on her. "We keep the pace we need to. But we work steady. Take your time and do it properly."

Her public reason was the inspectors. Her private reason was to remember Rose Turner and the fear of seeing another of her girls crumple to the floor.

"Every shell is perfect. We work fast, but we work *right.* We look out for each other. Understood?"

The words felt like ash in her mouth. *Work right?* The thought was a sneer in her head. How could she stand here and lecture caution when she'd told a bald-faced lie about the groaning press?

The hypocrisy bore down on her with immense force, threatening to buckle her knees. She was asking them to trust her with their lives, all while gambling on a machine that could kill them for four pounds ten shillings.

A succession of unique nods. Lucy's was quick and desperate. Sarah's was a sharp, almost impatient dip of the chin. June managed a shaky smile.

They all understood. The lure of the bonus, the gleam of those extra shillings, was palpable between them—a dangerous, unspoken promise that pulled against Eliza's words of warning.

Eliza gave a final grim nod, her eyes scanning over them one last time. She turned and put her hand on the heavy iron door handle of Room 42. She saw Lucy flinch behind her, that same raw terror shining in her eyes—one Eliza knew too well. *Steady, lass,* she mused, a quiet prayer for all of them.

Then she swung the door wide.

The familiar wall of heat and noise hit her—a hundred machines clanging, hissing, and groaning at once. It was a roar she tuned out, a rhythm she worked to, but tonight, with her nerves already frayed, it was like a punch to the gut.

Her eyes, already adjusted to the jaundiced light, immediately shot to a different part of the room. And her stomach dropped.

There, on the hard surface directly beneath the main pressure valve of her press, was a small, dark, glistening patch. A fresh leak. It wasn't there when she left this morning.

Tonight, the accustomed rhythm of the room was discordant, a half-beat too fast. A loose floorboard near the capping machine rattled with every passing trolley, a sound like chattering teeth.

The gaslight seemed to burn with a greener, more sickly tinge than usual, making the shadows leap and shudder in a way that felt predatory. The vibration wasn't only in the concrete floor; it was a living thing that worked its way up her bones, making her teeth ache with a deep, unsettling hum.

The other girls walked past her, their faces set, already absorbed into the room's brutal logic. She felt Lucy hesitate at the threshold and provided her a gentle but firm nudge forward, a silent command to keep moving.

Her gaze swept past the main corridor, and she glimpsed them—Finch and Harper—standing just inside the doorway of the supervisors' booth, two dark spectres watching, their clipboards glinting in the gaslight. They weren't looking at her. Not yet. But the sight of them sent a fresh wave of terror through her, a reminder that every movement was being measured, every second judged.

The door swung shut behind them, and the weighty iron latch dropped into place with a resounding, final clang.

17

Chapter 17 : The Ballad of Brass and Fire

5th December 1916, 10:00–10:04 PM, Barnbow, Room 42

Room 42's door slammed shut behind them. In a single, suspended moment, the seven women of Bench 12 stood on the precipice, the hushed calm of the cleanway already a distant memory.

Then, a piercing whistle from the factory—a shrill, absolute command that sliced through the murmur and unleashed a monstrous, metallic symphony. The floor shook, a guttural thrum that vibrated through the soles of Eliza's boots and lodged in her teeth.

Eliza took her place at the hydraulic press, her gut twisting at the memory of its grinding protest from the night before. She ran a hand over the greasy lever, feeling the phantom resistance of the jamming mechanism. The thought of Skinner's ultimatum—four pounds ten shillings by Saturday—pressed against her like a physical weight. Her children's faces, blue-lipped and turned out onto the frozen street, were a horror that choked her.

Her mind flinched from the image and fled to a memory—last Christmas.

Stan was home. The grey kitchen glowed with heat from the stove, where a small chicken roasted. Beth's newspaper chains drooped from the ceiling in crooked loops. Stan, clean of pit dust, lifted little Stanley to touch their bent silver star. He caught Eliza's eye and grinned—easy, familiar—and her heart skipped, just like always.

He launched into a loud, off-key version of "Good King Wenceslas," his booming voice filling the tiny house while Bobby rolled his eyes in mock embarrassment.

It was a memory of a life that had felt whole. A life of noise and warmth and laughter. A life worth fighting for.

The memory steadied her, hardening her fear into resolve.

"Right, let's make quota and then some." Her voice didn't waver—low and steady, too steady, a fragile mask over the fears that pulsed beneath. She guided the first shell into the machine's cradle, her fingers wrapping around the cool, greasy lever. The machine hummed beneath her touch, and a hard thud of her heart echoed against her ribs.

*****

The door slammed shut with a final, echoing clang. For Lucy, it was not the noise of a closing door; it was the sound of a tomb being sealed. A wall of intense sound and stifling heat crashed over her, a bodily assault that forced a small, choked gasp from her lungs.

As she stood there, paralysed by the sensory assault, the heat from the nearest Amatol kettle washed over her, and the instructor's stern words from her training week echoed in her tired, resigned voice. She remembered him holding up two jars of powder, his own hands tinged with a yellow hue.

"This one, girls..." He held up the fine, white ammonium nitrate. "...is little more than farm fertiliser on its own. But we mix it with this

devil's powder here..." He gestured to the pale saffron TNT. "...and it makes our supply go further. More bang for our bob. To do that, it has to be molten."

He tapped a diagram of the kettle, its pipes like a spider's web. "The steam pipes keep it like hot, thick treacle. Too cool, and it sets like stone, ruining the whole batch. But let that steam get her too hot..." He hesitated then, his gaze sweeping over their pale, nervous faces, a flicker of something that looked like pity in their depths. "...and the devil in it wakes up." He looked around at them to see the effect of his words. "One spark, one clumsy knock, and it'll be the end of you all. Your job is not to question it. Your job is to be careful."

The memory didn't soothe—it only deepened the fear. Machines clanged and hissed in a deafening chorus, the air heavy with scorched oil and the sickly sweet burn of molten Amatol. It coated her tongue like metal and dread. Under the flickering yellow gaslight, shadows stretched long, turning the room into a hellish cavern filled with frantic, blue-smocked ghosts.

Joe would've known what to say, she thought. *Something daft. He'd have told me the story about the farmer's runaway pig again, the one that ended up in the church vestry on a Sunday morning. He'd have whispered it in my ear right now, to see me smile. To stop the shaking.*

But Joe was gone, and the shaking was getting worse.

She followed the others to Bench 12, her movements rigid and jerky, like a doll made of sticks. Her station was a small, terrifying island of responsibility between Eliza's groaning press and Nora's fusing bench. On it lay the tools of her new life: a neat stack of wiping cloths, a tray of brass Gaines glinting like oversized bullets under the sickly light, and a trolley of freshly pressed shells waiting for her attention.

Each one looked impossibly heavy, a considerable weight of purpose and danger.

Her task was simple. Wipe the fuse hole clean. Take a Gaine. Seat it. Push the shell to Nora along the line. Simple. But her hands, slick with a cold, nervous sweat, felt like they belonged to someone else. She took hold of a rag; the rough texture scraped against her raw knuckles. She wiped the first shell, her movements clumsy, her entire focus narrowed to that one small, dark circle. *Don't smear it. Don't be slow. Drop nothing.*

A sudden, sharp clang from a dropped tool on an adjacent bench made her jump, her breath catching in her throat. The sound, so like the shriek of a ricochet from the stories she'd heard, shattered her fragile concentration. Her heart pounded, a frantic drum against the roaring machinery. The world wasn't sunlight and salt from the Bridlington shore; it was noise and danger. The sweet memory of aniseed rock on a summer beach was replaced by the bitter, chemical tang in her throat. And Joe was gone.

She grabbed for a new Gaine, her trembling fingers fumbling on the cold brass. For a horrifying, elongated second, it slipped. The world seemed to slow down; the noise of the factory receded to a distant hum.

She watched, eyes wide in a silent scream, as the brass cylinder skittered across the bench with a sudden jarring clatter. It spun, a glinting top of pure terror, before tumbling over the edge and landing with a soft, metallic thud among the Amatol-filled shells on the trolley below.

For one long, suspended heartbeat, no one moved. The air seemed to vanish, leaving a vacuum behind. One spark—one grain of grit between brass and steel—and they'd be nothing but ash.

All she could make out was the rush of blood in her ears, loud and frantic. Her breath sat like a heavy weight resting in her chest.

In the stillness of her mind, her mother appeared, turning from the kitchen sink, a dishrag clutched in hand. Her father, glancing up from his newspaper, had a sad smile ghosting his face.

The telegram boy came next, walking down her street.

I've killed us, she thought, panic swelling. *Oh, Joe. I'm sorry. I'm so sorry.*

Then, a voice, sharp but laced with a strange, panicked humour, sliced through her paralysis.

"Whoops-a-daisy, our Luce!" It was Sarah Jennings. The sound of her voice was a shock, a sudden crack in the suffocating dome of Lucy's fear.

"Next time, try juggling 'em. It'll be quicker for the tally! Don't send us all sky-high before payday, there's a love. Some of us have plans for that bonus money!"

The words, raw as they were, were a lifeline. A few nervous titters broke the surrounding tension. The factory's loud noise rushed back in, and Lucy realised she could breathe again.

A wave of relief, so powerful it almost made her knees give way, swept through her. She fumbled to retrieve the Gaine, her fingers clumsy, her cheeks burning with a shame that brought tears to her eyes.

She looked up and saw Eliza, her face unreadable, give the briefest, indiscernible nod. It wasn't forgiveness, but it wasn't condemnation either. It was an order: '*Refocus. Now.*'

Shaking, Lucy returned to her station. The fear was sharper now, personal. Not just the room, but her. Her mistake. Her hands trembled, exhaustion and the echo of brass hitting steel taking root. She reached for the next cloth, but her fingers felt numb, useless.

Suddenly, another hand gently covered hers, stilling the tremor. The touch was warm, firm, and startlingly human in the cold, mechanical roar. It was Nora Kershaw.

Lucy looked up into Nora's kind, steady eyes. Nora leaned in close, her voice a quiet breath against the overwhelming noise, meant only for Lucy. "Steady, love. One at a time. Just think of the one in your hand. Nothing else matters."

Nora gave her hand a final, reassuring squeeze before turning back to her own station, her thumb instinctively brushing over the worn gold of her wedding band. The small, private gesture was a prayer for her Will and a comfort for the terrified girl beside her.

Lucy took a deep, shuddering breath. The warmth of Nora's touch lingered on her skin. She looked at the shell in front of her. *One at a time.* The words were an anchor. She grabbed the cloth, her hand still shaking, but a little steadier now.

Pick up the cloth. Don't snag. Wipe—slow, but not too slow. He's watching. Put it down. Gaine next. Fingers, hold steady. Please don't drop it. Please don't drop it. Steady. Seat it. Push.

Each step was a battle; each breath was a prayer. As she worked, her movements stiff and robotic, she saw Nora Kershaw beside her. Her movements were a portrait of quiet, steady grace. Nora caught her eye momentarily and gave her the smallest, briefest of smiles.

Lucy completed five more shells without error. The victory was minuscule, a single drop of water in an ocean of fear, but it was hers. Her hands still trembled, but they obeyed. *I'm still here, Joe,* she thought, the tear-stained promise sent out into the roaring dark. *I'm still here.*

*****

At her station, Sarah's world narrowed to the Amatol kettle—a hissing, steaming brute she wrestled night after night.

A mustard-coloured vapour curled into her hair, clinging to her skin like apparitions. She leaned in, heat needling through her smock, and shoved the iron ladle deep into the thick, dragging sludge.

It fought back—slow, heavy, unforgiving.

Too thick? Or was it just these wrists again? The ache had shifted from a dull complaint to something sharp and grinding—a constant reminder of the factory's toll. Every turn of the ladle sent a splinter of pain up her arm, a harsh, brief report from the front line of her own body. But she pushed through it. She had to.

Push on, Sarah. Show them London men what you're made of. Show them you deserve that flat in Leeds. Two clean rooms. A window for Cecil. A place without Thomas Brown's shadow—that was the dream fuelling her every pour. His threat still echoed from that afternoon: "Out by week's end." The bastard meant it. She clenched her jaw, the muscle jumping, and put her weight into the stir, forcing the thick liquid to yield.

"This batch ain't pouring right," she grumbled, loud enough for those nearby to hear over the din, the words a release of pressure.

From her station, Hilda Morton replied without looking up, her back straight as the ruler she must have once used to rap knuckles. "This batch *isn't* pouring right, Sarah," she corrected, the schoolmistress in her stepping in to fix the grammar.

Sarah saw a wry smile touch Hilda's lips. A flash of fond annoyance went through her; even here, in this hell, Miss Morton was Miss Morton.

"Aye, well, they aren't paying us a bonus for our grammar, are they, love?" she shot back, the effort of the banter a welcome distraction from the fire in her joints.

Her gaze swept down the line for a second, just as a sharp clatter cut through the general roar. She saw the little mouse, Lucy, freeze like a startled rabbit. A brass Gaine lay on the trolley floor, nestled among the live shells. Sarah's mind didn't leap to the danger of an explosion; it leapt to the threat of the stopwatch. A dropped component. A delay. She saw Mr Finch's head snap up across the room, his attention zeroing in on their bench.

Christ, the little mouse. He's seen her. Break the tension. Now.

"Whoops-a-daisy, our Luce!" she said, her voice a sharp, deliberate shockwave. "Next time, try juggling 'em. It'll be quicker for the tally! Don't send us all sky-high before payday, there's a love. Some of us have plans for that bonus money!"

She watched the girl, white-faced and trembling, retrieve the Gaine. She saw the flash of gratitude in Lucy's terrified eyes before the girl turned back to her work, a little steadier now. *That's it, lass.*

She returned to her work, but the brief surge of adrenaline had cost her. A hot flush blurred her vision. The air swam, the yellow gaslights warping into sickly, smearing green. The roaring of the machinery seemed to recede for a moment into a dull, watery drone, the sound of being underwater. She braced herself against the kettle's edge.

The metal was scorching hot, even through her gloves, but the sharp, genuine pain was a welcome grounding in the disorienting fog. Her knees felt weak. For a horrible second, she thought she might be sick.

She wouldn't fall. Not here. Not now. Not for him to see.

The thought of Rose Turner, crumpled on the floor, shot through her mind—*and this is how it starts?* But then furious, pure anger flooded in to replace it. She wouldn't be another piece of damaged stock to be carted off and forgotten.

She would win. For Cecil. For her mother. She gripped the ladle again, the ache in her wrists a muted, familiar throb. The dizziness subsided, leaving behind a brutal fury. Every shell filled was a brick in the wall of their new life—every damn penny.

*****

The relentless pace, driven by quotas, frayed every nerve almost immediately. Eliza's eyes swept the bench. Sarah's shoulders were high and taut, the posture from biting down on pain. Lucy's hands—red raw—moved like they were trying to remember composure. June's shoulders slumped with exhaustion. Mary Sutcliffe paused at the capping machine, her face an unreadable mask.

Mary caught Eliza's gaze across the roar and gave a subtle, barely noticeable shake of her head, a silent, maternal warning aimed at Sarah: '*Go easy on her, Lize. She's running on fumes.*' The message was every bit as plain as if she'd shouted it. A long, hard, fresh wave of guilt washed over Eliza. Mary was right. She was pushing them all too hard—but what other option did she have?

Not now. Don't jam now. The thought of Skinner's smug face fuelled her more than any bonus. She pulled the lever again. Every second counted.

The pressure changed again when the men from London drew near. A prickle of awareness danced up Eliza's spine as Mr Finch and Inspector Harper zeroed in on her gang. Finch's stopwatch glinted. Eliza watched as their gaze fell upon Nora Kershaw. She saw Nora's back straighten, her movements taking on a strange, sharpened precision. Through her thin glove, Eliza saw Nora's thumb press down on the simple gold band of her wedding ring—a desperate, silent prayer for steadiness.

She remembered Nora showing her a letter from Will just the week before. In it, he'd told her he kept a smooth grey pebble they had found together at Filey last summer.

"*It's you, that stone,*" he'd written. "*Soft round the edges, but solid right through. Won't crack, no matter what.*"

Eliza knew that for Nora, each carefully fused shell was a prayer. And now, these men, armed with their stopwatches, threatened that ritual. Eliza saw Nora's gloved fingers, so sure, suddenly seem to falter as the inspectors watched. A cold panic must have seized her. The fuse slipped. It hit the floor with a metallic clatter that sliced through the noise like a blade.

"Damn and blast it!" Nora said.

Before the girl could bend, Eliza was there. "Leave it!" she said, her voice sharp with forced authority. "Get another from the tray, Kershaw! Keep the line moving!" She snatched up the fuse and flung it into the discard bin with a ringing clang. She saw the girl flinch, the hurt and fear in her eyes a fresh wound on Eliza's conscience. *And you, Eliza Wren—did you have to snap like that?*

Before the question could take shape, a calm, cutting voice spoke from just behind her shoulder. "A three-second delay on a dropped component, Charge Hand Wren."

Eliza froze, her back rigid. She turned to face Mr Finch, her movements weighted with care. He stood with his stopwatch in one hand and his clipboard in the other, his expression impassive behind his spectacles.

"Plus the time for your... reprimand." The slight pause was a deliberate insult. "And a wasted fuse. We are tracking all material wastage and inefficient movements. See that it doesn't become a pattern for your bench."

A hot, furious shame washed over Eliza. He spoke as if Nora were a faulty cog, not a terrified woman. She felt the eyes of her entire crew on her, saw their movements become even more strained and fearful. She clenched her fists, her stained fingers itching with the urge to say something she'd regret. Instead, she forced her next words out through a tight jaw. "Yes, sir. It won't."

"See that it doesn't," Finch said, making a neat, deliberate tick on his sheet.

It was then that another presence became apparent. "Is there a problem here, Mr Finch?" Miss McDowell had arrived, her posture as unyielding as the factory's iron pillars.

Finch gave a thin smile, condescending and without warmth. "Just observing a lapse in efficiency, Miss McDowell. A costly one."

"What I see," Miss McDowell said, her voice quiet but clear and commanding—a ring of authority, "is a good worker who made a mistake under scrutiny. These women are not machines, Mr Finch. They are tired, often underfed, and they are doing their patriotic duty. A little humanity goes further than a stop-watch in my experience."

Finch's smile vanished. He stared at Miss McDowell for a long, tense moment, the air crackling between them. The din from the factory seemed to recede, leaving only the sound of their silent battle of wills. He gave a curt, dismissive nod.

"Your experience has been noted, Miss McDowell," he responded before turning on his heel and continuing his patrol, Inspector Harper trailing in his wake.

Miss McDowell watched him go, then turned to Eliza. Her expression softened, but she spoke in a hushed rush: "He's right about one thing—they're watching every move. Keep an eye on Jennings. Her skin's worse. And the new girl—she's wound tighter than a drum. No more mistakes tonight, Eliza. Not from any of them."

Eliza's chin dipped. "I will, miss. Thank you." It was more than thanks for the warning—it was gratitude for standing with them.

Miss McDowell gave a single, firm head-bob, a quiet understanding of their shared burden, before continuing her rounds.

Eliza wasn't just watching the clock anymore. She was watching her girls: Sarah's fevered fury at the kettle, Lucy's trembling focus, Nora's silent prayer, June's fatigue-shaken shoulders, Mary's maternal watchfulness, Hilda's disciplined stance.

"Stay calm, please, girls," she said, the words lost to the din. "Steady and right."

They tried. Shell by shell. Pour. Cool. Press. Wipe. Gaine. Fuse. Cap. Hope. Repeat.

And somewhere in that never-ending pattern, forged of brass and fire, they found the strength to keep going—one penny, one shell, one breath at a time.

10:05 PM

Room 42 throbbed with a rhythm too fast, too tight for comfort. Each station in the trolley line strained to turn out a shell every forty-five seconds. It was constant. The main drive belt for the conveyor let out a low, steady groan, a bass note against the sharp, metallic clank of the presses. A fine yellow dust of Amatol, kicked up by the shuddering machinery, spun in the beams of the gaslights, catching in the throat and coating every surface with a greasy film.

The air was thick with the smell of hot oil and the sharp, acrid sweetness of the chemicals. Eliza felt the floor's vibration not just in her feet but in her teeth. It was the sound of a system being pushed past its limits. The heat in the room wasn't just from the machinery; it was the friction of too many bodies moving too fast in a space that felt ready to snap. She watched her girls, hunched over their stations like surgeons in a desperate, frantic battle. Every gesture was a risk, every drop of sweat a prayer.

10:08 PM

Eliza's gaze shot to the head of the line, where Sarah Jennings poured molten Amatol into empty casings. The hostile heat from the kettle flushed Sarah's face a painful, mottled red, a stark contrast to the deepening yellow stain of her skin.

Her focus was brittle, her movements sharp with a familiar, angry energy. Every pour was a brief, fervent battle, and Eliza knew what fuelled that fire: a desperate dream of a flat in Leeds, a safe harbour for her son.

Suddenly, Eliza saw her pause, the heavy ladle hovering over the kettle. Sarah's nose twitched, her head tilting as though trying to place a sound—or a scent. Her eyes darted up and down the line with a flicker of confusion. Eliza followed her gaze to the kettle's thermometer.

The needle was creeping just past the red danger line. *Too hot.* The thought was cold and instant. She saw Sarah tapping the gauge with a gloved knuckle—a useless gesture. The damned thing had been sticking all week. The faint, burnt-sugar smell that pricked Eliza's nostrils confirmed it: this batch was wrong.

For a heart-stopping second, she considered calling for Mr Parkin, but Sarah had already returned to her work with a look of grim endurance. She poured too fast. A splash of Amatol hit the concrete, too close to her boots.

Eliza's heart shot to her throat.

Sarah jerked back, eyes squeezed shut, jaw clenched tight. It was the look of a woman fighting to block out panic, to silence the image of everything she could lose. Then her eyes snapped open, sharp and steeled. *No room for fear. Not tonight.*

10:10 PM

Then, there was a subtle shift in the atmosphere. The low hum of chatter from other benches died down. A sudden feeling of awareness shot up Eliza's back. She saw heads turning, then quickly turning back to their work, their movements becoming even more rigid.

It was Finch and Harper. They were moving from the cleanway, their path deliberate as they steered the cramped space between the benches. Their dark suits parted the sea of blue-smocked women like sharks gliding through a school of fish. They weren't just observing anymore. They were hunting.

They stopped just behind Bench 12, right behind Lucy.

Eliza's heart hammered against her ribs. Finch raised his stopwatch, the silver glinting in the gaslight. He didn't speak to Lucy; he didn't even seem to see her as a person. He watched her hands as she reached for a pressed shell.

A sharp *click* as she began her task. Lucy froze, terror flashing in her eyes. *Don't look at him, lass,* Eliza pleaded in her mind. *Just do the work.*

Lucy fumbled with the wiping cloth, her movements suddenly clumsy. She wiped the fuse hole, her hands shaking so badly that Eliza could see it from ten feet away.

She reached for the Gaine. Her fingers trembled as she slotted it into place. The moment it was done, Finch's thumb came down with another, louder *click.*

He made a neat, precise note on his clipboard, then turned his cold, spectacled gaze to Eliza.

"Charge Hand Wren," he started, his voice devoid of humanity, "your new girl. Her cycle time is three-point-two seconds over the optimal benchmark. Her movements are hesitant." He paused before adding, "See that she improves. We are looking for uniformity."

He gave a curt nod and moved on, Harper following close behind, leaving a poisonous silence behind them. Eliza watched Lucy's face, which had drained of all colour. Her knuckles were white where she clutched the bench's edge, her whole body trembling.

A hot, protective fury surged through Eliza, so strong it made her dizzy—a rage against this man, this system, that measured a terrified, grieving girl's worth in fractions of a second. She wanted to scream, to hurl a shell casing at his back.

Instead, she forced her voice to be steady. "Next shell, June," she called down the line, her tone a fragile shield against the layered onset of fear that now gripped her team.

10:14 PM

Eliza's eyes snapped to Lucy Atkinson. After her near-disaster with the dropped Gaine, the girl's fear had taken on a new shape. The frantic, jerky movements were gone, replaced by a painstaking slowness that was, in its own way, just as dangerous to their rhythm. Every wipe of the fuse hole was deliberate and meticulous. She aligned each Gaine with the precision of a watchmaker before pushing the shell down the line.

The shells were backing up.

"For God's sake, Luce, shift it!" Sarah's voice barked from down the line, sharp with impatience. She gestured with her ladle towards the logjam at Lucy's station. "Are you polishing 'em for the king's inspection? That bonus won't wait for you!"

Lucy flinched at the tartness in Sarah's tone, her movements becoming even more hesitant. Eliza saw the terror in the girl's eyes—the fear of a dropped Gaine now warring with the fear of slowing them all down.

"Atkinson," Eliza called out, her voice firm but even, cutting through Sarah's frustration, "pick up the pace. Steady, but faster. We need you."

She's drowning, Eliza thought. *Drowning in fear.* Seconds dragged. The calm she'd worked so hard to build was gone.

10:17 PM

Eliza, stationed at her hydraulic press, watched, her chest tight. *Too fast,* she thought, a silent scream beneath the machinery's roar.

As if to underline the thought, her hydraulic press, troublesome all week, stuttered gravely as she released a shell. There was a jarring clank of protesting metal, followed by a deeper, groaning vibration she felt not just in her arms and teeth but coming up through the soles of her rubber boots from the concrete floor.

Her heart slammed against her ribs. *Not now, damn you. Not now!*

There was a faint wobble in the press's heavy iron frame, a shudder that wasn't there last week. Her eyes shot to the greasy joints, where the oil looked thin and inadequate. The grating of overworked metal was now part of the factory's rising chorus of failure.

What is that smell? A sharp, burnt tang that tasted of ruin. The machine's falter threw her rhythm off—a beat that felt entirely, horribly, her own. She saw the sickly sheen on Sarah's forehead and caught the frantic glint in Lucy's eyes.

The air thickened, hotter with every rushed cycle. The machinery's roar was a physical blow, making the floor tremble. The thought of failing—of that door slamming shut on her family—was a cold horror.

But beneath the fear, her undercurrent of furious anger continued to burn brighter. The lie she'd told Mr Parkin echoed in her ears, but it wasn't guilt she felt now. It was a pure, hot fury at the man whose smug, well-fed face was the reason she stood here, praying over a failing machine. She pictured Skinner's soft, nourished hands that had never known a day of real work.

How dare he hold their lives, their warmth, their very survival in his grasp? The injustice of it was a metallic taste in her mouth, more bitter than the Amatol. The anger didn't erase the fear, but it gave it a hard, sharp edge. It was fuel.

Her grip on the press lever tightened, her knuckles white. She would not let that man win.

The press let out another high-pitched shriek. Eliza flinched, but then Skinner's voice echoed in her memory: *"Out on the street."* Her jaw tightened.

She slammed the lever home, forcing the machine through its cycle. Another penny. Another step from the cold pavement. The shriek of the machine was awful, but the thought of her children's cries in the bitter December wind was worse.

10:21 PM

The seconds ticked by on the big wall clock above the watchers' table, each one a small, brutal hammer blow. Eliza kept her rhythm at the press, her movements economical, born of a fatigue so deep it had become a part of her. The cold knot of stress in her stomach was a constant companion now.

Pour. Cool. Check. Press. Her mind chanted the litany, a desperate prayer for focus.

She scanned her team. The girls worked like clockwork, yes—but a clock wound far too tight, its mainspring on the verge of snapping. June's usual cheer was gone, her face a pale mask of worry. Sarah's movements at the kettle were sharp, almost violent, her anger a visible heat shimmering around her. And Lucy... the poor lamb looked like she might shatter if someone spoke her name too loudly.

Keep it steady, girls, she thought, the words a silent plea against the roaring din. *We'll make the count.*

And God forgive her—they would.

Suddenly, a new sound sliced through the familiar symphony of the factory. But this time, it came from the capping station. The conveyor belt carrying shells to Mary Sutcliffe shuddered, jerked, and stopped dead, the motor letting out a low, angry hum.

"Not again!" Mary said, striking the side of the machine with the flat of her hand. With a protesting groan, the belt lurched back into motion, shoving two shells dangerously close together.

Mary deftly separated them, her expression a picture of grim frustration. It wasn't a groan or a hiss. It was a high-pitched shriek, followed by a deafening, cascading clatter—terrifying in its discordance.

Eliza's head snapped towards the sound. Across the cleanway, near Bench 18.

A trolley piled high, its wheels likely caught on a warped floorboard, had toppled over. A dozen 4.5-inch shell casings had spilt, skittering across the concrete like panicked metal beetles.

For a single suspended heartbeat, the entire room seemed to freeze. The roar of the machinery faded to a dull hum in Eliza's ears. All she could see was one of the heavy brass casings rolling, spinning, arcing in a slow, graceful, and horrifying curve directly towards the glowing-hot base of a nearby Amatol kettle.

Her breath caught in her chest, a stone of pure, white-hot terror. "*A single spark.*" The instructor's words from their training echoed in the sudden, ringing silence of her mind. "*One spark, and it'll send you all to meet your maker.*"

She saw Sarah flinch beside her, hands flying up to shield her face. She saw Lucy's eyes flood with fear, her mouth opening for a scream that never found its voice. Every woman on every bench was a statue carved from fear.

Then a watcher, his face purple with rage, shattered the silence. "You stupid, bloody girl!" He stormed towards the girl from Bench 18, who stood with her hands clamped over her mouth, her body shaking with fear. "Do you want to kill us all?"

But before he reached her, another voice cut through the panic—not loud, but sharp and clear as a headmistress's bell. It was Hilda Morton.

"Stay back!" she commanded, pointing a steady finger at the gawking girls nearby. Her face was pale, but her voice was unwavering. "Everyone, away from the kettle. You." She locked eyes with a terrified girl from another bench. "Get a sand bucket. Now. Do not run."

Her calm, decisive order momentarily broke the spell of fear, a small island of control in the chaos. It was then that Miss McDowell swept in from the main cleanway, her presence a wave of cold, absolute authority.

"That's enough!" she said, her voice cutting through the watcher's tirade like a blade. He stopped short, his mouth closing with a click. "You two." She gestured to the charge hand of Bench 18. "Create a cordon. No one goes near until the casings are cooled." Her eyes swept the rest of the room. "Everyone else, back to your work. *Now.*"

The incident was over in moments. The mess was contained. The watcher led the weeping, hysterical girl away, presumably to be sacked. But the damage was done. The air, which had been heavy with tension, was now saturated with a new, lingering dread. The near-miss had been a warning dress rehearsal.

Everyone's pushed too far, Eliza thought, her own heart thumping a sick, nervous rhythm against her ribs. *One more near-miss, one more slight mistake, and this whole place could go up.*

She returned to her press, her hands feeling clumsy and foreign.

10:25 PM

At her station, Eliza received the cooled, inspected shell from June. She guided it into the cradle of the press. The memory of last week's jammed lever flickered through her mind. Any delay now could mark them for the cull. She pulled the lever, released it, and shoved the shell onto the track towards Lucy—faster than she dared.

Her eyes met Mary's as Mary loaded a capped shell onto the trolley. Their shared glance spoke of the unbearable tension.

Lucy's voice was a thin thread, almost lost in the din. "Eliza?"

Eliza didn't turn but flicked her eyes towards her.

"We're doing alright... aren't we?"

Eliza forced her own hands to remain steady as she pressed the lever for the next shell, then nodded once, firm and final.

"You're doing grand, pet," she said, her voice louder than she intended. "You're still standing. That's more than most."

A trolley rattled past from another gang's section, its wheels wobbling on the loose floor planks—a clear sign of haste and risk everywhere.

10:26 PM

Cheers erupted from a distant gang that had moved through another trolley—a sound more desperate than triumphant—which died quickly into the thick, anxious silence. A watcher passed by Bench 12, his eyes scanning without stopping, his boots landing with soft, judgemental thuds on the boards. Eliza stiffened but kept her pace going.

Pour. Cool. Check. Press. Wipe. Gaine. Fuse. Cap. Hope. Repeat.

Her ears strained against the roar, trying to isolate the sounds of failure. She could hear the shrill cry of her press with every cycle, the angry hum from Mary's stalled conveyor, and saw the unhealthy, shimmering heat rising from Sarah's kettle. That peculiar, burnt-sugar scent stung her nose again, more intensely now. The entire room felt like a machine wound too tight, its gears groaning, ready to snap.

The seconds ticked forward on the big wall clock—brutal, relentless—each tick a hammer blow on the fragile barrier holding back chaos.

Then, that strange smell pricked her nostrils again, stronger this time, threading through the acrid air like a whispered warning. Her eyes darted around. The strained groans from her press. A frantic shout from another corner of the room. A glance at Sarah's station—the kettle was running too hot.

And on Bench 12, Lucy Atkinson, her head bent in intense concentration, reached for the next shell, deaf to the symphony of disaster Eliza could hear building all around them.

18

Chapter 18 : The Sky Ripped Red Over Room 42

5th December 1916, 10:27 PM

And then...

A crack, high and sharp as a whip, ripped through the roaring silence. It sliced through the cacophony, leaving a vacuum of stunned silence in its wake.

For a heartbeat, an infinitesimal sliver of time, every woman on Bench 12 looked up, their breaths caught in a single, collective gasp of primal dread.

Lucy! No!

The thought, stark and agonising, pierced Eliza's burgeoning terror. A blinding flash of white heat erupted from the processing trolley at the exact spot where young Lucy Atkinson was fitting the treacherous Gaine.

And with it came the smell—that strange, sweet scent of burnt sugar and stressed metal, now magnified into a sickening, all-consuming wave that emitted the smell of annihilation itself.

Eliza saw Lucy's small hand, still clutching the fateful brass, seeming to glow in the sudden inferno.

Joe?

The thought, bright and brief as the flash itself, pierced Lucy's terror as the world dissolved into searing light, igniting all around her with a brutal, instantaneous force that twisted and buckled the heavy trolley like a discarded toy.

Jagged shards of shrapnel exploded outwards, a deadly rain slicing through the air with the sickening whisper of scythes through wheat. The blast wave slammed against the atmosphere, a monstrous thunderclap that ripped apart sound, thought, everything. Metal shrieked, a tortured cry that echoed Eliza's silent scream.

Her gaze darted to the side, witnessing the horror as Nora Kershaw, who had been reaching for the very shell Lucy handled, recoiled at the white-hot burst. Eliza saw the shock etched on Nora's face, a fleeting moment of terror before a wall of unimaginable heat and force engulfed her. Her small world collapsed into a blinding flame in an instant.

Then, in less than a single breath, the adjacent shell detonated.

The second explosion was different—deeper, more ravenous. An orange-red flame, bright and hungry, surged outwards, swallowing that section of the line in a howling, irresistible rush.

Eliza watched, her heart seizing, as Lucy, at the very epicentre, vanished.

Her eyes, bulging with horror, snapped to Sarah. Her friend, so close to the initial explosion, was hurled sideways and slammed against the unforgiving metal of the empties line.

Eliza watched as Sarah's body twisted with the impact, a fragile doll in a furnace of debris. *Cecil... The flat...* The thought—her guarded dream—shattered in the roaring heat before she, too, was consumed by the fire.

Beside her, Eliza saw Hilda Morton, who had just called out a casing, stiffen, her mouth open in a sharp cry—perhaps a prayer, her brother's name—as the blast wave crushed her, erasing her quiet order and insistent duty in a horrifying blink.

Eliza's stomach lurched as she glimpsed June, closer to the cooling trolley, caught in the fiery tendrils of the expanding inferno. She saw June's face contort in fear as she raised an arm—a futile shield.

The concussion hit June with the force of an iron hammer, and Eliza watched her head snap back against the unyielding concrete floor. June's body crumpled, her friend, the woman she had convinced to come work here for the sake of her children, gone instantly.

Further down the line, near the capping machine, Mary Sutcliffe's stoic mask broke as she witnessed the firestorm rushing towards her. *Sam...* His name left her lips like a silent, desperate prayer as the wave struck, bringing with it shrapnel, unimaginable force, and unbearable pain.

Then, it came for Eliza.

She was thrown with brutal force against the cold, unyielding bulk of the hydraulic press. Her arm took the full brunt of the impact, a sickening crack echoing through the receding roar. A high-pitched whine, deafening and endless, filled her head, blotting out the surrounding screams.

She slid down the press, the rough metal scraping against her skin, until she collapsed onto the cold, greasy floor.

Stars exploded behind her eyes, blurring the horrific scene into a kaleidoscope of fire and shadow. Her last thought, a desperate, useless command, echoed silently: *Get down!*

Then the names of her girls—Lucy, Sarah, Nora, Hilda, Mary, June—flashed through her mind, a silent, desperate farewell etched into her skull as the inferno devoured the very space they had occupied just heartbeats before.

Above her, the thick factory roof buckled and folded like flimsy paper, revealing a night sky ripped open and bleeding red. The sturdy brick walls groaned and burst outwards, coughing forth plumes of thick, black soot and choking fumes that clawed at Eliza's throat.

She heard screams, sharp with raw terror, piercing the suffocating smoke, while the all-encompassing silence of death already swallowed others. She saw a watcher, his face a mask of grim determination, dragging a limp, lifeless form clear of the immediate wreckage.

Another voice, hoarse with fear, shouted, "Fumes! Out!" as the heavy cleanway door swung from its splintered hinges, hanging by a thread. Closer still, Eliza heard a faint but terrifying hiss—another shell on a nearby trolley, unstable and alive, threatening to unleash its fury and take the remaining survivors with it.

They had worked through exhaustion, through grief, under the crushing weight of lost husbands, lost homes, and the threat of being dismissed. They'd gambled with every second. Danger, always there, forever present, woven into the rhythm of the job.

Room 42 was now nothing but ruin—trolleys twisted like bones, machinery mangled, the air thick with poison—a factory gutted by its desperate purpose.

All for a penny a shell. That was all it took.

19

Chapter 19 : A Seashell Found in Soot and Sorrow

5th December 1916, 10:28 PM–11:59 PM

Across the corridor, in the time-recording office, Mr William Parkin had just set down his mug of tea, the warmth a slight comfort against the factory's ever-present chill. He picked up his pencil, ready to make another neat entry in his maintenance ledger, when the blast tore through the night.

The walls did not merely shake—they trembled, as if the very bones of the building clenched in pain. The overhead light sputtered wildly before snapping out altogether, plunging him into sudden half-darkness. Then came the sound: two enormous shocks. The first was a flat thunderclap; the second was deeper and hungrier, like the factory itself had split open and screamed.

Parkin lurched from his chair, tea splashing across his desk. Dust cascaded from the rafters. The clock above his head cracked. Smoke curled in thick ribbons beneath the door, carrying the unmistakable scents of fire, hot metal, and something fouler: seared cloth, scorched wood, and the acrid tang of burnt flesh.

Room 42.

He didn't hesitate. He didn't think. He ran.

Down the cleanway, its narrow timber-raised path now coated with falling soot, he charged into the choking blackness. Screams shattered the silence like glass. Girls ran past him, their eyes blown wide with disbelief, mouths gulping air like drowning fish.

Some stumbled, blood streaming from torn scalps or split lips. Others reached out blindly, clothes half-razed away, coughing so hard their lungs seemed to unravel. A few did not move at all.

The factory siren began—a slow whirring that built into a piercing, high-pitched scream of its own.

The doors to Room 42 had been blown outward, twisted off their hinges like toys, and flung against the walls of the corridor. Smoke poured from the opening in great heaving breaths. Beyond the room, flame and broken wood spat. The air snarled with heat, sputtering sparks like gunfire. Benches burned, their varnish bubbling and hissing. Sparks leapt upwards like fireflies in panic.

He entered.

Inside was a furnace. Thick smoke veiled the world in silhouettes and embers. The roar of the fire was constant, like a thousand forges working at once, mixed with the wail of the siren. Yet beneath it all, Parkin could hear the smaller sounds: the high, keening whimpers of the wounded, the crackle of burning aprons, the ping of cooling metal. And worse—the silence of girls who had taken their last breath.

Parkin pulled a girl—seventeen at most—from beneath a crushed bench. One side of her face was charred, the other ghostly pale with ash. Her blouse was torn at the collar, her arm twisted at an odd angle, hanging uselessly.

As he lifted her, he felt her ribs shift under his hands. Her eyes opened for a breath of a moment—and in them, he saw Alice, thirteen, feverish with scarlet fever, calling for him in that same thin, broken whisper.

He carried her into the corridor, talking, making sure she was okay, though he doubted she heard. "You're safe now, lass. Almost there." Her body grew heavier with every step. She had died before he reached the hallway. Her breath shuddered once, then was gone.

He laid her down with gentle care against the corridor wall and turned back into the flames.

He went back. Twelve times. Possibly more. He lost count. With each return, the world inside Room 42 grew smaller, darker. Smoke wrapped everything in its suffocating grip.

With every crumpled blue smock he turned over, a single, cold prayer repeated in his mind. *Not her. Please, God, not her.* He searched for every soot-blackened face, praying he wouldn't find Eliza Wren. Praying that her damned, groaning press—the one she had lied to him about—hadn't caused all this. The thought was a fresh, sharp guilt amidst the chaos, a terrible 'what if' that fuelled his frantic search.

Light from the cleanway glimmered like a dying star. He moved by memory—knew where the benches had stood, the Amatol kettles, the vibration plate.

But now they were rubble—burning wreckage. He tripped once on something soft and gave a broken sob when he realised it was someone's apron, still tied around a waist.

A watcher joined him—sleeves torn, face black with soot, a strip of shirt bound tight around a bleeding hand. They said nothing. Neither did the third man who came after. They moved, pulling arms from beneath beams, lifting torsos from smouldering piles of splinters and shell casings. No questions. Only motion.

A girl's hand clutched the edge of a crate. She was alive. Parkin pried the wood free, braced his back, and lifted her out. Her face was slick with dirt, eyelashes clumped with tears. She blinked once.

"Me mam," she mouthed, but the air was too thick for sound.

He carried her, too.

On his ninth return, his boot caught on something small and sharp among the splintered timbers where he knew Bench 12 had stood. But there was nothing there. Not a bench, not a trolley, not a single recognisable machine part. The concrete floor had been blasted into a shallow, blackened crater, the splintered floorboards around its edge still hissing with embers. It was a void. A space of total obliteration. He stared at the emptiness, and the cold, final certainty settled in his gut: no one here could have survived. Not a soul.

He paused, reaching through the ash to lift a tiny seashell—pale and scalloped, its edge browned with flame—a keepsake. Carried in a pocket, maybe kissed for luck. It looked absurd in his scarred hand. He slipped it into his coat and pressed on.

He found them everywhere: beneath collapsed beams, behind overturned cloth bins, under benches they'd ducked beside in reflex. Some huddled in pairs. Others curled up like sleeping children. One had her arms folded over her face, as if she thought she could hide from the fire.

The in-house fire station put out the fire, with thirty women and six men among the first to respond. The fire was not extinguished, just tired, as if the factory had burned through its rage.

Parkin's body ached from within. His lungs burned with every breath. His gloves had worn thin at the fingertips, the skin beneath raw. His shirt clung to him, soaked with sweat and soot. But he moved as if bewitched—his hands no longer his own but extensions of duty pulling at debris.

When the work ended—when the fire surrendered and the tally was taken—he collapsed onto a broken beam, black with ash. Someone pressed a tin cup of water into his hand. He did not drink.

He looked at his palms.

They were charred and shaking. Not from fear. From sorrow.

In the lull that followed, in the hush settling over the ruined corridor, a memory pierced through: Sarah Jennings, hair tucked back, grin wicked.

"That moustache needs wax, Mr Parkin. It's floppin' like a dead cat!" she'd said, eyes dancing.

He had laughed. Everyone had.

And now she was gone.

That night, William Parkin did not go home. He sat in silence beside the ruined threshold of Room 42.

That night, William Parkin kept company with the dead.

20

Chapter 20 : The Silence Between Wires

Late 5th December 1916, Barnbow Special

The carriage was a coffin on wheels, reeking of smoke, blood, and scorched fabric. Not the sharp, clean smoke of a coal fire but the bitter, chemical kind that clawed at Ann's throat, a taste like swallowed pennies clinging to her tongue. It settled on her skin in a greasy film that soap would later struggle to lift.

The windows, cracked open a mere inch despite the biting December cold, did little more than stir the foul air, making the stench of fear and burnt wool swirl like a malevolent spirit. Each jolt of the train induced a further attack of nausea through her.

Ann sat stiff-backed on the far bench, her body a ramrod of forced composure, tucked deep into the shadows where the flickering oil lamps couldn't quite reach her face. She didn't want them to see her. She didn't want to see them. Around her, a dozen other girls—survivors, they'd later be called, a word that already felt like betrayal—hunched in their seats.

Some whispered, their voices dry and raspy, like leaves skittering across cobbles. Others stared blankly ahead, their eyes wide and vacant, reflecting the lamplight like shattered glass. Too shocked for words. Too rattled for the mercy of sleep.

Ann pressed her lips together into a thin, hard line. *Don't look. Don't meet their eyes.*

She hadn't spoken since Mr Parkin's soot-blackened hands had pulled her from the brink of the inferno, his voice rough and quiet—a calming rumble in the roaring chaos. She'd walked wherever a watcher, his face pale beneath the grime, had pointed.

One nurse, her uniform singed at the hem, had cleaned the gash on Ann's forehead, dabbing it with something that stung like nettles, then wrapped her hand—too tightly—in white gauze. The scorch along her forearm, where the sleeve had vaporised, throbbed with a dull, insistent heat.

The doctor, a tired man with eyes that had seen too much already, had nodded. "Nothing broken, nothing deep. You're a lucky one, lass. Away to your home."

Lucky.

The word sat in her gut like glass. Her bench, her station in Room 42, had been at the far end—almost shielded by a stack of empty shell crates, opposite the blast. That, and the devil's luck, was what had saved her. Saved her, while Sarah...

She clamped her eyes closed, but Sarah Jennings burned behind her lids—grinning, jabbing a finger across the canteen table only hours before: "Only gang in Room 42 worth their salt is mine!"

Ann's scarf, a bright blue wool her mother had knitted, was drawn tight around her neck, almost choking her. Her hands—one bandaged, the other clenched white—were knotted in her lap. She kept her head down, greasy hair falling like a curtain across her face. The other girls kept glancing at her. She could feel it. Their eyes, like tentative fingers, prodded her silence.

They probably thought Ann Price—sharp-tongued, always ready with a boast—would have something to say. Something to explain the inexplicable.

Ann had nothing.

The words had burned with the rest of it, leaving only a hollow space filled with roaring silence and the stench of singed hair.

Some girls were more heavily bandaged, hands swaddled in white linen already blooming crimson like grotesque poppies. One, no older than sixteen, younger than Ann, had a dark, sticky patch across her temple where blood matted her hair. She whimpered softly with every lurch of the train, a sound like a trapped animal.

Another, still in her factory smock, stared at her soot-covered palms as if they held the secrets of the universe—or perhaps the names of the dead. A few had angry red burns—not deep, not like the ones Ann had seen on the bodies carried out—but bubbling welts across wrists and cheeks, powdered with filth and streaked with the clean trails of tears.

Coats had been handed out in haste at the factory gate—rough army surplus or thin woollen shawls from the guard post. Some wore only ripped work clothes, the fabric stinking of the blast. In the mad rush to get them away, some had left with nothing but what clung to their backs.

Beneath the grime, the faint yellow of TNT clung to exposed skin—a ghostly mark of their trade. Now it was the mark of Cain.

The oil lamp sputtered above them, casting long, writhing shadows that turned familiar faces into grotesque masks. No one cried now. That had come earlier, in the first awful minutes outside, huddled at the back of the factory, the night air doing nothing to cool the images seared into their minds.

Captain Miller had been there, grim and unreadable. The watchers, stripped of authority, looked as lost as the girls. Now, in the train's belly, there was only the clatter of wheels on iron, boots shuffling on grit, and sharp gasps whenever someone moved wrong and pain flared.

"How'd you get out then, Polly?" a girl with a scorched eyebrow asked, her cracked voice sounding like it cost her everything.

A girl near the door, pale as death, shook her head. Her voice was a breath, nothing more. "Was... was carryin' a tray from the inspection table. Felt the floor... lift like a wave. Next thing I know, I'm on my back, out on the cinders. The sky was red. Thought I were deaf. Couldn't hear nothin' but ringin'. Like all the bells in Leeds gone mad."

Another spoke, a voice flat and empty, like she'd memorised the words. "The fire door... it wouldn't open. Jammed shut. Florence—little Flo from Dotty's gang—she kicked it. Twice. Hard. Got it loose. Dunno where she is now." Her voice trailed off. She stared at her hands again.

A heavy silence fell—thick, suffocating—broken only by the name no one dared to speak aloud.

Ann said nothing. She hadn't screamed. Not then. Not when the world turned inside out, the air wrenched from her lungs like bellows pressed by some malevolent force. She'd moved on instinct alone and crawled over something soft that might have been a body. Someone had stumbled into her in the smoke, swearing.

Then, Mr Parkin's hands were under her arms, his voice steady, a solid hush beneath the storm: "Let's get you up, love. Get you out."

He'd smelled of pipe tobacco and something gentler—tea, faint and sweet, the kind he always brewed.

She blinked hard, trying to focus on the smeared train window. Across from her, the girl with the head wound hummed—a broken, trembling melody. It might have been Keep the Home Fires Burning, or maybe just some lullaby her mother used to sing. No one told her to stop. Fragile though it was, the sound was better than the silence.

The train jolted around a bend. Several girls grabbed at the seat rails, a collective gasp escaping them. One cried out as her bandaged hand slammed into the wooden bench. Ann's arm throbbed in answer—the scorched skin a brand of survival.

Outside, the first faint lights of Cross Gates pierced the snow-fogged night. Home. The word felt foreign now. It didn't belong to her anymore. None of them was going home, not really. They were carrying something back with them, something unnamed, something that would follow them into every room, haunt every dream, for all the years ahead.

She wanted to go back.

Back to the moment before she'd opened her foolish, competitive mouth in the canteen. Before she'd turned the promise of a bonus—and the desperate urge to impress those factory scrutinisers—into a battle of pride. Before her gang, and possibly Eliza's as well, started measuring their worth not in care or craft but in speed. In shells that flew down the line like bullets.

She dreamed of Sarah now. But not laughing and jeering. Standing still by the Amatol kettle, shoulders slumped, her face smudged with yellow powder. Exhausted. And terribly, hauntingly still.

Was it my fault?

The question—a coiled tormentor—gave her no peace.

6th December 1916, Barnbow, Leeds, 5:50 AM

Nell Clark stepped off the train into a silence so complete it felt as though the world itself was holding its breath. A windless hush hung over Barnbow Halt—a jarring contrast to the usual clatter and chatter of arrivals. The platform, alive with weary banter and the scuff of boots, was quieter than she had ever known it.

It was still dark—the deep, smothering dark that clung to the end of a December night. A fresh layer of snow, ghostly under the platform lamps, muffled what few sounds remained: the crunch of her boots on grit, the distant hiss of the cooling engine.

She joined the subdued trickle of workers heading towards the factory gates. Each step of the half-mile walk felt heavier than the last, as if her boots were filling with lead. *The slowest walk*, she thought, a tight knot forming in her gut.

Rumours had travelled fast on the train—whispers spreading like an infection.

"The entire factory's gone up," a girl from Selby had said, her face chalk white, staring as if the words themselves had scorched her.

Nell had tried to shake it off. Rumours. There were always rumours. But now, this silence—the absence of laughter, of song—felt like confirmation.

At the gates, the crowd had gathered as usual, but something was wrong. No girls linking arms, no voices rising in jest. Only pale faces and hunched shoulders in the flickering gaslight, a line of women staring at the iron poles as if they led to purgatory. No one seemed sure whether they would open—or what horror lay behind them if they did.

Nell's breath caught in her throat, tasting cold and something more nameless. Dread.

She thought of Eliza. Wondered if she'd heard anything on her way home last night. Eliza, always so steady.

And then, with a reluctant groan, the gates creaked open.

The whispers swelled—shapeless fear hardening into terrible fragments:

"The blast—they said it was like the wrath of God..."

"Carried out in sacks, what was left of them..."

"Limbs—lodged in the roof beams, can you imagine?"

Nell squeezed her eyes shut, willing the images away. But the fear had already taken root, and then came the smell.

It wasn't the usual metallic tang of the cleanways, nor the faint scent of oil and polish from the machine sheds. This was different; this was a disaster. Thick, oily smoke burned her throat. The sickly sweet stench of scorched flesh. The electric reek of burnt hair. And underneath it all, the damp, earthy rot of churned mud and fractured wood. The truth arrived not in words but in air poisoned by grief.

Nell followed the others in silence, a slow procession of shadows moving towards the changing rooms. Her heart thudded against her ribs like a trapped bird. Beyond the familiar cleanway, where Room 42 had once stood, all that existed was a gaping void—a cratered shell, still smoking.

The air here was raw. Bitter. Every breath like a wound.

Timber—splintered, blackened—jutted from the ground like broken ribs. The eastern wall was gone, ripped away in the blast. Bits of twisted metal lay scattered like bones. Snow, once white, was mottled with soot and ash.

Someone gasped behind her—a strangled sob. Another girl bent double, vomiting onto the frozen grass. Nell's stomach lurched. She reached for a charred post, her gloved hand trembling as she steadied herself.

Then she saw it.

Half-buried in snow and soil, a single, rubber-soled boot.

Small. Delicate. Scorched at the heel.

A child's boot. Or near enough.

Nell felt her knees give way a bit, weakness rushing through her. Her mind flashed to her lost boy, and tears burned behind her eyes, fierce and unbidden.

None of the night shift girls were there. Of course not. The factory had sent them home—those who could still walk. When Nell glanced towards the changing rooms, they were empty. The canteen, which should have been full of noise at the start of the day shift, stood in stillness. Girls were present, but not truly there. The clearways, once echoing with footsteps, had fallen silent.

Nell turned, bone-deep weariness settling over her. It wasn't the kind that sleep could cure.

She walked back towards the group of women now huddled near the canteen. Their faces reflected her own—shock, fear, disbelief.

"Room 42's gone. Where are we even supposed to go now?"

"Why bring us in?" someone said. The voice trembled, marked with rising anger. "To see... this?"

A man stepped forward from the cluster of officials—Captain Miller. His uniform was crisp, but his face was ashen. Haunted. He cleared his throat, trying for command, but the ruin behind him swallowed any authority.

"Ladies," he began, "you will be reassigned. Room 41. Room 17. Room 5." He hesitated. "Production must continue. We have orders to fill for the Front."

A pause.

Then, without conviction: "Room 42 will be rebuilt. It will be operational again by the end of the day."

By the end of the day? Nell stared, disbelieving, as if a new floor and a few planks of timber could erase the horror. As if wood and nails could patch over lives shattered here.

No one moved.

The women stood frozen, their faces pale ovals in the dim light. The silence stretched thin—taut, brittle, ready to snap. Then, slowly, with the hesitant movements of sleepwalkers—or the condemned—they turned. One by one, they followed the watchers, who had directed them into the canteen, assigning them to new workrooms.

Nell moved with them, a body carried along by a silent, shuffling current. She didn't make a conscious choice to go, but the thought of being left alone beside that smoking void was worse than being part of this procession of shadows.

The canteen felt like a chapel—silent, stunned. The usual clatter and chatter had vanished, swallowed by a thick, muffled quiet. Women sat hunched at the long wooden tables, their eyes fixed on nothing, not speaking.

Only the scrape of a bench and the steady hiss of the tea urn broke the stillness, its steam rising like a phantom into the cold air.

A woman in a clean apron, her face pale and set, was handing out enamelled mugs of milk—the so-called TNT tonic. The act was so routine, so very normal, that it felt like madness. Nell took a mug, her hand moving automatically.

The milk was chalky and lukewarm. The taste reminded her of yesterday morning, right here, when she'd shared a laugh with a night shift girl named Mary Gibson over the state of the tea. A girl from Castleford. Just a bairn. The memory was a sharp, physical pain so intense it made her flinch.

She sat at the end of an empty bench, cradling the mug for warmth it didn't possess. At a nearby table, she heard the first whispers cut through the hush.

"To see it..." one woman said, her voice trembling with a rage close to tears. "He brings us in to see their graves and then tells us to get on with it? Like we're just another part of the bloody machine he can replace?"

"I don't want to go back in," another voice replied, thin and reedy with terror. "Not to Room 17, not to any of them. What if it happens again? The whole place is a death trap, I'm telling you."

Nell listened, the words washing over her. Her cold fury at Captain Miller's speech, "Production must continue," merged with the familiar, hollow ache of her grief. She thought of her son, John, and the telegram that had gutted her life just two months ago, killed *"in action at the Somme, for King and Country."* They had told her his sacrifice was for a greater cause—to hold the line and keep the home front safe.

She looked around the canteen at the frightened faces—women and girls, though what was the difference now?

The boys were fed to the trenches, to mud and bullets. The girls came here, to poison and fire, fuelling the same endless war. Different fronts, same fate.

The line they held in this cold, reeking shed was no less real. No less deadly.

And the realisation didn't burn—it settled cold and quiet, with a strange, unshakeable calm.

The factory whistle shrieked.

The sound was a brutal, physical thing, slicing through the quiet and making half the women in the room jump. It was the sermon of the war machine, calling its congregation to work. Nell watched as, one by one, the women rose, their movements stiff and slow, like sleepwalkers. Their brief, silent rebellion was over. Necessity, sharp and unforgiving, was herding them back to the line.

For a moment, Nell remained seated. She could stand up, walk out the door, and never return. The thought was a wild, desperate bird fluttering in her chest.

Then she looked down at the faint yellow stain that would never truly leave. She thought of the rent, of the price of coal, of a world that had no place for a grieving woman with no wage. Her son was gone. She was still here. Her war was not over.

With a sense of grim, final clarity, she raised the mug to her lips and drained the chalky, lukewarm milk in three long, determined swallows. It tasted like bitter medicine. She placed the empty mug on the table with a soft, definitive click. Then, with a deep, shuddering breath that tasted of ash and despair, Nell Clark stood up and joined the silent procession of women shuffling back to the factory floor.

21

Chapter 21 : Killed by Accident

16th December 1916, Barnbow

The silence that followed the roar was a different beast altogether. It wasn't peace; it was a void—heavy, cloying, sucking the truth into a well of unspoken horrors. What twisted alchemy of error had birthed such devastation?

A whisper of a faulty fuse, like a serpent's hiss? A stray grain of crystallised TNT—a tiny, malevolent seed of destruction? Or a shell malfunction, its volatile heart turned murderous? No authority ever truly said.

Official lips pursed, offering words as smooth and cold as mortuary slabs. The papers, when they dared speak at all, called it an accident: a sterile, blameless word. The factory, a hulking, soot-stained beast that had devoured their girls, called it regrettable, a mere sigh of inconvenience.

But the women who survived, the families crossing a land of sudden, brutal emptiness, tasted the truth on their tongues, bitter as bile: this was the cost-the price of pennies, paid in flesh and bone.

No headline screamed their names from front pages. No bold ink mourned their passing. The city's pulse beat on, all but oblivious—no photographs captured their last smiles—now frozen only in memory's fading light. No solemn procession of black-draped carriages wound through Leeds' cobbled streets, no public artery of grief.

The Yorkshire Evening Post, in its funereal columns, bore witness—its pages rustling like dry leaves in a graveyard. Over the next week, dozens of death notices appeared—clipped, clinical, cold as the December wind whipping through the city. Each was a tiny, black-bordered tombstone pressed into cheap newsprint:

"Killed by accident."

The words were a shroud—thin and inadequate—thrown over a chasm of unanswered questions. No place, as if they had ceased to exist in a vacuum, untethered from the grimy reality of the factory floor. No cause, as if the blast were an act of God, not a consequence of human endeavour, quotas, and pressure. No factory named, as if naming it would admit a wound too grievous for the nation's morale.

The city's air, saturated with coal fumes and the metallic tang of industry, carried no public lament, only private, muffled sobs behind drawn curtains. But from a trench line in France, amidst mud and cordite's stench, Field Marshal Sir Douglas Haig, the man orchestrating death on an industrial scale, found a moment to issue a despatch Order of the Day.

His words, like polished brass, commended the *"devotion and sacrifice of the women in our munition factories."*

He didn't say where these brave, devoted women had made their sacrifice. He didn't need to. The girls at Barnbow—those who returned to the remaining sheds, faces pale, hands still trembling—understood. Their sacrifice was a number, a statistic, a footnote in the grand, bloody ledger of war.

Two days later, the silence was pierced by the timid, official voice of the War Press Bureau. A statement, bland as unsalted porridge, was released:

EXPLOSION IN A NORTHERN FACTORY. 26 WOMEN KILLED AND 30 INJURED. SPLENDID BRAVERY OF THE WORKERS.

(From the War Press Bureau) London, Wednesday, 7:30 PM

In the dim kitchen on Bell Row, the words transmitted across telegraph wires felt distant and sanitised. Agnes Atkinson, hands raw from gripping Lucy's small, unopened tin box, read them in the dim kitchen light, the newsprint blurring through fresh tears. Harold sat beside her, the paper trembling in his calloused grip.

"The Ministry of Munitions regrets to announce that an explosion occurred last night at a national factory in the north of England."

Regret. Another word as hollow as the ache in Agnes's chest.

"According to reports, 26 women workers were killed and about 30 were injured."

The numbers fell like stones into the vast well of grief—each one a life, a story, a future extinguished. Lucy wasn't even a whole number yet, her fate suspended in the fog of official confirmation.

The statement continued, a masterpiece of detached understatement:

"Prompt and effective steps were taken to deal with the emergency, and the damage done to the factory was slight."

Slight. Agnes pictured the raw, gaping wound she imagined Room 42 to be, of lives vaporised, and cold fury settled in her heart.

"The great majority of the workers in the factory are women, and their behaviour is deserving of the highest praise. They displayed the greatest coolness and perfect discipline both in helping to remove the injured and in continuing to carry on the work of the factory in spite of the explosion."

Coolness. Discipline. Was that what they called the terror, the desperate scramble for life, the courage born of sheer animal instinct?

"The effect of the accident on the output of munitions will be negligible."

Negligible. A final, brutal epitaph. Their daughters, their wives, their sisters—their loss was *negligible* to the insatiable hunger of the war machine.

A few days later, in Captain Miller's hastily cleaned office, the official inquiry began. The room felt airless, the lingering scent of stale pipe smoke unable to mask the new, oppressive silence.

Captain Miller sat behind his desk, his face grey and etched with lines of exhaustion. Mr Finch, the staunch man from the Ministry, stood beside him, his expression impassive, his clipboard ready.

Their first witness was Ann Price. She was a shadow of the sharp-tongued girl from the canteen, her face pale, a fresh scar on her forehead. She sat with her bandaged hands knotted in her lap.

"Miss Price," Finch began, his voice smooth, "you were the charge hand for Bench 17. Your gang's output was exemplary. Would you say the atmosphere in Room 42 was... competitive?"

Ann stared at her feet. "We all wanted the bonus," she whispered, her voice unsteady. "Me dad's out of work now. We needed the money."

"So you were all working at speed? Did you notice the girls on the adjacent bench—Bench 12—making any errors? Rushing their work?" Finch pressed.

Ann's head snapped up, a flicker of her old fire in her eyes, now tempered with grief. "We were all rushing. You wanted us to. Everyone was tired. Sarah Jennings... she was a good worker. They all were." Her voice broke on the last word. "It happened so fast. Just... a flash. That's all I saw."

She was dismissed. Next, they called William Parkin. His hands were bandaged, his face still smudged with soot that seemed to have settled into his skin.

"Mr Parkin," Captain Miller said, his voice heavy with genuine respect, "your bravery has been noted and will be commended to the highest authorities."

Parkin gave a slow, weary nod, his eyes fixed on Finch.

Mr Finch consulted his notes, his expression impassive. "Mr Parkin, you were the chief mechanic on duty."

"I was," Parkin said, his voice heavy. His bandaged hands rested on the table.

"In your expert opinion," Finch continued, his tone smooth as polished stone, "was there any sign of mechanical fault that could have contributed to this... incident?"

Parkin's gaze was unwavering. "The machines were being run too hard. The press on Bench 12—Charge Hand Wren's bench. It had been making a noise for a week. A high-pitched shriek under pressure. It wasn't safe."

Miller looked up, startled. Finch, however, merely nodded, as if expecting the answer.

"Yes, the press," Finch said, producing a thin document from his folder. He placed it on the desk, the paper a stark white against the dark wood. "According to the official maintenance log, that very press was inspected and cleared for service on the morning of the fifth. Signed off by a day shift foreman."

He slid the paper across the desk towards Parkin. "For the official record to be complete, Mr Parkin, we need your countersignature here, confirming the log's accuracy as chief mechanic of the night shift."

Parkin stared at it as if it were a snake. He leaned forward, squinting at the spidery signature at the bottom. A long silence stretched, broken only by the ticking of the wall clock.

"No," Parkin said, his voice quiet but absolute. He pushed the paper back. "That machine was screaming. I spoke to Charge Hand Wren about it myself that night. And that signature... it's not right. This log is a lie."

Finch's eyebrow raised a fraction. He made a slow, deliberate note on his clipboard. "I see. Your... *opinion*... on the official record has been noted. You may go, Mr Parkin."

Parkin stood, gave Finch a look of pure, unadulterated contempt, and walked out without another word.

After Parkin was dismissed, Miss McDowell was summoned. She sat ramrod straight, her hands clasped in her lap.

"Bench 12," Miller said, consulting a sheet of notes. "Eliza Wren's team. A good gang, you said. Competent."

"The best," McDowell corrected him, her voice quiet but firm. "Eliza Wren was the best charge hand I had. Cool-headed, meticulous. Her girls respected her."

Finch turned from the window then, his spectacles glinting in the light. "Their efficiency numbers were high. Very high. Was Charge Hand Wren pushing them too hard to meet the bonus targets, Miss McDowell?"

The question was a carefully placed trap. McDowell met his gaze, her own as cold as his.

"My charge hands push for the targets set by the Ministry, Mr Finch. The same targets that came with the bonus scheme you spearheaded. The same targets that, as Mr Parkin noted, left no time for essential maintenance."

Finch's expression didn't change, but a muscle twitched in his jaw.

"Miss McDowell," Miller said, his own voice strained.

Finch did not wait. He picked up the falsified log. "Miss McDowell, your chief mechanic seems to be suffering from a rather... unreliable memory. I was hoping you could provide some clarity."

He held the paper out to her. "The official record states the equipment was perfectly safe. It suggests the cause was therefore a worker error. Perhaps a lapse in judgement from a team being pushed too hard by their charge hand for a bonus?"

The trap was laid. He was asking her to choose between supporting her mechanic and implicating her charge hand or accepting the official lie.

McDowell's gaze was glacial. She didn't even glance at the paper in his hand.

"What I can clarify, Mr Finch," she remarked, with chilling precision, "is that I trust Mr Parkin's assessment of his machinery more than I trust a conveniently produced report. He warned me about that press. I requested it be taken offline. *You* were the one who insisted it remain in service to meet quotas." She paused, letting the accusation hang in the air. "My girls were not careless. They were exhausted. And they were let down."

Finch's thin smile vanished. He slowly retracted the paper and returned it to his folder. "Your testimony has been illuminating, Miss McDowell. Thank you."

Miller cleared his throat, intervening. "There was a report of a dropped Gaine at that bench before the main incident."

"There was," McDowell confirmed. "Handled immediately and correctly by the charge hand, as per procedure."

"And a dropped fuse?" Finch pressed, stepping away from the window. "A component wasted. A delay of several seconds. Was this standard for Bench 12?"

McDowell thought of Nora Kershaw, of her quiet, prayerful dedication. "The women were under immense pressure, Mr Finch, as I noted in my reports to Captain Miller for days prior. Pressure from increased quotas, and pressure from being observed and timed like components in a machine."

Her words hung in the air. It was as close to an accusation as she dared. Captain Miller shifted in his chair, uneasy, his eyes locked on the reports before him. Finch, however, was unmoved.

"So, you would characterise the working environment as... stressful?" he asked, the question slick with false empathy. "And in your opinion, this stress led to worker error? A fumbled component, perhaps? An overfilled shell?"

McDowell's hands tightened in her lap. She saw what he was doing—building a neat, straightforward narrative for the Ministry. A story of careless, hysterical women cracking under pressure. A tale that ignored the very policies and quotas that had created the pressure to begin with.

"I would characterise the environment as one where dedicated women were doing their patriotic duty under brutal conditions." Her voice was as precise and cold as a winter morning. "They were not careless. They were exhausted."

She stood up then, her audience with them over. "If that will be all, Captain?"

Captain Miller nodded, refusing to meet her eye. "Thank you, Miss McDowell."

As she walked out, the only sound was the scratch of Mr Finch's pen on his clipboard, reducing the lives of Eliza, Sarah, Lucy, and all the others to a neat, blame-deflecting footnote in a report that would be filed, stamped, and forgotten.

He finished his note with a decisive flick of the wrist, then looked at the ashen-faced Captain Miller, his tone flat and business-like.

"The new production targets for the remaining sheds will be issued in the morning, Captain."

But even those curated numbers told only part of the story—a fractured reflection of the true devastation. In the inferno that had been Room 42, Eliza Wren's team—all seven—had been obliterated. Their worktable, close to the ignition point, offered no shield.

Sarah Jennings, her laughter silenced forever, never stood a chance. Lucy Atkinson, small hands still wiping down a shell, dreams of stories and a life beyond, vanished into searing heat and flame. For some, no bodies remained—only fragments, memories, and the chilling emptiness where a loved one used to be.

Others returned to families not even recognisable; the fire stole their very identities.

A second blast—a sympathetic detonation—ripped through the next team. Nine more women would succumb to horrific injuries in the agonising days that followed—their passing often unrecorded by swift initial reports. Others were carried out, blackened, lungs blistered, choking on poisonous smoke that clung like a shroud.

Some would never walk again, their limbs twisted or lost beyond repair. Some would never speak again, the horror stealing their voices.

By dawn's first grey light, creeping over Barnbow's scarred landscape and casting skeletal shadows from the still smoking timbers of Room 42, another team of women was already assembling. Faces pale, etched with dread and grim necessity, their movements stiff and silent as they stepped to lines in adjacent sheds.

Their hair was pinned beneath caps. Their hands were still trembling, though they tried to hide it.

Room 42 itself—a horrifying void of twisted metal and charred wood—was declared operational before the next night's sun set. Machinery was repaired or replaced at a rapid pace. Floors were swept clean of the most visible traces of the immediate past.

The never-ending drive for production roared deafeningly, overriding all grief, all caution. The factory was indispensable; its workers—the working-class women of Yorkshire—individual cogs in its vast, grinding mechanism, were, in the cold calculus of war and industry, perhaps less so.

Like the new batch of shells they filled, their futures remained balanced, worth measuring by unseen hands; their lives hung by threads as invisible as the 'efficiency men', silent, constant, and demanding.

22

Chapter 22 : The Ghost of Yellow

28th November 1916, Selby

The last thing she remembered of Room 42 wasn't the noise but a sudden, gentle silence that had bloomed in her head as the floor rushed up to meet her. There had been no fear in that final second, only an immense, boneless relief as the world dissolved into a quiet, welcoming darkness. Then, nothing.

She woke to the smell of carbolic acid. The Leeds Infirmary's whitewashed walls pressed in, thinning the air around Rose.

Her memory was a blur of noise and yellow dust. She recalled the roar of the machinery, the weight of a shell in her trembling hands, and a wave of dizziness so profound it buckled her knees. The last thing she truly remembered was the look of alarm on Eliza's face, her charge hand's voice cracking through the din to stop the line as Sarah and June rushed to her side.

Carbolic acid stung her nostrils over the faint scent of illness, soap, and sun-starved skin. Beneath stiff hospital linen, Rose lay still. Some days, her lungs clenched like a fist; others, air slipped away before filling her. Her breath was never strong.

The doctor, a man whose face seemed permanently etched with weariness, spoke little. They seldom did. He lifted her hand and pressed his thumb to her pulse, brow furrowed in a frown that offered no comfort.

On the second morning, as a watery grey light seeped through the tall, grimy window, she heard him mutter to the nurse, his voice low and distant, "Liver swelling... significant." He scribbled something onto the chart at her bedside, his eyes avoiding hers as if her gaze might tarnish his clinical detachment.

Liver swelling. The words echoed in the sterile silence of her mind. *Is that what the Amatol did? Did it bloat you from the inside out before it claimed you?*

When she'd arrived, three other girls occupied the ward—pale faces, coughs ringing in the high-ceilinged room. Whispered stories of Barnbow passed between them in the dark: hushed tales of near misses and the ever-present yellow dust. But within a week, Rose was the last one left.

The others had been discharged one by one, their belongings bundled. Their steps were hesitant but hopeful as they walked out, leaving behind the odour of carbolic and the rustling paper sheets. They left Rose with silence and the slow tick of the ward clock, each tick a reminder of time she felt she hadn't earned.

Her chestnut hair never regained its vibrancy; blonde tips—cruel reminders of the poison rooms—clung to the weak fresh growth. Her skin still carried a pale-yellow tinge, not the deep jaundice of an overworked shell-filler but a faint shadow in morning light or a sparkle in the bedpan's reflection. The nurses, always brisk, promised it would fade. They called her a canary—a living warning. And she was still here.

The news, when it came, was not spoken. It seeped into her consciousness like damp creeping up the infirmary walls.

It was a week after admission. As the evening shadows stretched long and distorted across the ward floor, voices drifted in. Rose lay still, the linen calm and rough against her feverish skin, listening as a nurse changed her bedding. The nurses whispered, hushed and careful, but the thin partition offered little privacy.

"Barnbow... that big place near Leeds..." she said, the sound gentle, almost a whisper. "Room 42. They're saying... all of them. Gone."

The rustling of sheets paused. The other nurse made a soft, distressed sound.

"Poor things. Poor, poor things. Said it was... an awful mess. Twenty-something dead, and more by now. Blown apart, most of them, God rest their souls. Happened a few days later—a week at most—after that one came in."

That one. The words—sharp and impersonal—lanced through Rose. *That one. Me.* The air in her lungs solidified. The walls swam before her eyes. She turned her face to the cold, unyielding plaster, a silent scream trapped in her throat.

Scalding tears broke free, soaking the pillowcase—each one evidence of a life spared, a life that felt stolen from others. Her body shook, a tremor rattling the iron bedframe. Still, no one came. They likely thought it was a fever returning or the familiar chills of recovery. It wasn't. It was the ice of understanding, the jagged edge of unbearable truth.

She didn't speak for two days. Food went untouched; grief coated her tongue in metal. The nurses' cheerful greetings struck a wall of silence. Words felt like a betrayal. When her mother arrived—hat in hand, coat scented of camphor—Rose embraced her like a frightened child, not a woman of twenty.

The journey back to Selby by cart blurred, jolting wheels over countryside too green, too alive. Rose stared out at the fields, her eyes wide but unseeing, her mouth tight and grim. Her mother, bless her, filled the silence with gentle chatter—about the price of eggs, Mrs Carlton's rheumatism, the broth she'd make when they got home. Rose heard the words, but they slipped through her fingers, meaningless.

Days blurred into weak sunlight and long shadows. She sat on the back step, wrapped in her mother's scratchy blanket, legs folded like paper, eyes fixed on the overgrown herbs. The pale sun offered no warmth, yet she remained silent and still for hours.

The khaki-shirt job at the local depot came later, much later—only when her mother, patience worn thin by Rose's inertia, insisted, "Do something to keep your hands from turning to stone, lass. Life has to go on." But Rose's mind wasn't idle. Oh no, it was a hive of persistent activity, churning day and night, replaying, remembering, regretting.

Each night, when the house lay still and the wind sighed, she saw them: faces laughing in the canteen's smoky haze or locked on the dangerous glow of Room 42.

She saw Mary, standing with a stiff back and a tongue as sharp as a new knife, steady at her station even as the floorboards trembled.

She saw June, who always had a bit of barley water to share, her pockets seeming bottomless, her stories of little ones painting brief splashes of colour onto their grey days.

She saw Hilda, humming a quiet hymn as a shield against the factory's roar, her fingers that once handled chalk now stained a damning yellow.

She saw Nora, red-haired and sweet-faced, her gentle smile a balm, her lips moving silently as she wrote a letter to her Will.

She saw Sarah, *God, Sarah*, always loud, full of brass and swagger, her laughter a defiant roar against the gloom, hiding her heartbreak behind a barrage of jokes.

And Eliza, their charge hand, their rock, her voice calm and steady. "Keep your pace, Rose," she'd said, eyes kind but firm, "and I'll keep you safe."

A promise broken by fate that Rose had somehow sidestepped. She had fallen, succumbed to the poison they all breathed. And a week later, while she lay in a clean, white bed, the rest of them—her gang, her friends—had burned. The irony was a bitter acid in her soul.

She thought of going back. Not to Barnbow—the very name branded on her memory, a place of nightmares. Never Barnbow. But to Leeds. To the streets where families lived. To doors where mothers waited for daughters who would never return, where sisters washed black armbands, where children asked questions with no answers, their small faces clouded with grief too heavy for their years.

She imagined herself standing on a stranger's doorstep, hat clutched in trembling hands, skin still bearing the faint, ghostly stain of yellow.

"I was there," she'd say, the words tasting like ash in her mouth. "I worked with her. I lived." But what words could follow such an admission? What solace could she offer?

"I'm sorry." Pathetic. Meaningless.

"She died well." A monstrous lie. No one died well in such an inferno.

"She said your name." An invention, a cruel comfort.

"I should have been beside her." The truest words, perhaps, but ones that offered no comfort, only shared her unbearable burden.

None of it would be enough. Worse, far worse—what if they looked at her, at her living, breathing form, and their grief-darkened eyes screamed the question that haunted her waking hours: *'Why you? Why you and not my lass?'*

So she stayed in Selby—a ghost in her own insignificant life. Wrote no letters to families she'd never met. Lit no candles in churches that she no longer felt worthy to enter. She folded fabric in the quiet, dusty depot, hands moving with mechanical precision, stitching seams in endless silence. Each stitch was a penance. Each shirt was a shroud.

But in the pocket of her worn apron, tucked away like a forbidden relic, she kept a scrap of linen—torn from the hem of her old factory smock the day her mother burned the rest.

It lay on the edge, yellow and worn thin by time and washing. In the dead of night, she took it out and folded it smaller and smaller, pressing the fabric with desperate focus until it became a knot too tight to shrink—a tangible shard of her guilt, her survival, her unending grief.

And when the war ended, when bells rang and strangers danced in the streets, no one in Selby, Leeds, or anywhere else spoke of Room 42. The factory, the explosion, the names—all swallowed by the collective remorse, the urgent need to forget, to move on.

She sometimes wondered if it was the shame of it, a disaster at home, that made them so quick to turn away. Or was it something worse? Perhaps, in the grand, terrible calculus of the war, the loss of thirty-five girls in a factory was simply a rounding error, a footnote lost in the endless casualty lists from the Somme that filled the papers each day.

Their deaths were not on a foreign field, not listed under a glorious battle. They were just... an accident. She knew, with a certainty that was as cold and hard as a shard of shrapnel, that had it been peacetime, the whole country would have mourned them. But in a world already drowning in death, their small tragedy was just another drop of rain in a storm.

But Rose remembered. How could she ever forget? And every stitch of her life from that day forward, every careful fold of fabric, every silent, waking dawn, she made for them.

23

Chapter 23 : A Debt of Ash

6th December 1916, Castleford

The world had gone quiet. That was the first thing Robert noticed. Since his mam hadn't come home from her shift, the usual morning clatter of the house—the scrape of the poker in the grate, the clink of mugs, her humming that always went flat on the high notes—had been replaced by a thick, listening silence. He sat at the kitchen table, spooning cold, lumpy porridge into his mouth, his gaze riveted on the dead stove. It was a chilly December morning, and the cold was winning.

His grandmother sat opposite, her hands worrying the frayed edges of her shawl, her eyes locked on the front door. Every creak of the floorboards, every shout from the street, made her flinch.

Then came the knock. Not a neighbour's friendly rap but two sharp, official thuds that seemed to shake the air in the cramped kitchen.

His grandmother's head snapped up, her expression a mask of pure dread. She shuffled to the door, her hand trembling as she lifted the latch. A policeman stood on the step, his helmet held awkwardly in his hands. He was young, with a pale moustache that looked out of place on his nervous face, and he couldn't seem to meet her eyes.

"Mrs Wren?" he began, his voice low and full of a terrifying discomfort. "I'm afraid I have some difficult news. There was... an incident at the Barnbow factory last night. An explosion."

Robert watched as the policeman's words became just shapes in the air, sounds without meaning. His grandmother made a noise—a choked, tearing sound like a snapped rope—and collapsed back into a chair by the door.

"I'm afraid Eliza was... among them," the policeman finished, his gaze fixed on a crack in the floorboards. "I'm sorry for your loss."

Robert froze, the spoon halfway to his mouth. The world came to a complete halt. The taste of porridge turned to ash on his tongue. He looked from the policeman's polished boots to his grandmother's crumpled form, and a single, cold thought pierced through the fog of shock. *Mam's gone.*

The policeman mumbled something about official notice and support from the parish, but the words were a distant hum. The only thing Robert could hear was the terrible, practical question already forming in the silence: *What do we do now? How do we tell Dad?*

The hours that followed were a thick, grey fog. At three o'clock, after the factory let out the shell-shocked day shift, another knock came. It was Nell Clark, her face pale and etched with a sorrow that mirrored their own. With her was the vicar, a kind, stooped man whose hands fluttered nervously as he entered the grief-stricken house.

Nell didn't speak at first. She placed a small parcel wrapped in newspaper atop the table and began making tea, her movements practical and sure in a house that had lost its rhythm. The vicar sat with Robert's grandmother, his voice a low, gentle murmur of condolences that seemed to do little to pierce her silent shock.

It was Nell who broke through. She stared at Robert, her eyes clear and direct. "Robert, love." Her voice was steady. "Getting a soldier home... It's not simple. They won't just send him because we ask."

The vicar emitted a slight cough. "She's right, son. We must follow the channels. I will write a letter to the War Office myself, explaining the circumstances. That you children have no other guardian. But they'll need proof. An official death certificate once it's issued."

The words landed like stones. *Bureaucracy. Letters. Proof.* Robert surveyed the cold kitchen, at his weeping grandmother and his baby brother asleep in the cot, and the problem suddenly felt vast, an impossible mountain to climb. The idea of his father walking through the door tomorrow, or the day after, dissolved into a distant, uncertain hope.

The next day, Robert put on his father's good coat, the sleeves too long, and walked with the vicar to the Town Hall. The administrative office was a drab, cold room that smelled of damp paper and disinfectants. A tired clerk with ink-stained fingers listened as the vicar explained the situation. Robert stood beside them, his cap clutched in his hands, feeling small and useless.

"He has to come home," Robert declared, his voice sounding thin and young. "There's no one else."

The clerk sighed, his expression not unkind, just drained. "I understand, lad. Truly, I do. But there are procedures." He pushed a set of forms across the counter. "A request for compassionate discharge must be filed. We'll need a copy of the death certificate when you have it. We'll pass it up the chain of command." He paused, looking at Robert with a flicker of genuine pity. "But you must understand, son. The war effort takes priority. There are no guarantees."

Robert left the Town Hall with the useless forms in his coat pocket. He hadn't brought his father home. He had just been told, in the kindest way possible, that the great, grinding machine of the war didn't stop for one dead mother in Yorkshire. The weight of his family's future felt heavier than any sack of coal he'd ever hauled.

The week that followed was a slow, grinding torture of uncertainty.

Robert went back to the pit, his body moving on instinct, his mind a numb haze. Every shilling he earned was now the only thing keeping them from utter ruin. He'd come home, black with dust and exhaustion, to a house that grew colder each day.

The coal scuttle was empty by Friday. The food the neighbours had brought was gone by Sunday. His grandmother tried, but her grief made her frail. She would sit for hours, staring into the dead hearth, Baby Stanley fussing in her arms, her memory drifting.

On Monday, Robert saw John Skinner walking down Albany Terrace. He felt his blood run cold, and he pulled his grandmother back from the window, his heart hammering against his ribs. But Skinner didn't stop. He walked right past their door, his face set in a grim line. The threat was still there, a wolf circling just out of sight.

Hope, which had flickered briefly, died. The letter from the vicar had been sent. The forms had been filled out. And then, nothing. Just silence from the War Office and the deepening, bitter cold of a house without a mother and a winter without end.

By the morning of December 12th, the house had settled into a rhythm of quiet despair. Robert was getting Beth ready for school, his fingers fumbling with the ribbons for her hair, when a knock came at the door. Simple. Unassuming.

***

9th December 1916, Castleford

Across town, on what should have been Eliza Wren's eviction day, John Skinner sat at his kitchen table, the gas lamp casting a yellow glow on the open pages of his ledger. He tapped the entry for Number Seven Albany Terrace with an impatient finger. *Wren, S. Loan Account & Rent. Balance Due: £4 10s. Payment Demanded: Dec 9th.*

His wife, Mary—a woman whose quiet observations often carried more weight than she was credited—placed his lukewarm tea beside the book. "You're not thinking of going over there today, are you, John?" Her voice was almost neutral, but her eyes, missing nothing, warned him.

Skinner snorted without looking up from his figures. "A debt's a debt, Mary. It's the principle of the thing. You let one slide, and they all think you're a soft touch. Stan Wren knew the terms when he came begging after that fool strike. Business is business. The house needs to earn its keep."

"And what about our place in this town, John?" Mary's voice sharpened, losing its gentle edge. "Have you not heard the talk? It's all anyone speaks of."

She was right. He had heard it. Whispers in the street, hushed conversations that stopped when he approached. He'd dismissed it as idle gossip, women's sentimentality. But Mary's tone told him it was something more.

"I was at the baker's this morning," she went on, her voice low and steady. "No one was talking about the price of bread. They were talking about the girls from this town. Young Maggie Barker, who used to deliver for them... gone. Polly Booth, from down near the river... gone. A list of them. Their mothers are inconsolable, their fathers walking around like ghosts."

She paused, letting the weight of her words settle in the quiet kitchen.

"Eliza Wren bought her sewing thread from my sister's shop not two weeks ago. She was a good woman, John, working to keep a roof over her children's heads while her husband fought for the king. If you turn up on that poor woman's doorstep today—or what's left of her family—demanding money before they've even had a chance to mourn, your 'principle' won't matter a damn. You'll be the talk of every pub and chapel from here to Pontefract. 'Skinner the Ghoul,' they'll call you. No one will want your custom. No one will forget."

Skinner's face tightened. He hadn't grasped the depth of the town's collective grief, the raw, personal anger that simmered beneath the surface. He had only thought of the money. He looked down at his ledger, at the neat columns and balanced figures. They felt logical, safe.

The messy, unpredictable world of public opinion was a different matter entirely. A poor reputation was terrible for business. *Damn the woman*, he thought. To die in such a public, sentimental fashion was the worst possible inconvenience.

"She owed it," he muttered, but his conviction was wavering. "Am I to be the villain in this?" he snapped, his voice rising. "I'm to lose out because she was careless enough to get herself blown up? It's not my fault!"

"And her children owe you nothing but decent shelter—the shelter their mother died trying to provide," Mary retorted, her voice sharper than he'd heard it in years. "Let it be, John, for a week or two. Let the man come home from France. Let them see to their dead. There'll be compensation from the factory. You'll get your money. But not today. Not like this."

He slammed the ledger shut, the sound sharp and final in the quiet kitchen. He hated it when she was right, especially when her reasoning was better than his own.

"Fine," he muttered, voice edged with irritation, the word tasting like ash. "A little time. For appearances."

Mary gave a sharp nod, picked up her sewing basket, and walked out, leaving him alone with his lukewarm tea and unfinished sums.

He stared at the closed ledger, unmoving.

The principle of the thing. The words echoed in his mind, his own father's voice. He remembered his father, a man with a heart too soft for business, nearly losing their small haberdashery because he'd let a debtor slide for too long out of pity. "Pity doesn't pay the bills, John-boy," he'd said, his face grey with worry. "A debt is a promise. You forget that, you lose everything."

Skinner had never forgotten. He'd built his life on that hard lesson. He wasn't cruel; he was a realist. He was a man of property in a world that was always trying to take it from you. He picked up his tea, his eyes already calculating.

A brief delay wouldn't hurt his bottom line much, not if it kept his reputation from being dragged through Castleford's muck. And Mary was right about the compensation. The factory would pay out. A tidy sum, most likely. The debt wasn't lost; it was merely deferred. He could afford to wait. It was just good business.

***

12th December 1916 – Castleford

The train lurched into Castleford beneath a sky the colour of soot, hung heavy and close. The platform was a crust of packed snow and cinders, churned by boots into a patchwork of grey slush.

It was December 12th, and the cold bit deep—sharp as razors against the back of Stan Wren's neck as he stepped down from the train in his Sappers uniform. The weight of his body jarred his knees; his breath came in visible bursts. Frost clung to the station windows like bone dust, etched in delicate skeletal veins.

He carried no trunk. Only an army kit bag, worn thin at the strap, and the dense, immeasurable weight of loss that bowed his shoulders. A week had passed since the notification was received from Command HQ.

A week without Eliza.

The army had said little. A flat statement: his duty was now at home—three children, no wife. He had expected a fight, some cold logic to argue against. But the captain nodded once, eyes shadowed and voice flat.

"Go home, Wren. War's done with you."

Done with me. Just like that.

He moved through the grey streets, his boots grinding on the frozen road. Every step felt unfamiliar. The Wren house stood halfway down—with its slate roof, the blue door, the crooked garden gate. But something was different. It looked thinner somehow, as if it had exhaled and forgotten how to breathe again.

He knocked once. Habit. Then, he forced the door open.

Warmth met him.

Beth sat at the table, small hands wrapped around a chipped enamel mug. Her hair was loose, her face pale and open. She looked up—and for a long second, nothing moved. Her eyes, rimmed with tears, caught the light like glass.

Then she ran.

"Dad!"

He dropped his kit bag and crouched just in time to catch her, her slight frame folding into his chest with desperate force. Her sobs were muffled against his coat, hot through thick wool, as if she were trying to press herself into him, to prove he was real. His arms curled around her; his gloved hands cradled the back of her head. His own eyes blurred.

She was smaller than he remembered. Or maybe he was seeing her with fresh eyes.

Her grief shook in time with her breath—silent at first, then hiccupping into gasps. He pressed a kiss to the crown of her head; the fragrance of soap and smoke clung to her curls. Warm, beautiful life living here.

On the stairs, a figure appeared—tall, lean, too old for fourteen but too young for the burdens he carried. Robert. He stood like a shadow halfway down, fists clenched at his sides, jaw set tight. His face was carved with something heavier than resentment—a wariness, perhaps, as if unsure whether his father was flesh or ghost.

Stan rose, every joint stiff. He met his son's eyes. No words, not at first. Only a long, searching look between two people who had both been forced to grow up too fast.

Then he stepped forward and wrapped the boy in an embrace neither had prepared for. Robert stiffened, resisted—and then relented, his arms awkward yet strong around Stan's back.

Stan held him, feeling the sharp bones of the boy's shoulders, and understood. This wasn't just his son; this was the man of the house, and Stan was a stranger who had just walked back into a world that had moved on without him.

"All right, Bobby," Stan said. "I'm home now, son."

There were no tears from the boy, but Stan felt something give way—a slackening in the shoulders, a tremor in the breath.

Not forgiveness, not yet. But something approaching it.

From the back kitchen came the creak of floorboards and the soft rustle of wool. The old woman appeared, holding the baby against her chest like a bundle of firelight. Baby Stan stirred, one mittened hand reaching towards the air. He blinked, then focused his tiny fingers, stretching them towards his father with absolute trust.

Stan crossed the room in two strides and bent his face to the baby's head. The scent struck him like a blow—warm milk, soft wool, the faintest trace of rose salve from Eliza's old tin. The smell was so full of life it hurt. The boy gurgled once, then stilled against him.

The old woman didn't speak as she passed the child over, but her hands trembled once their fingers touched. She looked smaller, her eyes sunken, her dress too loose at the shoulders. The tiredness in her wasn't the kind you slept off—it was carved deep, like a name in granite.

"You're home, then," she said at last.

Stan nodded, pulling off his cap with one hand and cradling the baby with the other. "Aye, Mam. I'm home."

The fire held her attention rather than him. "I've done my best," she said. "Kept the place right."

He swallowed hard, throat thick. "I know," he said. "And I'm grateful."

His eyes scanned the room—the dented kettle, the stew pot still simmering, Eliza's shawl hanging on the back of the door. Her absence was felt everywhere. In the shifting air. In the quiet corners.

This is home, he thought. And it isn't, not without her.

After supper—the stew reheated and thickened with scraps, the bread returned to its tin, the mugs washed and dried—the house exhaled.

Beth had fallen asleep on the settee, curled like a kitten with one thumb resting on her cheek, her hair half-unpinned. Robert had gone up early, with very little said between them—a quick "Night, Dad" and the creak of stairs under his growing weight. A 5 AM shift loomed for him. It always did now.

The baby slept in the cot beside the stove, one arm flung across his face in the universal gesture of peace, tiny snores rising and falling in rhythm with the flames.

The house was quiet, not only in volume but in tone. Quiet as an empty jar. Quiet like breath held too long.

Stan climbed the stairs, one hand trailing the bannister like a blind man feeling for home. The upper hallway was dim; the air was cooler here. He pushed the bedroom door open. It didn't creak. She'd oiled that hinge last winter.

The room smelled of her—not perfume, nothing like that. It smelled of lavender soap from the sachet in her drawer and the faint, clean scent of the cold air coming through the slightly warped window frame. Still their room. Still hers. The bed was made—not with the crisp corners she always folded sharp as an envelope, but smoothed over.

Robert's work, he thought. Her nightdress lay folded atop the pillow, soft and clean. He reached out a hand, his calloused pit man's fingers hovering over the worn cotton, before pulling back. He couldn't touch it. Not yet.

His gaze drifted to the dresser. Her brush rested beside the chipped enamel cup with its faded blue rim. A few of her long, dark hairs were still caught in its bristles, and the sight of them, so mundane and so full of her, was like a physical blow. He saw her sipping from that cup, her face pale but smiling after Beth was born.

And then came the ghost of another child, a memory that was theirs alone, a wound they had dressed together. Judith. Their bonny lass was stolen by pneumonia before her first birthday. He remembered Eliza's silent, shaking grief, a sorrow so deep they felt it as hard as a pit collapse. But their love, forged in that shared darkness, had held them fast. It was another promise they'd kept: to endure, through owt and all.

A life in objects, still warm with presence. He pulled open the top drawer with a deep breath. The odour of lavender was stronger here. Her aprons were folded in a careful stack. A small tin of buttons she'd saved. A half-used bar of soap wrapped in cloth. He ran his thumb over its smooth surface. Small things. The small things that made up a life. And beneath them... he found the bundle of his letters, tied with a strip of faded green curtain ribbon.

On top was the final one. His last letter from France. The envelope slit cleanly.

He perched near the edge of the bed, the mattress sinking beneath him with a sigh. The page felt heavier than it should, like it knew it had arrived too late. He unfolded it slowly, fingers thick and clumsy with dread.

It wasn't long—three short paragraphs in his cramped hand.

"...You're doing more than most generals, love... Tell Bobby I'm proud of him... I miss your hands. Your laugh. The sound of you banging pans when you're cross..."

His own words clawed up through his throat. He should have said more. Should have told her everything—how she tethered him to the earth, how her letters steadied his shaking hands, how he imagined her voice when the shells fell too close.

But he hadn't. And now she was no longer there, and paper couldn't carry what his chest now held.

He pressed the letter against his face.

And broke.

Not a sob. Not yet. Just a sound—thin, caught in his throat. Raw, ripped from the depths of his lungs. His body bent forward with it, curling around the ache like something wounded. The bedframe creaked beneath the weight of his grief as he rocked, the letter crushed against his cheek, eyes shut tight against the unbearable.

From the hallway, his mother paused, watching through the crack in the door—one hand bracing the frame, the other clutching her chest. Her son unravelled. Her daughter-in-law was gone. Without a sound, she closed the door.

***

15th December 1916 – Castleford

After the initial shock of Stan's return settled into a quiet routine of shared grief and the daunting task of rebuilding, his mother-in-law—her sorrow etched deep—spoke of Skinner's visit that terrible Tuesday. She told him about the ultimatum—the demand for the full sum. Stan listened, face grim, as the fragments of Eliza's final desperate days fell into place.

The seventy-pound compensation from the Ministry, along with Eliza's last week's wages, sat heavy in a tin box—blood money, every penny.

The next morning, Stan Wren walked to John Skinner's house. He did not wait to be summoned. The air was sharp, the snow underfoot frozen into treacherous ridges. He knocked firmly on Skinner's door once, twice.

Skinner opened it, a flicker of surprise in his hard eyes masked by a calculating look as he took in Stan's discharged soldier bearing.

"Wren. I didn't expect you. Come about the... outstanding matter, I presume?"

Stan stepped into the narrow hallway without invitation, his presence filling the space.

"Mr Skinner. I'm here to settle our account. Which was always *my* account." His tone was quiet, stripped of warmth, but each word landed with precise weight.

He pulled a small purse from his coat and counted out four pounds ten shillings, the coins clinking coldly onto Skinner's side table.

"That's the sum you demanded from Eliza. The balance of the loan plus interest. It's cleared."

Skinner's eyes flicked between the money and Stan, a shrewd glint assessing him. He scooped up the coins without a word.

Then Stan produced a thicker roll of notes from his coat.

"And this..." He set it firmly on the table. "...is fifty-two pounds. It covers the rent for Number Seven Albany Terrace for the next two years, from today. I'll have a receipt for all of it, Mr Skinner—clearly stating the debt is cleared, and the rent paid in full."

Skinner stared at the fifty-two pounds, his composure momentarily shaken by the sum. He glanced from the money back to Stan, whose gaze was unwavering, implacable. Mary Skinner appeared in the doorway without a sound. Her expression was unreadable, but she brought a silent, undeniable weight to the space behind her husband.

Skinner cleared his throat. "That's... a substantial sum, Wren." He made no move to protest, his mind racing.

"It is," Stan said, his voice steady. He waited.

Skinner moved to a small desk, pulled out a ledger, and took out a pen. The nib's scratching was loud in the tense silence. He wrote two receipts with a startling steadiness, then pushed them across the table. Stan reviewed them carefully before pocketing the thin scraps of paper.

He met Skinner's gaze one last time. "I hope this satisfies you, Mr Skinner." It was no question.

Skinner grunted, eyes on the money. No condolences, no parting words.

Stan Wren turned and walked out, shoulders a little straighter. The debt was paid. Eliza's struggle on her front was over. His children had a roof.

He walked back through the cold streets of Castleford, the weight in his pocket now only of coins and paper, no longer the crushing burden of a predator's hold.

By the following Monday, he was signing on at the Prince of Wales Colliery, his name added back to the roster of men wrestling coal from the unforgiving earth. The tunnels awaited.

24

Chapter 24 : A Father's Stand

16th December 1916, Castleford

The morning after was colder, somehow. The fire in the grate was a sullen, reluctant thing Stan had coaxed to life in the pre-dawn dark, and it offered little more than a flicker against the kitchen's gloom.

The silence in the house had taken on a new shape now, a hollow carved out where Eliza's bustling had once been. There was no clatter of pans, no scent of brewing tea filling the air. There was only the quiet rhythm of the clock on the mantelpiece, measuring out time he no longer understood.

I have to get the children ready. The thought was simple, a plain fact, but it landed in his gut with the weight of a dropped pit prop.

He started with the porridge. Simple enough, surely. He'd watched Eliza do it a thousand times. Water, oats, and a pinch of salt. But his mind was somewhere else—down a tunnel, maybe, or back in the mud of France—and the smell hit him too late.

Bitter, sharp. *Burnt*. "Damn it," he said, scraping at the bottom of the pan with a wooden spoon. A thick brown sludge clung to the metal—simple porridge, and he'd ruined it.

He salvaged what he could, spooning the lumpy, slightly scorched mess into two bowls, adding a splash of milk to hide the worst of it.

Beth came downstairs then, dressed for school, her hair a wild tangle down her back. She carried a brush and two thin blue ribbons. Eliza's ribbons. She held them out to him without a word.

Stan stared at them. His hands, caked with a lifetime of coal dust beneath the nails, more used to the rough handle of a shovel than the slip of silk, felt far too large and clumsy.

"Right then, love," he said, his voice rougher than he intended.

He sat her on a stool by the fire and took the brush. He tried to be gentle, but the delicate strands of her hair snagged and pulled against the coarse bristles. He fumbled with the parting, his fingers like clumsy sausages trying to tame a spider's web.

He divided the hair into three sections. He could picture Eliza's hands—quick, nimble, weaving the strands into a neat, tight plait in seconds. He felt useless. The braid was loose, lopsided, a sorry, unravelling thing. He tried to tie the ribbon at the end, but his thumb got in the way, and the bow ended up a graceless knot.

He finished, and for a moment, there was just the crackle of the fire. Beth didn't move. Then, she slowly raised a small hand and touched the messy plait. Her lower lip trembled.

"That's not how Mam did it."

The words were quiet, a statement of fact, but they hit Stan with the force of a blast wave, knocking the air from his lungs. He saw Eliza's face then, clear as day, laughing at him from across this very kitchen, her hair pinned up in a perfect, neat coil.

The immense crushing weight of her absence, of all the thousand tiny things she *was*, descended on him. He didn't get angry. He couldn't. He just felt a profound, bottomless failure.

He knelt in front of Beth, his bad knee groaning in protest, and pulled her into a hug, burying his face in her hair.

"I know, love," he said, his throat thick. "I know it's not. I'm sorry." He held her tight as a small, hiccupping sob escaped her. "But I'll... I'll get better. I promise. We'll learn how to do it together, eh?"

She nodded against his chest, her small arms wrapped tight around his neck. He let her go gently. She wiped her eyes with the back of her sleeve, sniffing once, hard.

Then, with a look of fierce concentration that was pure Eliza, she took the ribbons from her hair, undid his clumsy knot, and tied them herself. Her little fingers fumbled, but the bow was still askew. She pulled it tight with a determined tug.

She looked at her work, then up at him, not with a triumphant smile but with a simple, solemn nod. A minor act, that was all. *We will manage. We have to.* In that moment, Stan's heart ached with an unfamiliar pain—loss, but a fierce, swelling pride dwelt there, too.

She wasn't just his daughter; she was Eliza's, too, and that stubborn spark could never be extinguished.

The sound of heavy boots on the stairs broke the moment. Robert appeared, ready for the pit, his bait box under his arm. The sight of him, of a task Stan understood, was a strange relief. Stan stood, giving Beth's shoulder one last squeeze.

He turned to the counter, where he began the familiar ritual of slicing a hunk of bread and adding a wedge of cheese. This, his hands knew.

The solid weight of the loaf, the sharp edge of the knife. This was something a man could get right. It was a small island of competence in a sudden, frightening sea of domestic failure.

He wrapped the food in a piece of waxed paper and inserted it into Robert's tin with a quiet, final snap of the lid.

Later, after the older children had left for the pit and school, the house fell into a heavy quiet.

Nell Clark from down the road, who used to trade shifts with Eliza when a child was ill, knocked quietly and stepped inside. She sat on the edge of the kitchen chair, hands folded, eyes drifting to the coat hanging by the door—Eliza's.

"I hope it's not too soon," she said. "Folks've been asking. Wondering how the little ones are holding up."

Stan nodded. "A lot've been round already," he rasped, considering his appearance for the first time with his steady churn of visitors. He hadn't shaved in days.

He rubbed his knee—the old ache stirring louder now, without distraction. "We're getting by," he said. "Bobby's working most days. Beth's kept up with her schooling. It's... quiet."

Nell's smile was small, tentative. "Too quiet, I expect."

Stan nodded again. "Aye, she filled the house."

Nell looked down. "I was thinking about her last night. Could still hear her shouting both of them back in from the ginnel."

His mouth twitched—almost a smile. "Aye. She had a way of carrying on, didn't she?"

"You were kind to come," he said after a pause. "If you hear anything from the factory, the girls that were there—I'd be grateful." He glanced again at the coat. "Thanks for bringing her things back. I don't know what I'll do with 'em. Not yet."

Nell stood after a moment. "You'll know. When you need to, love."

Their eyes met then, and in the kitchen's quiet, there was no need for more words. She had lost her John at the Somme; he had lost his Eliza at Barnbow. They were two members of the same terrible club, and they both knew it.

It was the physical weight pressing on his chest that made it hard for him to breathe. He felt adrift, untethered.

A happy, sudden gurgle cut through the gloom.

Stan looked over at the cot. Baby Stanley was awake, but he wasn't crying. He lay on his back, his small legs kicking gently. A sliver of weak winter sun cut through the grimy windowpane, landing on the cot, and Stanley was wholly transfixed.

His gaze was fixed on his own hands, which he held up in the beam of light. He opened and closed his tiny fists, watching them as if they were the most fascinating, miraculous things in the world.

He knew nothing of loss, nothing of debt, nothing of the roaring noise that had stolen his mother. He knew only the warmth of the blanket and the light on his hands.

The sight was so pure, so uncomplicated, it pierced Stan's sorrow like a ray of sun through storm clouds. This tiny, perfect life. This was his anchor now. This was the reason to face the tunnels, to face the mornings, to face the world. This was the hope.

18th December 1916

Pontefract pit needed men. The war had thinned their numbers, and the coal didn't care about grief. The shifts had returned to six days a week, and there was always overtime.

At 5 AM, Stan kissed Beth and Baby Stanley lightly, buttoned his work coat, and stepped into the December dark with Robert at his side. The cold was brutal—the kind that cracked your breath in the air and set your boots burning. The snow had deepened, clean and cruel.

The sky above was still tucked in, the sun nowhere to be seen—not for hours, maybe not at all.

They walked three miles to the pit without speaking much, their steady footfalls crunching through the snow. Their breath misted between them like threads that refused to tangle.

Halfway there, Robert turned his head to his father. "You sure you're up to it?"

Stan didn't answer, not at first. "Not really," he said at last. "But the coal won't dig itself. And the house needs the money."

The boy nodded. "Feels different now. Since Mam..."

"Aye," Stan said. "A lot of things do."

"She kept us going," Robert said. "Even when she was knackered. Never let on how bad it was."

Stan's jaw tightened. "I know."

"I never said thank you."

"She knew."

Ahead, the winding gear's outline rose black against the dark horizon. Stan placed a brief but firm hand on Robert's shoulder.

"We keep going, son," he said. "For her. For Beth. For the baby."

"You too, Dad," Robert said. "You watch yourself."

They nodded—men now, both of them—and crossed into the yard.

Because the coal still waited.

Because grief had no shifts.

Because her letter, tucked away in the drawer upstairs, had told him to.

And now it was his turn to hold the line.

25

Chapter 25 : A Tin Box Buried

6th December 1916, Leeds

The morning frost clung to the back steps like spilt flour, sharp beneath Agnes Atkinson's boots as she stood at the scullery window. Her apron hem was damp from wiping the condensation. It was nearly eleven, and Lucy should've been home by now—pale, blinking, smelling of soap and powder, ready for tea and a slice of toast before bed.

But the street stayed empty. Milk boys and coalmen trudged through the cold, but not Lucy. Agnes's chest tightened, a knot of unease growing with each tick of the clock.

She'd heard it last night—a deep crack, like thunder dragged across iron. She and Harold had sat up in bed, the walls giving a soft tremble. "Quarry work, could be." His voice was rough with tiredness. But Agnes hadn't believed it. Not entirely. Now, with no Lucy, the sound haunted her—a warning she couldn't shake.

Turning from the window, she glanced at the cold teapot stewing on the counter, the tea now beyond saving. She gripped the edge of the sink, willing her hands to steady.

At half-past eleven, a knock shattered the silence—sharp, official, like a judge's gavel. She opened the door. A telegram boy, no older than John from across the way, stood with his cap too big and gloves unravelling at the fingertips. He didn't meet her eyes.

"From the War Office, missus." He held out an envelope. Agnes took it wordlessly, the letter stiff in her fingers. She firmly closed the door. Her knees buckled as she sank into the scullery chair, the envelope trembling in her hands as if it might burn through the paper.

She stared long at the seal before tearing it open. The words swam across the page.

"The Ministry of Munitions regrets to inform you that Lucy Margaret Atkinson, employed at His Majesty's National Filling Factory No.1, Barnbow, was killed by accident on the 5th of December, 1916 ..."

Killed by accident. Not in battle. Not at sea. Just gone and snatched from the world like her brother before her. A scream tore from Agnes's throat—raw and singular, sharp enough to split the air. She stumbled to the back step, the telegram crumpled in her fist, and howled into the frozen yard, the sound bouncing off stone and ice like something feral.

Mrs Daley heard it through the wall.

She came without a coat, no words, a cardigan thrown over her shoulders. She stepped into the scullery and grabbed the kettle. Agnes hadn't moved. Her gaze was locked onto the envelope, now curled on the table. Mrs Daley lit the stove, measured the tea, and added the sugar.

They'd been saving that sugar—a few spoonfuls tucked in a paper packet. Lucy had brought it home from the canteen, shy but proud.

"For Christmas, Mam. We'll have proper tea, not that watered-down stuff." Agnes had tucked it away, planning to use it on Christmas Day with the good cups.

Mrs Daley used it now.

She poured the tea, placed the mug down gently, and squeezed Agnes's shoulder once before leaving. She said nothing. She had no need to. The silence was heavy enough.

An hour later, a neighbour hurried to the mail centre and called Harold at the Yorkshire Electricity Company. The call was brief—a death. *Come home.*

He arrived before noon, his work cap in his hands, eyes already red. Agnes couldn't bring herself to voice the words.

She handed him the paper.

He read slowly. His jaw clenched, then loosened. He sat beside her and reached for her hand. They held each other like driftwood in a tide, saying nothing, not even crying, just holding on.

He looked around the small, silent kitchen—at the cold teapot on the counter, at Lucy's empty chair tucked under the table—and the finality of it hit him like a sledgehammer. This was real. His daughter was gone.

He could still see her sitting in that very chair just last week, her head bent over a book from the library, one foot tucked under her, a smudge of ink on her cheek. That memory was so clear, so present, it was a physical pain.

"Our lass," he said, his voice a rough, broken sound in the stillness. "Our little Luce."

Agnes didn't reply, her grief too vast for words, but her grip on his hand tightened, a quiet recognition of their shared, unbearable loss.

Hours passed in the grey, silent kitchen. The world outside the window seemed to move on, but inside, time had fractured, leaving them stranded on the single, sharp moment of the telegram's arrival. They just sat, hands clasped on the worn tabletop, like two figures carved from stone.

A quiet, hesitant tap rapped at the door.

Harold looked up, his expression hollow. Agnes didn't move. He rose slowly, his joints stiff, and opened it. It was Mrs Daley from next door again. This time, she wasn't alone. Mrs Hirst from two doors down stood with her, clutching a small meat pie wrapped in a clean tea towel. The aroma of hot pastry and gravy—a scent of ordinary life—wafted into the stagnant air of the kitchen.

"We won't stay, Agnes, love," Mrs Daley said, stepping just inside the doorway. "We just... We heard. And we wanted to bring you something. Don't you be worrying about cooking now."

Mrs Hirst looked at Agnes, her own eyes brimming with a sympathy that was deep and true. She seemed to search for the right words, the ones that could bridge this impossible chasm of grief. The usual condolences felt thin, inadequate.

"I was just thinking..." Mrs Hirst began, her voice thick. She took a small, shaky breath. "I was just thinking about Lucy. Last summer. I saw her out in the back ginnel with my little Tom."

Agnes looked up at the mention of her daughter's name, her eyes clouded with a pain that made Mrs Hirst falter momentarily before she pressed on.

"She was attempting to teach him how to make a daisy chain," she said, a watery, faraway smile touching her lips. "And he—you know how he is, all thumbs—he kept breaking them. But she didn't mind a bit. She had more flowers tucked in her hair than she managed to get in the chain and grass stains all up her arms. And she was laughing."

Mrs Hirst's gaze met Agnes's. "A proper belly laugh, you know? The kind you don't hear often enough. My Tom was wrapping the broken ones around his muddy boots, but she just gave a loud laugh. Said he was making 'ogre's jewellery'."

Only after Harold had walked through the door did a sound escape Agnes's throat. It was a choked, broken thing, half-sob and half-laugh, a sound of profound pain and a flicker of remembered joy. Harold's hand tightened on hers, and he looked down at the table, his mouth twisting into the ghost of a smile. He could see it. He could hear her laugh.

Mrs Hirst placed the warm pie near the edge of the counter. "She was a good lass, your Lucy. A bright one."

With a final, sympathetic squeeze of Agnes's shoulder from Mrs Daley, the two women slipped back out, closing the door softly behind them, leaving the scent of warm food and the even warmer memory in the quiet kitchen.

Agnes looked at Harold, her eyes still swimming with tears, but the hard mask of shock had cracked. The memory didn't take the pain away, but it sat alongside it—a reminder that their daughter's story wasn't just about a factory and a telegram. It was also about laughter, sunshine, and daisy chains in the grass.

That evening, after the neighbours had come and gone—bringing flowers wrapped in newspaper, a pie neither touched, and condolences spoken too softly to matter—Agnes stood at Lucy's door, Harold at her side, keeping her brave. They hadn't entered since Lucy had left for her shift the night before.

We've already done this once.

In the room, the air still smelled of rose soap. The bed was half-made, the pillow crumpled, the blanket tucked hastily in the way Lucy always did.

Agnes sat on the side of the bed and let her hand drift over the worn quilt. She caught the corner of something beneath the bedframe—a tin, familiar, dented on the side.

She pulled it out and opened it.

As the lid lifted, a faint, sweet scent rose to meet them—the smell of rose soap and old paper. Lucy's smell.

Inside was a life, folded with quiet precision.

The first thing Agnes saw was Joe's letters, dozens of them, tied with a bit of kitchen string.

Harold reached out and took the bundle as he settled beside her, his calloused, work-worn hands gentle as he weighed them. So many words sent, so much hope carried across the water, all of it ending here, in this dented tin box.

Beneath the letters was a photograph, already fading at the edges. Agnes picked it up. The two of them were at Bridlington, squinting into a summer sun that seemed a lifetime ago. Her thumb traced the outline of Lucy's laughing face, then Joe's, so young and alive. She remembered that day so clearly—the sharp smell of salt, Joe teasing Lucy until she shrieked with laughter.

A world away.

A world that was still whole.

Her fingers brushed against a pressed poppy, its petals brittle and fragile as a butterfly's wing, and a theatre stub from the Grand for a pantomime two Christmases ago. Each object was a small, sharp stab of memory.

At the bottom was a sheaf of papers—Lucy's own stories. Agnes lifted them out with reverence. The handwriting was neat, the pages filled with tales of clever mill lasses and magical creatures found in the back ginnels of Leeds.

"She never stopped, did she?" Agnes said, her voice thick with a mix of pride and unbearable sorrow. "Always had her head full of stories."

Harold took the page from her. The last one was unfinished. "*The Girl with the Seashell Heart.*" He read the title aloud, his voice cracking on the last word. He looked at Agnes, his eyes full of a pain she knew mirrored her own. "She was still writing them, Aggie. Right to the end."

It was a story about a girl who could hear the ocean no matter how far she was from the shore. The words, so full of innocent imagination, were an unbearable contrast to the grim, noisy reality of her last hours.

Agnes clutched the pages to her chest, breath catching. Harold came and sat beside her. They didn't read Lucy's stories. Not now. It was too much. Instead, Harold untied the string from Joe's letters, and together, they read the one folded on top.

Dated 5th Dec 1916:

I am glad you were with your friends.

You didn't say anything about the fear.

Were you scared? Did you die alone? Were you in pain, Joe?

I hate that I don't know.

I hate that no one does.

They didn't speak. They didn't need to. Each word was a wound and a balm.

Agnes wept silently, her tears soaking into Lucy's quilt. Harold sat with one letter pressed between his hands like a prayer.

The tin was Lucy's heart, her grief, her dreams—all bundled into one box they hadn't known existed.

And now, with no body, it was all they had left to bury.

The funeral was a quiet, brittle affair, as wartime directives demanded—no procession through the streets of Leeds, no headlines. Just a handful of neighbours scattered in the cold, damp air of St. Hilda's chapel, their hushed condolences sounding like a language from another country.

Agnes sat beside Harold on the hard pew, hands clenched in her lap. She didn't hear the vicar. His words were smooth, worn down by countless funerals—useless against the sharp, jagged edges of *this* loss.

A child of God, taken into His arms. Her mind recoiled from the sentiment. Lucy wasn't taken; she was ripped away, consumed by a fire born of greed and haste. Agnes focused instead on a crack in the pew's varnish in front of her, a dark line like a frozen river, and tried to breathe.

When it ended and the few neighbours filed out, offering awkward, sympathetic glances, Agnes's eyes drifted to the back of the chapel.

A young woman stood alone near the oak door, half-lost in shadow. Agnes didn't know her. She was thin, pale, and dressed in a plain dark coat.

Grief sharpened everything: the fresh pink scar across the girl's forehead, the white bandage around one hand, the manner in which her shoulders sagged under some unseen weight.

The girl didn't approach them, nor did she attempt to offer the usual condolences. She just stood there, a ghost at the feast of sorrow, her eyes glued to the small, plain coffin at the front of the chapel. As Harold helped Agnes to her feet, their eyes met for a brief second across the cold space.

The girl's gaze held no pity. It held something far more harrowing. It was a look of shared, unbearable knowledge—a look of someone who had seen the same fire.

Agnes felt a jolt of profound confusion. *Who was that girl?*

The question followed her out into the graveyard, where the December wind whipped at her scarf. It was just them now—Agnes, Harold, and Mrs Daley, a few steps behind, a silent, steadfast presence. They stood by the raw, open wound in the earth as two groundsmen, their faces impassive, lowered the small wooden coffin on ropes.

Inside was the tin. Agnes had placed it there herself that morning, nestled in the soft folds of Joe's baby blanket. It held the letters, the faded photograph, the pressed poppy, and the last story Lucy had written. There was nothing else to lay to rest.

The first shovelful of earth hit the lid with a dull, hollow *thud*. The sound was brutal. Final. It was the echo of a door slamming shut on a life full of stories yet to be told. Harold's arm came around her, his grip tight, anchoring her as her knees threatened to disobey her. He said nothing. He didn't need to.

Agnes wept—silent tears that froze on her cheeks in the biting wind.

She thought of Lucy's laugh, of daisy chains, of the girl with the scar—a stranger, yet grieving like family.

Agnes didn't know who she was or why she'd come—only that Lucy's death had sent sorrow rippling far beyond their small, broken home.

There was no body to kiss goodbye. Only memory. Only silence.

A week later, the silence in the house on Bell Row had become a heavy, suffocating blanket. Harold sat staring into the cold hearth, the newspaper unread in his lap. Agnes stood at the window, watching the grey street, her hands twisting the fabric of her apron. On the mantelpiece, a small notice from the parish church, brought home by Mrs Hirst days ago, sat curled and ignored. It was an appeal for the Soldiers' and Sailors' Families Fund, requesting donations of baked goods for the upcoming sale.

Agnes's eyes drifted to the notice. She read the words without really seeing them, until her gaze caught on the phrase *"for the families of our brave boys." Joe.* The thought was a familiar, sharp pain. And Lucy, who had died serving the same vast, hungry war. An idea, fragile but persistent, formed.

She turned from the window. Her movement was slow, as if she were wading through deep water. She walked to the pantry and took out the small bag of flour.

"What're you doing, Aggie?" Harold asked, his voice rough from disuse.

"Baking," she said simply, not looking at him as she tied a fresh apron over her black dress. "For the church sale. For the fund."

The act of kneading the dough was familiar, mechanical. Her hands, still clumsy with grief, found an old rhythm. It was a purpose, however small. Harold watched her for a long moment. He then rose from his chair and reached for his coat and cap from the hook by the door.

"I'm going out," he said.

Agnes paused, her knuckles white in the dough. "Harold..."

"Just for a bit," he clarified, understanding her fear. "To the club. Saw Jack Albright at the yard yesterday. His lad... he was in Joe's battalion. Never came back either. Thought I might just... sit a bit."

He didn't say he would talk to the man. He didn't need to. Agnes nodded once, a silent understanding passing between them. She went back to her kneading as he quietly closed the door behind him. The house was still silent. But now, it was the silence of two people taking their first, impossible step forward.

26

Chapter 26 : The Cost of a Mother's Life

2nd January 1917, North Atlantic Convoy Patrol

The North Atlantic in early January was a study in grey—a grey, heaving sea met a grey, indifferent sky, and for weeks, the only change in the view from HMS Warrior was the shape of the clouds. Life had settled into a monotonous, soul-grinding routine of patrol: watch-keeping, drills, the endless, bone-aching cold, and the ceaseless vibration of the engines. The war was not a thing of battles out here; it was a war of waiting.

Then, one morning, the smudge on the horizon condensed into a shape. A lookout's call echoed across the deck: "Supply ship sighted, port bow!"

A current of life, sharp and electric, shot through the weary crew. It wasn't the thought of fresh provisions or fuel that animated them but the promise of the most precious cargo of all: mailbags. For men cut off from the world for weeks on end, a letter was a lifeline, a tangible piece of home.

Cecil Jennings stood with his shipmates, a knot of fragile hope tightening in his chest. He scanned the approaching vessel, sharing in the desperate, collective prayer that there would be a letter from his mam.

The mess deck erupted into a chaotic, hopeful roar as a petty officer, mailbag slung over his shoulder, began the sacred ritual. "Henderson! Davies! Macleod!" he yelled, tossing letters amongst a multitude of eager hands.

Men whooped in triumph or slumped back to their hammocks in disappointment. The air was thick with the smell of home—of ink and paper and perfume—a stark contrast to the usual smell of bilge water and stale tea.

"Jennings!"

Cecil's head snaps up. He pushed through the crowd, his heart thumping against his ribs. The officer handed him a single thin envelope. He recognised Annie's handwriting immediately, but it was wrong. Where it was neat and controlled, it was now a shaky, spidery scrawl.

The envelope itself was grimy, softened, and worn from its long journey. The postmark was weeks old, and a dark, blurry smudge marred the corner, a remnant of what could only have been a tear.

He knew. In that single, stomach-dropping moment, before he had even broken the seal, Cecil Jennings knew that something was wrong.

He retreated from the noise, seeking refuge on the upper deck. He found a stolen moment of privacy in the lee of a massive gun turret, the wind whipping past, tearing at his coat. The steel was bitingly cold against his back as he leaned against it, his fingers fumbling with the envelope.

He pulled out a single sheet of paper and unfolded it. The letter was brief.

My dearest Cecil,

I don't know how to write this. Something terrible has happened. There was an accident at Sarah's work... a terrible accident.

Oh, Cecil. Our Sarah... she is gone from us...

He read the lines once, then again. The words seemed to float on the page, refusing to form a coherent thought. *Gone from us.* The phrase was a gentle, impossible euphemism for a reality he couldn't grasp. *Accident.* The word was meaningless. His mind, frantic and horrified, raced through a hundred different scenarios—a machine, a fall, a fire.

The not knowing was a unique kind of torture. He clutched the St. Christopher medal around his neck, the cool metal a useless talisman against the inferno of his thoughts. The thunder of the sea, the cry of the wind—it all faded to a dull, distant hum. His entire world had narrowed to the shaky, tear-stained words on the flimsy page in his trembling hands.

He didn't know how long he stood there, frozen, before a quiet voice beside him said, "Son?"

It was the ship's padre, his face etched with a gentle concern. Someone must have seen him. Cecil couldn't speak; he just held out the letter. The padre read it, his expression softening with a deep, practised sorrow.

"I am so very sorry, Jennings." He put a hand on Cecil's shoulder. "I will speak with the captain on your behalf immediately. We will arrange compassionate shore leave for you as soon as we next make port. That will be Portsmouth, in March. Until then..." He paused, his grip firming. "...if you need to talk, my door is always open. Do your work, son. We will get you home."

After the padre left, the numbness gave way to a storm of emotion. A hot, furious anger surged through him—anger at Thomas Brown, a man whose petty cruelties had surely driven his mother into that dangerous factory in the first place. Then came the guilt, profound and gnawing, for having left her there to face it alone.

He looked out at the vast, indifferent ocean, feeling impossibly small and far away. A shipmate walked past, whistling a tune, and the mundane sound was a physical blow, highlighting how Cecil's world had stopped while the ship's ground on.

His grief and rage hardened, only to cool into a single, sharp point of purpose. He carefully folded the old, tear-stained letter and placed it in his breast pocket—a sacred, terrible relic. He was no longer just a sailor on patrol; he was a son who must go home.

He turned from the rail, his face set like stone, and headed below deck. His war had just changed.

11th March 1917, York

The train from Portsmouth carved a path north through an England Cecil no longer recognised, its engine sighing like a weary beast.

Almost three months since the stark, brutal telegram had found him aboard HMS Warrior. Compassionate leave, they'd called it—a cruel irony, for there was little compassion in the hollow ache lodged deep in his chest.

He sat stiffly in the third-class carriage, his naval greatcoat feeling thick and foreign in the close air heavy with civilian scents—stale tobacco and the faint peel of oranges. Scattered soldiers and sailors filled the carriage, some boisterous with drink, others sunk into the same weary quietude that mirrored his own. He offered no conversation, his stare locked onto the fleeting green countryside, a scene so peaceful it felt like a personal affront.

As the wheels turned, memories of his mother flooded him. Her laugh—surprisingly hearty for such a small woman—when he'd tried to teach her a naval hornpipe in their cramped Warthill kitchen. The determined set of her jaw as she faced down Thomas Brown's endless petty cruelties. Her hands, always busy, stained yellow by her work, waved him off as he left.

With every turn of the wheels on the track, a single thought returned, sharp as a shard of glass: *I ran*. He could still feel the worn fabric of the railway carriage seat from the day he'd left Warthill, could still taste the bitter relief of his escape—a relief that now felt like poison. He flinched in his seat, a sharp, involuntary jerk, as if shying away from a blow only he could feel.

He had fled Thomas's tyranny, leaving her to bear it alone—and then to face the horrors of Barnbow. Now he was returning, not as a triumphant son but as a mourner, going back to the very place he'd sworn never to endure again.

It was early spring when Cecil Jennings made the walk from York Station to Warthill. The air, dense with the damp earthiness of thawing Yorkshire soil mingled with the ever-present coal smoke, was a shock after months of sharp sea winds.

The same six or seven-mile walk his mother had done a hundred times—trudging home in the dark, fingers numb, feet aching after a night at the factory—now lay before him like a penance.

Turning onto the empty sweep of Bad Bargain Lane, he remembered hiding behind the kitchen door as a boy, cups trembling on the dresser as Thomas's voice rumbled through the walls.

"A stain on this house," Thomas had spat, the words ugly, even if Cecil didn't understand them. "And what're you going to tell him if he ever asks about his father?"

Cecil hadn't known what that meant, not really. He just knew they were aimed at his mam.

He remembered his mam standing in front of him like a shield, her voice not loud but sharp enough to cut string. "He was born of love," she'd said, and Cecil knew, even then, that it was the truest thing in the world. He hadn't understood what that meant either at the time. But he knew it was the opposite of Thomas's growl.

He clutched the worn St. Christopher beneath his uniform—her last gift—its cool metal a small, insufficient anchor in a sea of returning dread.

The hedgerows remained stripped bare, black branches rattling in the wind like the bones of forgotten soldiers. The sky, bruised purple as the sun slipped low, offered no comfort.

A duffle slung over one shoulder, his dark blue greatcoat hanging loose around his frame, Cecil moved with the slow weight of someone bracing for something unnamed. The white tally on his cap—HMS Warrior—felt like a brand, marking him apart. He hadn't expected to leave so soon, but the Navy's terse compassion had limits: three days, then back to the grey Atlantic.

Each step on the rutted lane cracked open another memory. He didn't see the factory worker she became but the mother he'd left behind.

The memory of her surprisingly good—if infrequent—apple tarts; the impossible cheerfulness of her last letter. He'd read it on the heaving deck of the Warrior, the sea spray indistinguishable from the tears he refused to shed. Now, the familiar track beneath his boots seemed to mock him.

This lane... his mam used to sing here sometimes, a snatch of a music hall tune quickly stifled when Thomas was near. And just over that rise, Brown's damned pigs—creatures Thomas had always seemed to value more than his wife's sister or her son. Old anger, hot and familiar, churned alongside the cold dread of the homecoming.

He was walking back into the heart of his misery—and this time, she wouldn't be there to offer even the smallest, secret comfort.

Cecil's heart was heavy with regret, with guilt. He had abandoned her to Thomas, then promised to save her from him, but this was his first time back to her, and she was gone, and he would never see her again.

The cottage came into view as the sky turned blue-grey with dusk. Smoke rose in a thin, unenthusiastic ribbon from the chimney. Chickens pecked at the frost-hardened soil. The gate made its usual creaking sound.

Annie opened the door, gasping, her hand flying to her mouth. "Cecil!"

"Hello, Annie."

She embraced him fiercely, her arms tight, fingers clinging as if to anchor him forever. Thomas stood behind her by the stove, arms folded, face unreadable.

"You've grown," Thomas said, his voice rough and warmth absent.

"Still five foot seven," Cecil said, brushing imagined lint from his collar, aware of the man's appraising gaze.

But he had grown—the Navy had hammered some boyishness out of him, replacing it with a sailor's lean hardness, a tension around his eyes that hadn't been there two years ago.

They ate in silence, a thick, cloying quiet Annie tried to fill with nervous chatter about Lizzie's new schoolteacher and the price of eggs. Thomas didn't look up, his gaze fixed mainly on the scarred tabletop, as if the wood's grain held some grim message only he could read.

Cecil watched him over the rim of his mug—a man grown greyer, slower, but with the familiar hardness around his mouth, the coldness in his eyes. Yet, there was something else—a slackness to his shoulders, a profound erosion Cecil hadn't expected.

The old resentment coiled hot and acrid in Cecil's gut but was complicated now by this shadow of a man burdened by more than just the farm.

Mam did everything, Cecil thought bitterly—scrubbed his floors, mucked his yard, endured his tempers—all while working herself to death at Barnbow.

And he... he just let her. Thomas hadn't laid hands on her in ways that left visible bruises, but he'd made her life small, hard—a slow grinding down of spirit. He'd been the unspoken weight she carried long before the war and factory claimed her. And Cecil knew it. The guilt churned once more in his stomach. He'd left her here with him.

When the meal ended, Thomas spoke, his voice raspy. His hand hovered over the envelope on the dresser before he picked it up, as if it were a burden. He didn't slide it across the table but placed it with care before Cecil, his calloused fingers clumsy.

"From the Ministry," Thomas said, his voice flat and toneless. "Seventy pounds." He avoided Cecil's eyes, his gaze fixed on a knot in the wooden table.

Cecil didn't touch the envelope. *Seventy pounds.* The price of a mother's life. A cold, clean anger pierced his numbness. He stared at the stark white rectangle, then deliberately pushed it back towards Thomas.

"She was worth more than that alive," he said, his voice shaking with a rage he couldn't contain.

Thomas's head snapped up. For a moment, his old, familiar anger flared in his eyes. "Don't you take that tone with me, boy," he snarled, the words a bitter reflex. "It's what they sent. It's more than she'd have seen in ten years on this farm."

The cruelty was meant to sting, but it lacked its usual force. The fire in his eyes died as quickly as it had appeared, leaving behind something empty. He looked not at Cecil but through him, his focus lost somewhere on the smoke-stained wall. The anger was just a ghost, a hollowed-out habit with no strength left behind it. He seemed smaller, his broad shoulders slumped not with sorrow but with a profound, unnerving emptiness.

His chair scraped against the stone floor as he pushed himself away from the table. He stalked out into the yard without another word, the door closing with a quiet, defeated click rather than its usual angry slam.

The silence he left behind was a physical thing, thicker than the smell of boiled potatoes and stew that still hung in the air. Cecil sat motionless, his eyes focused on the stark white envelope on the table.

Seventy pounds.

His anger was a clean fire burning inside him, a single point of clarity in a sea of grief.

The clink of a plate brought him back. Annie was clearing the table, her movements a little too loud, a little too deliberate amidst the heavy silence. She didn't look at him, but he could feel her hovering, her grief a nervous energy filling the space.

Cecil finally looked up from the envelope, his eyes scanning the quiet corners of the room. "Where's Gran?"

Annie paused, a plate held halfway to the sink. A fresh wave of sorrow washed over her face. "Oh, Cecil, love," she whispered. "She's gone. The news about your mam... it broke her heart. She just... faded. Lasted another month, but her spirit had already left. She's buried up at St. Hilda's with me dad."

She placed the plate down with a soft, final click. "Thomas... he didn't even argue when the doctor came. He just stood there... paid the fee. I think it was one death too many for this house to bear."

She stacked the plates, the scrape of crockery grating his nerves.

She stopped. She came to the table not with a cloth but with two chipped enamel mugs, one of which she placed before him. Steam curled from it in a thin, questioning ribbon.

"He... he doesn't mean half of it, Cecil," she began in a whisper, uncertainty threading through her words. She sat down opposite him, wrapping her chapped hands around her mug. "He's just... broken. By this. By everything."

Cecil didn't reply. He just looked at the envelope, a muscle working in his jaw.

Annie sighed, a weak, exhausted sound. "I know what you're thinkin'. And you're not wrong. He was cruel to her. And I... I should've done more."

Her voice cracked, and she looked down into her tea as if the answers were there.

"I should've stood up to him more for her. But he wears you down, you know? A word here, a look there. After a while, you just... you try to keep the peace."

Her confession hung in the air between them. Cecil looked up from the envelope and met her eyes. He saw not an accomplice but another victim, trapped in this house just as his mother had been.

A ghost of a smile, sad and fleeting, touched Annie's lips. "She was never meant for a life like this, your mam. She had too much... spark."

Cecil frowned slightly. He remembered her spirit, yes—her sharp tongue, her defiance. But it had always seemed like a tool for survival, a shield she used to endure.

"You only ever saw the woman who'd already been through the wringer," Annie said, seeming to read his thoughts. "Sulgrave House, and then... well, then you. But before all that? When we were lasses? Oh, she was a terror."

Annie's eyes grew distant, a genuine warmth lighting them for the first time that evening.

"I remember one time, must have been fourteen, she was. Our dad had forbidden us from going to the Midsummer Horse Fair in Pocklington," she said with a little smile. "Said it was full of rogues, gypsies, and tinkers. Sarah just laughed. That night, after he was asleep, we snuck out the window like a pair of thieves."

Cecil could almost picture it: the summer moonlight, the hushed giggles.

"We ran the whole way," Annie said, her voice full of a memory so clear it was alive in the room. "She spent the only penny she had to buy us a toffee apple. We shared it while sitting on a fence, watching the gypsies trade horses in the torchlight, playing music, and dancing. It was so loud you could feel it in your bones."

Her smile grew, but a tear ran down her face as she reminisced.

"Even as a young girl, she wasn't scared of anything—not of Dad's temper, not of the dark, not of going to Sulgrave House. She wanted to taste all of life, not hide in a small village. 'You can't let them keep it from you, Annie,' she would say."

She looked at Cecil, her eyes pleading with him to understand.

"That's who she was. She was always the brave one, always the one ready to climb out the window. Thomas... he never knew what to do with a woman who sparked like that."

She glanced out of the window, then back at Cecil.

"It frightened him, I think. A man like Thomas—simple, knowing only this farm all his life. All he knows is how to stamp on a thing that shines too brightly, to snuff out the spark."

The story landed in Cecil's chest with a quiet, profound weight. The anger at Thomas didn't vanish, but it shifted, complicated now by a flicker of something like pity for a man so small he had to crush anything that made him feel smaller.

He thought of his mother. Her strength had always seemed like endurance—a rigid shield she held up against the world. He'd never pictured her as a carefree girl with sticky fingers, running towards music in the dark.

He was grieving the mother he'd known. But now, for the first time, he was also mourning the girl she'd been—and the vibrant, laughing woman she could never become.

He reached into his coat, his fingers brushing against the worn, folded paper of her last letter. *"A little place of our own... I want to live."* Her dream wasn't just an escape from misery; it was a means to find happiness. It was an attempt, he now realised, to find her way back to that moonlit lane, back to a life that was lived, not just endured.

That night, Cecil tried to sleep in Sarah's old room—a small, cold space tucked under the eaves that still clung to the faint, stubborn scent of her: lavender soap mixed with the sharp, chemical tang of Barnbow, a scent death hadn't quite erased. The bed was made with care—Lizzie had given up her corner for the night, Annie had whispered to him, her eyes full of sympathy. Cecil didn't know how to accept.

The St. Christopher medal his mother had pressed into his hand when he left for the Navy, the one he wore through storms and the fear of U-boats, still hung from its cord around his neck, silver cool against his skin.

But that wasn't what he reached for in the dark. He opened the rickety drawer of the small washstand, fingers searching for what he knew would be there. He pulled out a folded letter. The paper was creased and softened from much handling. The date was scrawled across the top in her familiar looping hand: 4th December 1916—the day before she died.

My darling boy,

I saw a sign in the Yorkshire Reporter—two rooms, city centre, deposit due Friday. I think I can do it. One more week of shifts, and it'll be ours.

A little place of our own. Nothing grand. But away from here. I want to make a home for us. A quiet one. No raised voices. No more cold shoulders. I don't want to scrub floors for the rest of my life, and I don't want you to walk back into that farmhouse when you come home. We've done enough surviving. I want to live. Only a few more nights at Barnbow. One more payday.

I'll write again on Friday.

All my love,

Mam x

Cecil stared at the page, the ink wavering—not from tears he hadn't shed but from the unbearable weight of her hope, her fierce, desperate love that had driven her into that hellhole day after day. A Leeds flat. For him.

A place free from Thomas Brown's shadow. She'd been so close. The letter trembled in his hand, and for a moment, the cramped, cold room under the eaves dissolved. He was seven years old again, standing on a stool in the Warthill kitchen.

He'd been trying to "help" her bake a cake and had tipped the entire bag of flour onto the floor, creating a cloud of white dust that settled on everything. He had frozen, expecting a scolding. But she hadn't shouted.

She had looked at the mess, then at him with his flour-dusted eyebrows, and a laugh had escaped her—not a chuckle but a full, hearty roar of pure amusement that made her eyes crinkle and her whole body shake. She had scooped him up in a hug, not caring that they were both covered in white, her laughter the warmest thing in his world.

The memory—so sharp and full of life—was a fresh, brutal wound. *That laugh.* The war hadn't taken it. Thomas Brown hadn't crushed it. It had been there right to the end. And now it was gone forever. The thought was unbearable.

He folded the letter with meticulous care, the paper softening at the creases, and slipped it back into his coat pocket, as if it were something alive—a fragile, beating heart.

He hadn't cried. Not when the ship's padre, face full of gentle, practised sorrow, took him aside to speak the words no lad should ever hear alone on the vast, indifferent ocean. There was no room for grief aboard the Warrior—no quiet, no privacy. Only the unremitting clatter of engines, the endless grey sea, and the shared, rough comfort of men who knew better than to pry into another's pain.

Alone in her room, with the faint scent of her life around her, sorrow stayed buried. Anger came first—molten rage coursing through his veins. Anger at Thomas Brown's petty cruelties, at the factory and the war, at a world that crushed women like his mother, full of fierce love and sharp laughter, for a few meagre pennies towards a broken dream.

Most of all, anger at the seventy pounds lying on the dresser downstairs—the price of a mother's life.

The next morning, Cecil caught the early train towards Barnbow. The air hung heavy with coal smoke and the rattle of boots. Cross Gates Station swarmed with women in uniform, joking and singing, their arms linked on the platform as if nothing had happened. He walked the two miles from Cross Gates to the gates of Barnbow.

"Stop!" an armed guard shouted. "Workers only beyond this point."

"I'm not here to work," Cecil said. "I'm here because my mother died here."

The guard—a young man, not much past twenty—blinked. "Sorry, sir?"

"Sarah Jennings," Cecil said. "She died in the December explosion. Room 42."

The lad's face twisted in confusion. "Explosion? At Barnbow?"

Cecil stared. "You work here, and you don't know?"

"I've only been here since January," the boy said. "Didn't hear anything about that. All I knew was there were new rules—stricter checks, more watchmen." He looked genuinely lost. "There was an explosion?"

Cecil glanced past him. The factory grounds buzzed with routine—the low thrum of machinery, carts stacked with crates, women laughing as they passed security. The fence ran high and tight, topped with barbed wire, the sprawling factory behind it like a city of sheds and smoke.

"No names," Cecil said aloud. "No plaque. Not even a sign."

"Was she... close to the blast?"

"She was a blast," Cecil said with a wry smile.

The guard said nothing.

Cecil nodded. "Right. Well, I've seen enough."

He walked the fence line, a little way off the path, and dug a small hole in the hard, not-yet-defrosted earth beside the fence. From his coat, he took the St. Christopher medal she'd given him when he joined up at fifteen. He pressed it into the soil and covered it carefully, as if it were something sacred.

As he stood, he rested his palm against the cold wire. Then he turned and walked the two miles back to Cross Gates Station.

As he neared the halt, he passed a new group of girls heading for the gates. They were laughing, their hands already tinged with the telltale yellow of the poison, oblivious to the tragedy that soaked the very ground they walked on.

War was still waiting. But so was his memory.

27

Chapter 27 : A Question in the Ash

25th December 1916, Christmas Day

The roaring silence of Room 42 still rang in Ann Price's ears, louder now in the suffocating hush of her small bedroom than it ever had been in the blast itself, and a week had passed. A week of lying stiff in the narrow bed, staring at a ceiling that swam in the dark.

Outside, the world kept moving. Inside this room, time had stopped at 10:27 PM on the 5th of December. Her mother's raw sobs from the other part of the wall had thinned to exhausted, watery sniffles.

Her father, after his one night of cursing the war, the king, and the factory that had swallowed a generation of daughters, had said little at all. His silence was worse.

Sleep was a foreign country she couldn't find the papers for.

With a hand that still trembled, a faint tremor that started deep in her shoulder, Ann reached beneath the bed. Her fingers brushed against the cheap, lined notebook.

She'd bought it two days ago from the stationer's, the clink of the coins on the counter feeling like betrayal. Money she no longer felt entitled to. She opened the stiff cover. The blank pages seemed to mock her, clean and blindingly white. Slowly, deliberately, as if the act itself were a prayer, she began to write.

Sarah Jennings. Nora Kershaw. June Mitchell. Eliza Wren. Mary Sutcliffe. Hilda Morton. Lucy Atkinson.

They weren't just names. Each one was a stone in her gut. She could see their faces, hear their voices in the oppressive quiet.

She forced herself to jot down memories beside each name, a desperate act of penance before they slipped away from her like smoke.

But as she filled the pages, the scratching of her pen a slight noise against the hush of the room, she realised it was becoming something more. It was an act of defiance against the official silence that had swallowed them whole.

Sarah—that bark of a laugh, the flash of her teeth. June—the bright blue wool of her favourite scarf, a splash of impossible colour. Nora—humming a hymn under her breath, a sound that thrummed as persistently as the vibration plates themselves.

Every detail was a shard of glass she had to pick up.

Was it my fault? The question wasn't a whisper anymore; it had sunk claws into her ribs and refused to let go. She hadn't poured the Amatol too fast or seated a Gaine crooked, no. But she had been the one to spark the race.

She could feel the heat of the canteen, see the glint of the bonus in everyone's eyes. Her voice, loud and sharp, echoed in her head. A challenge. A jibe.

And now Sarah is ash. The thought was blunt, brutal. The laughter that had filled the canteen was gone, that cheeky grin, extinguished.

January 1917

The biting January wind felt different from the cold of December. Sharper, somehow. Less like a blanket of frost and more like tiny shards of glass against her cheeks. The walk back to Barnbow felt longer than she remembered. Heavier. Her mother hadn't wanted her to go.

"It's not right, Ann. Not yet."

Her father had just grunted something into his tea, something that might have been an approval of the wage or a surrender to a world that took everything.

She paused at the gate, her new pass feeling slick and foreign in her gloved hand. The guard, a different one from that night, gave her a passing glance, his face pinched with cold and boredom. She stepped through. And the world tilted.

It looked the same. That was the horror of it. The same sprawling city of sheds, the same maze of cleanways, the same plume of smoke dirtying the pale sky. But it was all wrong. A ghost of a place. Her feet, moving on their own, carried her down the familiar path, but her mind was a battlefield of then and now. Every crunch of her boots on the frozen cinders was an echo of a scream she hadn't made.

Her dread now had a new shape. It wasn't the vague fear of the unknown that she'd felt on her first day; it was a specific, intimate horror of the known.

Then she saw it.

Where the blackened wreck of Room 42 had stood, there was now a clean, brutal new shed. No evidence of the explosion, no evidence of the women who worked here. The factory hadn't just repaired it—it had erased the fact the explosion even happened.

New timber and corrugated panels formed a pale rectangle against the soot-streaked sheds. Brand new doors, the same heavy latch.

It looked wrong. Too neat. A wound stitched too fast, the scar still raw beneath a dusting of sawdust and denial.

No scent of ash or grief lingered—only sawdust and the sharp sting of chemicals.

The message was clear: *'Nothing to see. The machine still runs.'*

Ann stopped, her breath hitching in her throat, a physical pain lancing through her ribs. She could almost see them, the ghosts of Bench 12, their laughter and arguments swallowed by the new wood and clean lines. She saw Sarah leaning against a wall that no longer existed, a defiant grin on her face. *Was it my fault?* The question—her constant, coiled tormentor—hissed in the wind.

She forced herself to walk on, her heart a cold, heavy stone in her chest. She was a ghost here now, a relic from a different, more terrible war than the one these new girls, with their clean hands and unknowing eyes, thought they were fighting.

Inside her assigned workroom, Room 17, the air was colder, the machinery a different pitch. New girls, some looking barely old enough to be away from their mothers, stood in awkward lines around unfamiliar benches.

One glanced at Ann's bandaged arm, her eyes wide with morbid curiosity, then looked away just as quickly. Another whispered to her friend, the sound lost in the growing hum of the machines.

Then she saw her. Polly.

She stood at a bench across the room, pale as chalk, her expression locked down tight. She was alive. They shared a single glance across the cavernous room—quick, unsparing, and freighted with everything they couldn't say. There were no smiles. No nods. Just the grim, mutual recognition of a shared nightmare. *We survived. And no one else in this room knows what that means.*

The days that followed were a blur of mechanical motion. Ann's hands moved with practised rhythm—casing, charging, fusing—but her mind was in turmoil. She and Polly had found their silent orbit.

They worked near each other when they could, and now, during the ten-minute break, they sat on a back table in the canteen, a small island of quiet in a sea of raucous chatter. The other girls avoided their corner altogether, as though something toxic lingered there.

Ann stared into her mug of watery, chalk-like milk, the sour smell catching in her throat.

A new girl, only sixteen and still with the rosy-cheeked look of someone who hadn't yet breathed in the poison for months on end, walked past their table. She was heading for the tea urn, laughing with her friend.

She glanced over, her eyes met Ann's for a quick second, and the laughter died on her lips. Her eyes widened with a look Ann was coming to recognise—a morbid fascination mixed with raw fear.

The girl tugged her friend's sleeve and gave their table a wide, almost comical berth, hurrying away as if she'd seen a ghost.

Polly watched her go, a thin, brittle smile touching her lips. She leaned closer to Ann. Her voice came in a strained whisper, barely audible enough to carry over the din.

"Look at her. You'd think we had the pox." She took a slow sip of her milk. "Still," she said, her eyes glinting with a dark, sharp humour, "there is an upside."

Ann looked at her, her expression questioning.

"We don't have to queue for the lavvy anymore." Her thin smile didn't quite reach her haunted eyes. "They just... part for you. Like the bloody Red Sea."

A sound, rough and unused, scraped its way out of Ann's throat. It wasn't a laugh, not really. It was closer to a cough, or the sound of a rusty hinge giving way after a long winter.

But it was the closest she had come to laughter in weeks. The absurdity, the sheer, bleak truth of it, was a strange and bitter comfort. They were outcasts, marked not by sin but by survival.

She met Polly's gaze, and since the explosion, she felt a flicker of something other than grief or guilt for the first time. It was a shared, dour understanding, a fragile, two-person conspiracy against a world that didn't know how to look at them.

The whistle shrieked then, its piercing cry signalling the end of their borrowed time. The brief connection dissolved. As they stood up to return to the noise and endless line of shells, Ann felt the familiar dread settle back into her bones, but it was different now. It was no longer just her own. It was theirs.

A week after her return, it happened. The tension on the line was high. They were behind in the tally.

A shout cracked the air: "Pick it up, you lot! We're behind!" A foreman, his voice a gravelly bark.

Then a crash.

It wasn't even close to her. A metal crate, overfilled and unbalanced, slipped from a trolley at the far end of the room. It landed hard on the concrete floor with a CRACK that was not a clang, not a thud, but a sound like the world splitting open.

Ann was gone.

The factory dissolved. The walls of Room 17 bled away into smoke and roaring orange flame. The air was punched from her lungs, emitting the smell of burnt hair and something sweet and foul. There was a flash of white heat, then screams—was that her voice? Someone else's? She didn't know.

She only knew she had to get down. She dropped to the floor, arms clamped over her head, her body curled tight like a child waiting for a blow. *Get down. Get out.*

The girls on her bench froze, staring at her in silence. One shrieked. Another backed away, her expression one of terror.

But Polly was already moving. She scrambled around the bench, her own hands shaking as she knelt and touched Ann's shoulder. The touch served as a grounding point in the swirling chaos of memory.

"Ann! It's not real." Polly's voice was a fierce whisper right by her ear. "You're not there. You're here. You're safe. Breathe, love. Just breathe."

Ann sat on the narrow cot, the cold sweat of the panic attack soaking the collar of her smock. Her arm throbbed. Her heart had steadied, but something inside her had stilled in a different, more profound way.

She looked at the untouched mug of sweet, lukewarm tea. She thought of Sarah's last, defiant grin. Of Eliza's quiet, unshakeable authority. Of Lucy's shy, hopeful eyes. They had fought their war in that room. She realised her war was different now.

The nurse in the medical hut looked up from her ledger. "Nerves," she concluded, her voice brisk with impatience as she pushed a chipped enamel mug towards her. "Common enough, nowt to worry on."

Nerves. The word was a dismissal, a placid label for the roaring inferno that had just consumed her. She knew what would happen if she went back to the line. Every sharp clang would be the shriek of twisting metal. Every shout would be a scream for help. Every time she closed her eyes, she would see Sarah, not laughing but standing still and exhausted by the Amatol kettle. She would be a spectre in a factory of ghosts, and every day would be a fresh torment.

But what was the alternative? The thought of leaving sent a fresh fear—cold and sharp—through her veins. The wages, the best she had ever earned, money that put food on the table. What would she tell her father, a proud man already broken by the colliery laying him off? She, Ann Price, who had boasted and scrapped to be the best, would be a quitter—a girl with bad nerves who couldn't handle the work. The shame of it felt like its own kind of suffocation.

She weighed the two fears in the echoing silence of the hut. The terror of staying, of slowly losing her mind with each shriek of the factory whistle, versus the terror of leaving, of facing poverty and the judgement of a world that didn't understand. It wasn't about shells or shillings anymore.

A cold calm spread through her veins, extinguishing the last of the fear. Something inside her, something that had been coiled tight with guilt and terror since the explosion, stilled.

And then she stood.

The nurse blinked, startled, as Ann placed the untouched cup at the side of the desk with a steady, deliberate care that felt final. "Where are you off to, then? Your shift's not over."

"The main office," Ann said. Her voice sounded distant, calm. Certain. "I'm going for my leaving certificate."

She walked out of the hut into the pale, indifferent winter light, the factory's ceaseless hum already sounding like a distant memory behind her. She didn't look back. She wasn't going back in. Never again.

Ann Price had survived the blast. But walking away was the moment she started living.

The walk home from the gates felt longer than it ever had before. A knot of fear tightened in her stomach as she thought of her father's face, of the lost wages, of the hard, lean winter that now stretched before them.

The fear was real and sharp. But for the first time in weeks, the roaring in her ears had stopped. There was only the crunch of her own boots on the frozen road and the clean, biting air in her lungs.

The silence was vast and terrifying, but it was hers. And in it, she felt the first, fragile sense of peace.

28

Chapter 28 : The Lipstick Mark

5th December 1916, Barnbow, Room 42

In a stolen heartbeat—a sliver of time carved from Room 42's unyielding, seething cycle—Sarah Jennings paused.

Her fingers, nimble despite their chemical burns, slipped into a secret fold of her smock and emerged with a stub of lipstick, its crimson a shocking splash of defiance against the factory's monochrome misery. With a furtive glance, McDowell was a distant shadow; the other watchers were distracted. *Now.*

The cheap metal base twisted. A waxy, floral scent, incongruous yet achingly familiar, bloomed for an instant amidst the factory's foul breath of Amatol as she dragged the colour across her lips—a crooked, urgent slash of red. Her heart hammered. Then, with a defiant half-smirk—part bravado, part benediction—she leaned towards a newly capped 4.5-inch howitzer shell.

Cool, impassive steel met the fleeting warmth of her mouth. A perfect, startling crimson lip-print—a kiss, a brand, a tiny, human scar—blossomed on its grey flank. "That's for Fritz," she said, the whisper swallowed by the noise. Then, softer still, a breath against the metal: "And one for you, Cecil lad." With a swift wipe of her mouth, the lipstick vanished.

The shell, nudged along, was taken by Mary's gloved hand, which brushed the mark without notice as she loaded it onto the trolley. The lipstick print remained—a vivid, silent scream.

The trolley jolted across the pitted concrete, its iron wheels screaming. At the loading bay, men grunted, heaving munitions onto wooden pallets. A gloved palm, gritty with factory dust, smeared the vibrant crimson, dragging a greasy trail across the heart of the print, dulling its sheen to a bruised, compromised red.

Still, it clung. Outside, needle-sharp rain turned to sleet, slicking the shell's casing. The lipstick bled, the colour thinning like watery blood against cold steel. But it held.

Heavy arms lifted Sarah's shell into the goods wagon's echoing gloom. Coal smoke and the stench of engine grease filled the darkness—the crimson mark—now a muted, greasy smear pressed hard against another, invisible shell.

The train lurched, beginning its long, clattering journey south. Through hours of jolting darkness, the print was further abraded, grease seeping into the fading pigment. Night. Day. Another night. The train thundered on.

Portside: a cacophony of shrieking gulls, bellowing foremen, rattling winches. The air reeked of decaying kelp and diesel. Sarah's shell was slammed onto the granite quayside.

The mark—now a faint, dirty pink, a ghostly stain beneath grime—caught a fleeting breath of salty air before a stevedore's tar-blackened glove brushed it, oblivious. Then, into the transport ship's cavernous hold. Darkness again.

The cold, damp breath of the sea, the thrum of engines. The boat groaned against the Channel's chop. Sarah's kiss—her defiant mark—faded further, almost erased by the persistent damp and indifferent friction.

Dawn broke grey over the French coast. Shells emerged like ingots of cold, condensed violence, slick with sea spray. Unloading was faster here, driven by front-line urgency. A motor lorry growled over rutted, muddy roads towards the Somme, dust from shelled-out villages coating every surface, turning to grey paste in the persistent drizzle. The kiss—if any trace still defied erasure—was buried deep beneath layers of French mud and grime from its brutal passage.

The field battery was a raw wound in churned mud, a Dantean circle of despair. Camouflage nets sagged; gun crews, faces skull-like with exhaustion, moved like wraiths in the clinging mist.

Sarah's shell, one among a thousand anonymous grey cylinders, was dumped and stacked in a muddy revetment. Forgotten. She had poured her heart into it; Eliza's gang had touched it, played their part.

But their hands, fears, and hopes were ghosts here, lost to the guns' impersonal appetite. A corporal barked. A gunner pulled Sarah's shell, wiping it roughly with a filthy, oil-stained rag. If a smear of old wax, a hint of pigment, remained, his indifferent cleaning obliterated it. He didn't notice.

The 4.5-inch howitzer squatted, its muzzle gaping. A loader hefted Sarah's shell, arms straining, and fed it into the breech. Steel scraped steel. The breech block slammed shut with deafening finality—a whistle. A lanyard was yanked. *FIRE!* The gun convulsed, its roar a physical blow. A blinding orange-red spear of flame, then choking smoke. The shell screamed skyward—a spinning, incandescent speck, launched on its brief, terrible arc.

A glimmer of light against a distant, mud-brown horizon. A silent, blossoming orange flower of devastation. Then, a beat later, the sound—a deep, gut-thumping *CRUMP*—as the shockwave punched the air. Mud, shattered timber, twisted metal, perhaps unidentifiable fragments of men, hurled skyward in a momentary, violent silhouette. Then, only settling dust, drifting smoke, and the gun crew were already preparing for the next round.

The kiss was gone. The shell was gone—Sarah's defiant, human mark consumed. No one saw. No one knew. But for one infinitesimal, violent instant, in a blasted, forgotten crater on the Somme, death itself carried the faintest, molecular trace of a woman named Sarah Jennings.

A mark. A joke. A prayer. And that, in the grand, terrible calculus of war, was nothing. And everything.

The end.

29

Chapter 29 : The Silence Ends Where MemorySpeaks

That night at 10:27 PM, an explosion ripped through Room 42. Twenty-two women died on the spot. By dawn, eleven more had succumbed to their injuries. One lingered for two weeks before passing away, and another fought on for almost two years before shock-related complications claimed her. In all, thirty-five lives ended here, on the outskirts of Leeds, in a factory that appeared on no public map and whose work was guarded in secrecy.

Inside its high sheds, these women handled TNT and Amatol day after day. They did not wear the khaki and steel helmets of soldiers; instead, they arrived in overalls, cotton shirts, sturdy trousers, and rubber-soled boots. Some sang on the crowded early trains, their voices carrying through frost-cold mornings as they made their way to the gates. Others rode in silence, the yellow stain of explosives still clinging faintly to their skin from the previous shift.

In small homes across Leeds, York, Castleford, Harrogate, Normanton, Pontefract, and beyond, they kissed their children goodnight—often leaving behind the sharp scent of the factory's steam pipes and molten shells. Their hands, stained by the powder they packed so precisely, shaped instruments of war even as they prayed for peace.

When dawn broke over the smoking ruins of Room 42, there were no parades, no medals, no wreaths laid in their honour. By the following evening, the factory whistle blew again, and production resumed as if nothing had happened. Survivors—faces drawn with shock and grief—were moved to new stations before their tears had dried. Efficiency was the watchword. The war demanded no pause.

In the days that followed, the rebuilding of Room 42 was swift. Inspectors reported that the interruption to output was 'negligible'. Yet the same push for speed and quotas went on—and by March of 1917, as part of a workforce 'streamlining,' some seven thousand shell-fillers were declared surplus and dismissed. The cost of wartime demands reached beyond those who died in the blast: many more lost both their livelihoods and the sense of purpose they had found behind those factory doors.

Censorship and official reticence ensured that the Barnbow disaster faded from headlines almost as quickly as it had appeared. Two smaller explosions would follow in the months ahead—each mentioned only briefly in the factory logs—yet the risk remained ever-present in every scoop of mixed Amatol, every turn of a hydraulic press, every careful insertion of a fuse.

Not all victims perished in the blast itself. Some slipped into yellowed illness, their skin stained by daily exposure to TNT; others saw their lungs collapse or their livers fail in the weeks and months afterward. Compensation cheques arrived in brown envelopes: a few families received nine-and-a-half-dozen pounds, others only sixty-five shillings. No record asked what these women had been worth alive, nor what hopes and plans vanished with them.

For decades, their names were all but absent from schoolbooks and local lore. But in quieter corners of Leeds and York—among families, in small village memorials—some remembered. Below is the list of those whose last shift ended in smoke and ruin. Their names stand here, reclaimed from the long hush.

Barnbow Explosion Victims – 5th December 1916

Elsie Martha Atkinson, 18, Leeds
Mary Amelia Schofield, 42, Leeds
Florence Whiteley, 31, Leeds
Amelia Stewart, 28, Leeds (died 30 Dec 1916)
Kate Bainbridge, 40, Leeds
Edith Sykes, 15, Leeds (died weeks later)
Ethel Agnes Jackson, 20, Leeds
Emmie Keyworth, 26, Leeds
Martha Alderson, 27, Leeds
Katie Chapman, 41, Leeds
Gertrude Reid, 27, Leeds
Agnes L. Power, 36, Leeds
Ida Worslop, (age unknown), Leeds
Mary Jane Blackstone, 35, Leeds
Ada Glassby, 30, Harrogate
Jennie Blackmore, 21, Normanton
Mary Gibson, 14, Castleford
Polly Booth, 21, Castleford
Eliza Grant, 39, Castleford
Edith Levitt, 22, Castleford
Maggie Barker, 17, Castleford
Emily Sedgwick, 39, Harrogate (died two years later)
Olive Yeates, (age unknown), York

Charlotte Fox, 46, York

Maria Evelyn Rowley, 19, Halton

Helena Beckett, 33, Leeds

Jane Few, (age unknown), Pontefract

Kathleen Violet Eastment, 17, York

Mary Elizabeth Wortley, 38, York

Alice Smart, 45, York

Sarah Ann Jennings, 38, Warthill (York)

Mary Elizabeth Carter, 22, York

Elizabeth Mason, 41, York

Lilian Eva Ellis, 19, York

Eliza West, 53, York

Each name marks a woman who rose before dawn, who knew the hiss of steam and the tremor of presses, who left behind families, friends, and futures never truly lived.

When the armistice came on the 11th of November 1918, Barnbow's shed doors closed at last. An uneasy stillness settled over the empty conveyors and silent kettles. The women walked away with a final pay packet—an extra week's wages—and returned to lives forever altered: some into domestic service, others back to dusty looms or quiet shop counters, their TNT-stained hands a reminder of what they had built.

Newsprint celebrated the Representation of the People Act, which granted suffrage to women over thirty with property qualifications. For many of those who had worked late-night shifts at Barnbow, that milestone arrived too late. They had risked their lives and limbs but remained without a vote for another decade.

Year after year, the final production figures stood stark on factory ledgers:

Those numbers spoke of collective effort on an immense scale—but said nothing of individual sacrifice.

In the spring of 1985, a twelve-year-old boy wandered from his school group at York Minster and paused by the Five Sisters' window. There, carved into the wooden panels, were the names of women lost in that war—among them, "Sarah Ann Jennings." He traced the letters with his finger, sensing even then that this name held a story he would one day need to tell.

He would learn she was his great-grandmother, that she died at Barnbow, and that her son, Cecil Jennings, never spoke of her again. Cecil passed away in 1973, the same week that the boy was born, another silence passed to the next generation.

That boy grew up to tell this story.

If you would like to know more

A Penny a Shell tells only part of the story.

Many of the people you met in these pages — Joe, Lucy, Mary, Nora, Hilda, June, Ann — lived lives that could not fully be contained within a single novel.

On my website, I am slowly sharing additional companion pieces: short, self-contained stories that explore their lives before and after the events of Room 42, as well as historical notes and reflections drawn from the real records behind the book.

If you would like to read these, you can scan the QR code below.

Or Visit our website: **here** https://antonyjbell.com/books/a-penny-a-shell/after-reading/

There is no obligation, and no obligation to stay.
These pieces are simply there for readers who wish to linger a little longer.

Printed in Dunstable, United Kingdom

79110268R00160